The St Martin's Mystery

by

Neil Ewing

The Conrad Press

The St Martin's Mystery
Published by The Conrad Press in the United Kingdom
2025
Tel: +44(0)1227 472 874
www.theconradpress.com
info@theconradpress.com
ISBN 978-1-916966-88-8
Copyright ©Neil Ewing 2025
All rights reserved.
Typesetting and Cover Design by: Levellers
The Conrad Press logo was designed by Maria Priestley.
Printed and bound in Great Britain by Clays Ltd, Elcograf
S.p.A.

For Susan

1

The Scottish Highlands lay silent under the stars, icy and unforgiving.

The still sharp air above them was brutally cold. No life moved; every earthly creature was hunkered down, buried deep inside their snow holes, dug into the frozen white wasteland.

And yet, wedged into the hills, there was something; a few faint yellow lights showed themselves. The tiny settlement, a community spared the ravages of the 1830 Highland Clearances two years earlier, clung to the grey escarpment. Thin pencils of smoke pushed up into the crackling night air. Human habitation forged centuries ago had made a life amongst the rocky slopes, sheltered in the lee of the mountains.

But there was also another presence that night. The equine visitor was on its own, standing in the snow at the edge of the village, indifferent to the bite of rime frost in its mane.

The beast had set off weeks earlier. Its goal was a distant city, beyond these smoky primitive dwellings, and it had already travelled a long way from the crags in the far north, seeking new life. The animal had made light work of its journey over the jagged peaks and moved sure-footedly through the ravines, untroubled by the scree that bounced and rattled down the slopes under its tread.

There was still a long way to go, but for now the beast paused its journey. A storm was approaching and the chaos this would bring was something it could use to advantage. Head down, it studied the settlement.

It knew none of the inhabitants in the cottages would appear until daybreak, a long way off, so far north in deep winter. The beast, possessed of infinite patience, had never needed food or water, though. It took a few steps across the bridge that led into the settlement. In time the beast would make use of the waterway, but for now, winter held the stream captive, frozen hard into the rocks, waiting for the release of spring.

The visitor took in the cottages. A few pale shafts of light escaped through the heavily shuttered windows, and a narrow uneven track wound its way through the settlement.

The beast measured its tread carefully, and its hooves rang hard on the icy rock, but it felt no cold. The prints it left in the snow pointed backwards up into the hills even as it walked forward over the bridge.

The best thing about the bothy on a winter's night, Douglas MacGregor thought, was how warm and snug it felt. The windows were tiny, the walls were thick, and the door behind him battened shut.

He could hear the icy blasts of a highland storm chasing down the mountain slopes into the village. The full force of the gale descended on the tiny settlement. It buffeted and growled at the doors and whistled down the narrow passages between each homestead. But the crofter's homes stood resolute, and it could find no way in. It reached the other side of the cottages defeated and hurried angrily on down the valley.

Douglas was used to the banshee wail of the wind, and he ignored it. He hung the cast iron pot of potatoes and kale over the fire and settled down. The pot simmered and sang, and the aroma of artisan food filled the small warm room. He broke off some bread from a loaf and dipped it into the broth. He found the heat and flavour of the meal deeply comforting as the storm raged outside and he settled back into his chair. There was no movement in the room, save for the dance and crackle of the fire.

Douglas had almost fallen asleep when he thought he heard an extra sound, one new to him, something he couldn't place. He sat and listened, staring into the fire. The sound was indistinct and mixed up with the gale. There were pauses, but they were never long enough for him to assume it had stopped. Insistent but irregular, difficult to pinpoint, hard to identify, the noise, sporadically, continued.

He added a peat brick to the fire and sat back, idly mopping up the remains of the broth. And there it was again. It seemed part of the wind and yet it did not come and go in the same way. Sometimes it was there at the peak of the blast, but in other moments it followed when the moans of the gale receded. He fancied it was slightly louder than when he'd first heard it. Was there another quality to it now? To him the sound had seemed far away, and the storm and the distance had masked any details, but now it had a kind of texture. What had been anonymous had gained an almost animal-like quality. It had become an organic sound.

He moved to the window and peered out. The light from the fire reflected off the tiny glass plate and made it hard to see past the swirling snow outside. The flames sent shadows dancing high into the ceiling. They stretched and flung themselves crazily against the walls of the room, reaching for him while he stared into the night. It was hard to make out anything, but the snow picked up grains of light from the stars high above the storm and cast the palest of shadows. He scanned the uncertain shapes and silhouettes beyond the glass.

The storm wailed and groaned, and the snow spun in great spirals through the village. Douglas was about to leave the window when he noticed a movement out of the corner of his eye, slow and deliberate in contrast to the chaos of the gale. The shadow was indistinct, but then it moved. Whatever it was took a step closer toward his cottage.

Then the sound came again. High pitched, and now quite separate from the noise of the wind, with its own identity and purpose. As he stared, the shadow changed course toward him. The shape was huge now, filling the window.

And then it was there, an enormous black horse, with its head pushed hard against the glass. He peered at the animal through clouds of steam billowing from its nostrils

and was shocked to find a brooding malevolence in its coal
black face.

And then he realised it was not seeking shelter.

It had come for him.

2

August 1933, London England

The day had been a hectic one for Leonard Ash.

As someone who aspired to be a branch manager, it was his job to interview potential customers who came into the Swan Lane offices of St Martin's Bank. This was, he accepted, entirely reasonable. So relentless was this supply though, he sometimes wondered what his manager did with these recruits once he signed them up.

This afternoon was notable for one appointment. At three o'clock a Mr Colpach had arrived to discuss the opening of an account.

The gentleman spoke with a soft Scottish accent, probably from Edinburgh, Ash decided. The customer wore clothes that were smart, if a little dated. His lustrous hair was long enough to reach his shoulders, and his black shoes were a heavy design Ash hadn't seen before. The overall impression was of an artistic type, Ash thought, someone who didn't often come to London and had made a special trip, perhaps on the Flying Scotsman. This customer was probably a stranger to banking matters, although Ash wasn't sure. After all, for a man to make such a trip spoke of wealth.

At the beginning of the meeting, Ash nearly stopped proceedings and suggested the branch of St Martin's across the river on the south side of Blackfriars Bridge, which dealt with the trades.

The branch, closed following the General Strike of 1926, had reopened. But it was this last thought that stayed his hand. It wouldn't be the first time an individual had opened an account without drawing attention to himself, only for the bank to find their new customer was as rich as Croesus.

So, decided Ash, a *successful* artist then. He hadn't heard of the man and would have to look him up.

The exchange had begun with Ash setting out the bank's history before he moved on to what it could offer. As usual he asked for details of Colpach's circumstances, but Ash had found himself thwarted. Over the course of the meeting, the conversation had swung in favour of the visitor so that it was Ash who answered the questions. The process had been quite subtle, but afterwards, Ash had to admit, it felt as though *he* had been interviewed. That was something he hadn't experienced before and certainly not by a man with water weed in his hair.

Yes, that had been the strangest thing of all. The meeting over, Ash walked Colpach out to the foyer. He saw the traces of green as he left. He looked again, but there was no mistake.

The Crowfoot Ranunculus, flecked with white and yellow, were mostly hidden. Here and there though, the tiny flowers gave themselves away, drifting out from underneath the mane of hair as he moved. The impression was of weed moving in the current of a stream.

For the rest of the afternoon Ash was busy with other customers, but his thoughts kept returning to the unusual, softly spoken visitor. By now he had decided the man would never return. No doubt he was visiting several banks before placing his account, and although St Martin's was better than most, he told himself, an artist might prefer a more bohemian institution. That is if you could have an institution that was, well, bohemian. Perhaps, thought Ash, he should have sent him to Blackfriars after all.

Ash was looking forward to his annual holiday, an innovation the bank had recently granted to senior staff. With the last customer gone and the clock in the banking hall finally ready to release him, he closed the final file for the day. He walked through the foyer and paused outside. The August weather was warm, and the still of the evening was like a balm after the busy day. He decided to take the towpath along the river, before turning back up into the City, to the station, and the train that would take him home. Home for now he thought, but if things went well, he would soon be able to afford a much grander address.

There were some steps let into the side of the path, which went down to the edge of the river. At high tide, the bottom step was level with the water, and he made his way to the spot. From here he could watch the steamers and pleasure boats as they chugged their way along the Thames. Approaching, he saw, to his surprise, that a black horse standing on the towpath was blocking his way; as he got closer, he realised the beast was huge.

Ash stepped forward carefully, making encouraging noises. The animal appeared docile enough, though, and lowered its head as he approached. Ash patted it on the neck, murmuring quietly.

The beast moved forward and gave him a nudge, adjusting its stance on the towpath, creating room for Ash to pass. Close to the horse now, he saw it was suffering from a deformity in that its huge hooves were pointing the wrong way.

Ash gave the horse an extra pat on the head and slid his hand down over the beast's nose. He looked into its eyes and was unnerved to find something he was not prepared for, a malevolence in its gaze. The lines in its features were cruel, and its face seemed cast in shadow.

It was then he made a startling discovery. For some extraordinary reason he could not remove his hand. The fingers that had stroked the creature's face were stuck fast to its nose. This was so odd that initially, Ash did not even find it frightening.

Then the horse moved, and he was compelled to follow it or break his wrist. At first, the animal took only half a pace, and Ash followed the movement, protecting his hand. But then, to his horror, the beast deliberately began to withdraw down the steps towards the river. Ash pulled harder but there was no point. The beast seemed unaffected by the strain of his hand on its face, and the pain this must be causing. There was nothing in its expression other than the same darkness that unsettled him moments earlier. Still, it withdrew, further now, back down into the river itself.

The Thames lapped around the beast's body. Its head was level with the water and Ash, for a moment, took comfort that it could go no further. Arm outstretched, he stood on the bottom step, preserving his balance, the Thames breaking over his shoes in small ripples.

There was a pause as if someone had spliced two rolls of film together, then the beast disappeared below the surface, and Ash, shouting, then screaming, was pitched into the Thames.

A passenger on the pleasure steamer *SS Galadriel* watched events as the boat made its way upriver. As the steamer passed the now empty steps, he turned to his wife and pointed at the bowler hat floating towards them.

'Hetty, what was that, did someone just fall in? Should we shout, 'Man overboard' or something?'

'Nonsense, Charles, do pay attention, they're just going to tell us about the bridge.'

Charles returned to the guide's commentary and shook his head. Whatever would he see next? He hoped it wasn't his medication playing up again.

3

The boardroom of St Martin's Bank was typical of its type. A chestnut table stretched the full length of the vast space and gleaming chandeliers marched across the ceiling. Mahogany panels clad the walls and portraits of long-gone chairmen looked out across the empire of the bank's interests with satisfaction. Discreetly placed antique ornaments given to the bank down the years hinted at the wealth of the customers. Everything within the boardroom had a sense of order, of decorum, of well-being.

Except the people sitting in it.

The chairman and Sir John MacGregor, chief executive of St Martin's Bank, were silent. Their discussion, animated at the start, had fallen away, and they hadn't spoken for a while. Both were at a loss, reluctant to acknowledge the problem but knowing they needed to act. The boardroom clock's Westminster chimes announced 11:00; the chairman coughed.

'So that's the second, you say, at two different branches?'

'Yes. George Stevens from Embankment and Harriet Simpson from Hope Street, Blackfriars.'

'And gone, without a trace?'

MacGregor nodded.

The chairman hesitated. 'No money is missing, no accounts tampered with?'

MacGregor raised himself in his chair. 'Nothing, nothing at all. They were conscientious, hardworking employees.'

'Perhaps they've had to deal with something urgently and had no chance to ask for time off,' the chairman ventured, hopefully.

'Possibly,' MacGregor said. 'But then why wouldn't their families know?'

There was silence again. The chairman studied the portraits of his predecessors, as he'd done many times before. He looked around the room, taking in one impassive face after another, seeking inspiration. As he did, he drummed on the immense table.

Sir John shifted in his seat. The drumming stopped; the chairman's fingers held just above the tabletop.

'Have we reported all this to the police?' he asked. 'I assume we must have done.'

'We told them on Monday, but this being only Thursday, they'll begin their enquiries next week. Assuming no one returns.'

'Why the delay?' The chairman was drumming again. 'I can understand if one person goes missing, there may be an explanation, but two...' He tailed off, but the drumming continued.

'They take the view that where a man and a woman are missing, well it's more likely there are other reasons...' Sir John offered.

'Quite so, quite so.' The chairman brightened. 'Do we know if they were stepping out together?'

'We don't. And George Stevens is married. The bank's rules about that kind of thing are strict. One of them would have to find alternative employment if the relationship were a steady one. We know these things happen but...'

'But employees keep such matters secret for that very reason,' finished the chairman. 'Nevertheless, it might explain why the families were in the dark.'

The drumming stopped and the chairman straightened himself.

'I know these matters are for the police,' he began, 'but I think the bank should make some enquiry of its own. His Majesty's resources can only stretch so far, and we should do all we can to help.'

'We need to be discreet, but I agree, we can't stand by and do nothing.' Sir John's mouth tightened into a grim line.

'Let's review all this on Monday. We can think no more of it if they've returned. However, assuming that isn't the case, make an appointment with my secretary for 10:00.' The chairman got to his feet.

MacGregor took the cue and stood up.

'Let's keep our fingers crossed.'

Both men went their separate ways, lost in their thoughts.

***

The spirits of the bank lived high in its vaulted ceiling. They had absorbed the conversation and knew more than they could pass on. Time passes, stone weathers, chairmen and chief executives come and go. Nothing was new to them. For now, at least, they settled down to the business of the day.

4

On the following Monday, the two men met again. They were in a sombre mood.

'I'm still hoping for a romantic explanation, but have we heard anything?' the chairman asked.

'Sadly, nothing.' Sir John had thought hard over the last few days. 'Alastair, it's possible our two missing employees are involved in a tryst. But we need to make our own enquiries, for the benefit of the families and because we need to be sure there's been no damage to the bank. The police won't focus on this aspect for a while yet. As well as looking for the people we need a forensic analysis - to be confident of our position as a business.'

Sir John's comments received an encouraging nod.

'We should conduct a review of each branch where the missing people worked, to make sure there are no concerns. I think we should commission a third-party investigator to do this properly.'

Sir John could see his chairman looked perturbed.

'I understand the first step, but the second, are you suggesting a private detective?'

Sir John was ready with his answer.

'I understand. Hiring someone like that, it suggests something sordid, a mistress or the like. We need a more sophisticated type, someone with intellect, resource, and a degree of courage. A man who's able to understand the details but also see the full picture, who'll alert us to any embarrassment for the bank. He might not be an investigator by trade, but he'd have the skills for the task.'

'More Sherlock Holmes than Lone Wolf then,' said the chairman. 'Do you have anyone in mind?'

'No, I don't have a name, but I have a few customers I can talk to who will be discreet. They may have a suggestion for us.'

The chairman and Sir John had been together for a long time, and they trusted each other. This worked in Sir John's favour.

'If you think it'll help,' the chairman agreed. 'I'd like to meet the investigator too when you find him.'

Sir John continued. 'I'm going to visit George Stevens' wife and Harriet Simpson's parents; I want to assure them we're doing all we can. Having a plan to bring in our own investigator will give them some hope at least. I'm determined the bank should help if it can.'

The meeting broke up. Sir John, invigorated by the chairman's approval and pleased to be doing something about the situation, returned to his office.

The chairman was also in a better mood. He was not the only one.

***

High above, the spirits at the bank were careful to manage their emotions. Too great a surge could sometimes result in otherworldly sounds echoing in the old stone walls. Even the marble corridors might ripple with some faint draught if sufficiently stirred. For this reason, the spirits held themselves in check, but were it possible, the staff of St Martin's Bank might have noted a faint zephyr of approval drifting through its vaulted ceilings.

***

Sir John's afternoon was a busy one. The regular business of the bank needed his full attention, but now he also had to find the investigator promised for his chairman.

There was no shortage of people prepared to take on the task; he was sure of that. He knew though, finding the right person wouldn't be easy. If there was 'foul play' as the novels called it, the man would need courage too.

Sir John called his secretary into the office. The clack of typewriters intruded briefly. Miss Denby was a tall, elegant woman; her silhouette was triangular, with a suggestion of a shoulder pad in the jacket of her pale grey two-piece suit. She wore a fitted straight skirt finished at the knee and paired the outfit with stylish Oxford shoes. She had a formidable reputation.

Miss Denby entered, notebook in hand. 'Yes, Sir John.'

'Miss Denby, please could you draw up a list of our London based customers.'

'All customers?'

'Just holders of single accounts, not joint accounts, and just the male customers please.'

Privately, Sir John acknowledged, the possibility of danger influenced his plan. He already had a particular type in mind and had decided it would be wrong to place a married man at risk.

Miss Denby withdrew, leaving Sir John alone in the office. He tried to focus on the folder in front of him, full of papers for the bank's upcoming board meeting. This proved futile, and his mind repeatedly returned to the disappearances.

Most of the afternoon had passed when there was a brisk knock on the door and Miss Denby appeared.

'I have the list, Sir John,' she said, and stood waiting.

Sir John smiled encouragingly.

'Wonderful, Miss Denby, whatever would I do without you?'

The secretary stepped forward and laid a red folder on the desk. He saw it had a typed list of names that ran to two sheets of paper. They were all male and Miss Denby had added their date of birth.

'I wasn't sure what else you'd need, but I thought the date might be useful.'

'Thank you,' Sir John enthused, 'this is very helpful.'

'Will there be anything else today?'

Sir John glanced at the clock on the office mantlepiece. Such had been his concentration that, as was often the case, he'd missed the chimes on the quarter and half hour, and it was now approaching six. His faithful secretary had stayed late again.

'I am sorry to keep you,' he sighed. 'Please do go and take a late train in tomorrow.'

'Thank you, Sir John, that's very thoughtful of you.'

Both parties had played out the scene many times, Sir John knowing Miss Denby would be at her desk fifteen minutes before her start time and Miss Denby appreciating his offer, nonetheless.

Sir John slid the folder into his briefcase and clipped the brass catch shut. He was the last to leave. Walking through the foyer he looked around the cavernous hall, its marble cladding veined with black. Every so often these lines forked, and new seams began their journey through the stone. Sir John liked the flow of the veins which reminded him of geological strata.

He saw these threads every day, but he fancied that from time to time he found a new one. This was possible as the staff sometimes moved the stands advertising the bank's services, revealing previously covered parts of the marble wall.

It was also the case that the spirits in the bank lived and breathed through this geological circulatory system and sometimes made changes of their own.

Of course this was less well known.

In the street, the rush hour was at its height. Sir John had already decided to take a taxi home rather than use the train, as he wanted to study the list typed by Miss Denby without someone looking over his shoulder. He reached out into the traffic and summoned a cab. A taxi weaving between the trams, horse-drawn vehicles and cars, tacked its way across to him. Sir John stepped up onto the running board and swung open the passenger door.

'Richmond,' he directed.

The driver acknowledged with a brisk 'certainly guvnor,' and pulled back out into the traffic.

Used to the journey and grateful for the time it would give him, Sir John opened his attaché case. He tapped the typed sheets smartly together on the lid and settled back.

The taxi fought its way through Cheapside and past St Paul's. Sir John began to work his way down the list. He checked each name, pausing to recall the account holder. As he travelled down the list, he made notes against a handful of names, but there weren't many, and Sir John crossed out most of the entries after brief consideration. He also added a few handwritten notes where customers occurred to him that might be able to help in some way, even if they did not fit his original criteria.

Now on Western Avenue, the cab began to pick up speed. The light was fading, and Sir John switched on the yellow overhead lamp. The driver checked his rear mirror but said nothing. As the growl of the engine increased, Sir John adjusted his position, gave the driver an instruction and went back to his review.

By the time the cab reached Great Chertsey Road, Sir John had reduced the typed schedule to a list of possibles. All of these were customers to contact for suggestions, and he could find no candidate for the job itself. He sat back and relaxed for the last part of the journey, catching the occasional glint of the Thames through the trees.

The cab entered Richmond, and the driver asked for instructions. Sir John watched the lights of the houses from the taxi window and imagined the family lives inside. They passed the travelling fair set up on the green and The Slow Pony public house, which as always, was doing a great trade.

Turning right at a sign entitled *Redshanks*, the cab pulled into the drive of Sir John's house. He got out, paid the fare with a suitable tip, given the unproductive drive back for the cabbie, and entered the house.

Supper completed; Sir John retired to his study. He opened his briefcase and read his edited list again. Pouring himself a scotch and reaching for his address book, he picked up the telephone and began dialling.

Sir John's phone calls took up most of the evening. Some customers were at home; for some, he left messages, and in a few cases, calls went unanswered. These were rare as most of the bank's patrons ran houses with domestic staff, but he found one or two where there was no one home. The outcome was, however, a complete blank, and at around nine o'clock he stopped for the day.

Sir John arrived at the bank the next morning, ready to continue with the list. He now had the help of Miss Denby, who arrived at her usual time despite the previous evening's exchange. She made the first calls and put each customer through to Sir John. The morning wore on, and the regular commerce of the bank's day began to intrude on the schedule, until Miss Denby called through.

'I have Sir Patrick Knowlesby,' she said, and put the customer and Sir John's friend on the line.

'Patrick, good morning, I'm sorry to disturb your evening, I hope Ann has forgiven me.'

There was a short chuckle. 'Nonsense, John, there's no need to apologise, especially when the subject is so intriguing. I pretended we had an application for the club to discuss; Ann's used to that sort of thing. I was packed off to the study with my brandy to take the call.' Sir Patrick went on. 'Actually, that's why I'm calling. I drew a blank when we spoke, but I had an idea this morning. Do you have a moment?'

'Go on.'

'Last year I operated on a chap whose knee was injured in a mining accident. He was pretty smashed up and needed some specialist work. He came to me through someone I know at The Foreign Office.'

'I see.'

'I got to know him a bit as it needed three procedures before he was up and running again, so to speak.'

'Go on,' said Sir John. He valued his friend's views and wondered where this was leading.

'Well, it happened this chap was in the Transvaal for a while, and it was during this time he got injured. It was in the Komberley mining collapse, a dreadful affair. I don't know if you remember it?'

Sir John certainly did.

Sir Patrick continued. 'After the accident there was a lot of pressure for change in the industry. He was one of the people who helped drive through some big improvements in safety.'

'What's your thinking?'

'The industry is still pretty bloody, but back then there was resistance to any form of change. From what this chap said, it didn't stop at intimidation but included physical beatings and even threats on his life. But the key thing is he kept going and eventually won some substantial changes.'

'Just the kind of chap to follow through on an investigation?'

'Indeed, tenacity and courage were the qualities you were looking for you said.'

'That's right, but I also want discretion?'

'That's harder for me to say,' said his friend, 'but he's the closest I can think of to fitting the bill.'

'Thank you, Patrick, there may be something there for us - are you still in touch?'

'Not now, but I'm sure I can track him down.'

'Well please do and ask him to contact me. At the very least I should meet him, especially if he carries your recommendation...'

Sir John heard another chuckle.

'I'm not promising anything, but I think it's worth following up.'

'What's this fellow's name?'

'Erskine. Robert Erskine.'

The telephone call ended. Sir John thought for a minute and then called in Miss Denby.

'We may have unearthed someone,' he said. 'Carry on with the list, but if you get a call from a Robert Erskine put him through and hold any other calls.' Miss Denby was too experienced to ask what was going on, but she sensed its importance.

To their disappointment, no call came that afternoon, or the next day. By the afternoon of the third day, Sir John had finished the calls, and apart from a couple of half-hearted exchanges, he and his secretary had nothing to show for their efforts. During this time, he took Miss Denby into his confidence and told her the whole story. She prided herself on her discretion and being Sir John's 'ADC' as he called it. She enjoyed the feeling of being critical to the plan.

Sir John was at his desk on the fourth morning when a breathless Miss Denby knocked on the door and announced,

'There's a gentleman in the foyer who wants to meet you. He says his name's Erskine.' She paused. 'He's got some kind of accent.'

She regarded her boss hopefully.

Sir John gathered himself. 'Show him in,' he said, 'this should be interesting.'

***

High in the vaulted ceiling of the banking hall, the spirits listened intently.

5

'My name's Robert Erskine. Sir Patrick asked if I'd arrange to see you. I hope you don't mind the impromptu visit.'

The guest removed his hat, settled down in a chair with his legs out in front of him, and surveyed the office.

'I was happy to oblige Sir Patrick, I know you're a friend of his. I'm not much of a catch as an account, but is there something I can help you with?'

Sir John took in the visitor. Erskine was probably around forty, he thought, although it was hard to tell as the man's face, weathered by the African sun showed more years than he might have carried. His features were well set and open and his appearance was tidy rather than stylish. The man wore a steel grey coloured suit and a dark hat. He kept his shoes polished but his tie was slightly loose. The effect, thought Sir John, was of someone who was prepared to wear city clothes, but was more comfortable out of them with his sleeves rolled up.

'Has Sir Patrick explained anything to you?' asked Sir John.

'No, nothing at all. He said you would put me in the picture when we met.'

Sir John proffered the coffee Miss Denby had brought in. His guest took the cup and saucer and set them on his knee. Sir John watched the steaming coffee, it looked as if it was heating up on Erskine's suit.

'Patrick and I have known each other a long time,' Sir John explained. The visitor smiled back.

'His recommendation is worth a lot...'

'But you would like to know about my character and experience first-hand,' interjected Erskine. 'What should I focus on?'

Sir John thought for a moment.

'An ability to unravel mysteries, tenacity and,' he hesitated, 'and courage in the face of intimidation or danger.'

Erskine lifted his cup.

Sir John watched his visitor.

'Now, that *is* an interesting brief. Well, I'm an engineer by training. My speciality is mining and geology. I've been involved in mines and mining for most materials, including what you might call industrial metals as well as gold and platinum. I've mined in most regions of the world, particularly South America, South Africa, and Russia.'

Sir John motioned for another coffee; Erskine accepted with a nod.

'In terms of mystery solving I'm not sure what experience I can point to,' went on the visitor. 'But I suppose geological investigation and testing for mineral deposits is a mystery of sorts.'

Sir John made a conciliatory gesture.

'In terms of tenacity,' Erskine added, 'I can help a bit with that one. A colleague and I worked in South African mines after the war, gold mostly. The conditions were tough for everyone, and we weren't just surface engineers; we went down to the seams and got involved in the entire process. That's a dangerous business today, but a few years ago it was deadly. The dangers above ground, criminal gangs, heat, and disease were bad enough, but the safety measures below ground were non-existent. There were a lot of accidents. Some were minor, but there were also a fair number that claimed lives. My colleague and I put together a set of basic safety protocols.'

'What kind of steps?' Sir John asked, thoroughly absorbed.

'We championed a lot of changes, duration of shift underground, maximum heat levels in the shaft, minimum dimensions of pit props, other steps too.'

'Sounds like expensive research,' Sir John added. 'How did you fund your efforts?'

'We found ways.'

Sir John studied his guest.

'And did you have any success?'

'At first, no,' acknowledged Erskine. 'There was a lot of resistance. But we expected it. On its own, none of this was going to reduce expenses and improve profitability. We spent months travelling the mines and townships, talking to the operators, and lobbying the owners.'

'*At first,* no?' queried Sir John.

'At first. Then the Komberley collapse came. The worst mining loss in the history of Africa.'

'I remember. And that changed things?'

'The mine was out of action for almost a year and most of the technicians - the ones who were on-site at the time - left to find other jobs. It made a big dent in the company's operations.'

'That must've been tough. It was an awful business.' A vague memory came back to Sir John. 'Wasn't there an Erskine involved in the enquiry afterwards?'

'Yes, that was me I'm afraid.'

'The poor devils who got caught underground,' Sir John continued. 'Terrible, those last few moments for them, like entering the gates of hell.'

'Yes,' said Erskine quietly.

Sir John noticed Erskine was pale. The engineer's hand trembled as he picked up his cup. A dreadful realisation came to him.

'There was a lot of bravery shown that day. There were survivors as I recall,' he added hastily.

Erskine was silent.

'And the loss of life, some good did come of it. With what came out of the enquiry.' He hesitated. 'And you were the investigator?'

'One of them.'

'And the safety proposals, they got a more receptive audience after that,' Sir John ventured.

'They did,' said Erskine grimly. 'I'm not pretending the industry's motives were altruistic, but I was happy to accept any reason in the interest of getting things done. And it has made a difference.'

'Remarkable. Truly remarkable. Out of such things can come change for the better. Well, that covers tenacity,' Sir John encouraged. 'How about the last two?'

'Intimidation and danger, they're two sides of the same coin. Pushing for the safety changes created plenty of the first one. There were a lot of threats from mine owners and operators, even shareholders. Some of it was violent, beatings and so on, at the site or even underground. But it didn't stop me, and, in the end, it paid off. As for danger...'

'Try working underground in a gold mine,' finished Sir John.

Erskine raised his eyebrows in acknowledgement.

'Are you still involved in mining?' Sir John asked.

'Yes, but these days it's more of an advisory role. Geological prospects, test drilling, financing, or due diligence on potential clients.'

'So, a sort of mining investigator?'

'Sometimes. I like the project roles, although there are times when the work strays into, let's say, grey areas.' Erskine managed a smile and studied the bottom of his cup. 'So how can I help you?'

Sir John set out the issues for the bank. When he explained the disappearances, Erskine could see Sir John's distress for the missing staff was heartfelt. As his potential client finished, Erskine made up his mind.

'I may need access to the bank's records,' Erskine said. 'But let me start with some basic research on the missing employees, just to get a feel for their routine.'

Sir John picked up the phone. 'Miss Denby, would you come in for a moment?'

The ever-prepared secretary appeared in the door and Sir John beckoned her in. He dealt with the introductions and then added,

'Erskine, Miss Denby has been with me for years. She's briefed on all this; I trust her completely. If you can't get hold of me, you can leave messages with her at any time.'

The two conspirators acknowledged each other with a smile, and Miss Denby withdrew.

Sir John stopped. 'I haven't asked, Erskine; how much do you charge for this sort of thing?'

The engineer laughed. 'I haven't thought about that.' He grinned, 'I'd better let you know.'

'Can I call you here and at home?' Erskine asked.

'Of course.' An afterthought occurred to Sir John. 'How is your colleague, the one who worked with you on the safety measures, I hope he survived too?'

'Yes, but he's a she. Amanda is still in South Africa, as far as I know.'

'I see,' said Sir John slowly. 'Friendships like that, where you go through adversity together, they often last a lifetime.'

Erskine examined his gleaming shoes. He left St Martin's with his new brief and lost in thought.

***

Sir John took a taxi back to Redshanks in better spirits than for some weeks. Following his meeting with Erskine, he had asked Miss Denby to arrange visits to the homes of the two missing people. He knew these would be difficult, but he wanted to assure the families that St Martin's was doing all it could. His bright 'good evening' to the staff echoed through the banking hall and reached the other listeners high above. They were also pleased with the day's events.

6

'Robert Erskine,' the headmaster rumbled, he sounded like a volcano. 'Young man, you are in serious trouble. I will be speaking with your parents later. No doubt they will wish to recall you from the school whilst we review your conduct in this matter.'

I can still remember what happened after my first experiment at school. Standing in the headmaster's office, with Mr Trowbridge himself, looking at me over the top of his spectacles.

Grownups get mad. There is the first sort, which is ordinary mad, like when I forgot to pass on an important message to Father. He was cross but it didn't last long, and although he called me Robert not Robbie for a while, I wasn't worried. Then there is the red faced mad. That's a bit worse. Grownups shout a lot, go red in the face, and might even break something if it's close by. That's a bit worrying but it wears off in the end. Then there is the white faced mad. That's really bad. The grownup looks sort of pale, but with a kind of black shadow on their face. They can't speak or shout, they just shake. That's scary.

The headmaster was white-faced mad.

I knew Strachan and I were in for it. But it wasn't our fault. Well, not just our fault anyway. We'd learnt about alchemy in class. How chemistry started as alchemy and then became chemistry, absolutely yonks ago. They'd tried all sorts of stuff we used in our chemistry classes. Things like Sulphur and Mercury, and Salt too. But they couldn't get it to work, make gold I mean.

Anyway, Strachan and I had a plan. What if we could make gold? After all, hundreds of years ago they didn't have the modern equipment we have now, test tubes and Bunsen burners and stuff. We would be rich. We went through it all standing outside the tuck shop. I said I could buy the whole shop if it worked, and Strachan said I'd explode if I didn't give him some sweets too.

Father sent me postal orders every week. I saved and saved like mad until we had enough money to go to the village shop and buy a 'boys own chemistry set,' obviously we couldn't use the school's stuff. But we needed to get the Mercury. That was dangerous and wasn't in the kit. It was Strachan who had the idea of buying some thermometers from the chemist in the village. That's a chemist for medicines not the other sort. We broke them open. I cut my hand, but Strachan said it was all in the interest of science and I should be proud. The salt was easy as we got some from the kitchens and the sulphur and the equipment were in the set.

We wanted to be somewhere quiet, so we went to the cricket pavilion, after all no one goes there in winter, apart from the groundsman. Well, that's what we thought, but when we were doing a 'recky,' Mr Telfer and Miss Hobbs came in. We said we were looking for 'Tonks,' our school cat. They said they were too. Which was dead lucky as we didn't know he was actually missing. After they left, we set everything up and flipped a coin to see who would *light it. Strachan won. I went outside to stand guard just in case, and Strachan stayed to light the mixture.*

Strachan said afterwards, that at first it seemed like it was working. There was a kind of hissing sound and the stuff in the bowl sort of melted. But then the noise got really loud. I could hear it outside even though I was hiding behind the sightscreen. Strachan ran out and shouted and we both legged it. Good job too.

The headmaster was sitting down at his desk, but we were standing. If you leant forward, you could see the pavilion out of the window over his shoulder. The firemen were packing up, but if you looked carefully, you could still see a bit of smoke coming through the hole in the roof. I thought they were laughing especially the big one, but it was hard to tell.

And that's when I came to my decision. If I couldn't make gold, then I'd look for it, and that's what I've done.

7

By the time Erskine began his investigation, Sir John had told him of a third disappearance.

'Hubert Heath, he's a single man. The branch called to say he hasn't reported for work. He was in good spirits the day before and no one at St Martin's seems to know what's happened to him.'

Erskine's research work on the staff had turned up nothing. As far as he could tell, the three missing employees had no common background or interest, except they all enjoyed a reputation for working late. No doubt, he thought, this was usually a quality valued at the bank, but as Sir John made it clear to Erskine, he now actively discouraged the idea. All he knew was they left work after hours, locked up their branch offices, and he assumed, set off for home.

None of them arrived. Erskine found no trace of them on their regular routes, or the platforms on which they would have waited for their trains. Their fellow commuters, all regulars who travelled back and forth at the same time, hadn't seen them either.

Erskine was sure he would find a human solution to the disappearances, but Sir John also warned him of the perils of the City when left to its own company. 'There's a malice in those stones,' he said. 'So many fortunes lost, and lives broken, be careful.'

Erskine worked on developing an understanding of the missing people. All three were well regarded employees. He found their career records, although unspectacular, were sound. The first, George Stevens and the third, Hubert Heath, were men who had embarked on a steady progression through the ranks at St Martin's Bank. The second of the disappearances was a woman, Harriet Simpson, who unusually for the bank, had moved across from secretarial work to help in a more senior role at St Martin's. None had put a foot wrong. Both men, Erskine noted, had one or two bad debts on their loan records, but as Sir John explained to him, this was better than no customer defaults at all.

'An unblemished record probably means the manager is using too conservative an approach to lending, it suggests the bank's assets aren't being used enough. Of course,' Sir John assured him, 'we don't want lots of defaults, but a few, well it shows just the right commercial approach... there has to be a degree of risk for our reward.'

Having satisfied himself of their characters from the bank's perspective, Erskine spent several days walking the streets of the City. He equipped himself with sketches of the employees and spent time in coffee shops, newsagents, and sandwich bars, hoping for some recognition from the proprietors, but with no results. The owner of the Lunchtime Lovelies sandwich bar recognised one of the missing three, but this turned out to be pre-disappearance.

'That's Hubert,' the man confirmed, slicing through some rare roast beef. 'He's a regular,' Erskine's interest sharpened, 'but I haven't seen him for a while.'

Erskine tested the proprietor on the character of the missing Hubert, but other than knowing his sandwich preferences and agreeing he was a 'hard worker, who often just rushes in and out to get back to his desk,' the owner of the shop had nothing helpful to add.

Erskine left and walked back down the Minories. As he turned out of the door, he felt uncomfortable. He had noticed the feeling as his research took him around the old streets. There was no sense of danger; if anything, the impression was one of something with a benign interest, it was there from time to time, as if he was being watched. He glanced around but there was nothing.

8

Slow Pony regular Silus Tarbert cursed under his beard. The pub, his pub, was irritatingly busy. The regular customers in the bar had been joined by stallholders from the funfair, visiting the village on its usual autumn tour. The rides were set up and the coconut shy and tombola were ready for their hopefuls in the morning, but now the gates of the fair were closed for the day.

It was the same each year during fair week and Silus knew what was coming. Crammed elbow tight on the bar, shouting for service and uncompromising, the fairs' people, without intending it, took over.

He liked the pub. The regular patrons were comfortable in the place and the publican looked after them. Silus could rely on having his pint topped up and measures were generous. The food, although basic, was excellent and the portions sizeable. But he knew on fair week there were no such indulgences.

Silus studied the noisy bar morosely. 'I don't know why I bother,' he muttered. He was jammed in the corner, leaning against the fireplace, trying unsuccessfully to take the weight off his feet. He eased from one leg to the other, and as he did, the beer tilted in his glass, although it never quite escaped. Having checked first to make sure none of the other customers were likely to take it, he placed his half empty glass on the mantelpiece. He discovered that with some adjustment of his stance, he could watch his beer, keep an eye on the progress of food appearing from the bar and stay in contact with his friend, who now stood scarcely a foot from the end of his nose.

His companion was Lambourne Tucker. Like Silus, he was an artisan who made a living from the gardens and large houses that ran along the banks of the nearby Thames. They often worked alongside each other, and over time had become friends.

'You bother because there's nowhere else you'd get a pie like the ones here,' Lambourne grinned. 'Stop complaining and sup up. You know it's always like this fair week and Maggie gets a lot of extra trade.'

'If we ever get one it'll be burnt,' Silus said with melancholy satisfaction, 'or cold.' He gestured at the crowded bar. 'There's too many in tonight. It's worse than ever.'

'Maggie will see to it, you watch,' said his companion. 'She always looks after us. Have you ever known it different?'

Silus moved to recover his beer from a cluster of other glasses that had joined it. He eyed these new arrivals on the mantlepiece with suspicion. Both men supped their drinks and then Lambourne edged even closer. His voice took on a conspiratorial tone.

'You did some work for MacGregor?' His face was now just a couple of inches from Tarbert's ear.

'Yes, I did. Cleared the ditches for their gardener Knapp, they were in a right state, smelled awful too.'

'And when was that?' asked Tucker.

'Just last week,' Silus confirmed. 'Why, has anyone said anything?' He looked anxious.

41

'And,' breathed Tucker, 'have you been paid yet?' He rocked forward in the best dramatic fashion.

'No, but I wouldn't expect to be paid until the end of the month.' Silus, despite his grumbles was a supporter of the MacGregor's, having worked on casual jobs for the house over many years. 'Why?'

'I've heard times are a bit hard at Redshanks, that's all,' Lambourne took a pull at his pint. 'Just make sure you do, get paid I mean.'

A familiar face appeared through the throng. Hands held high above her head and expertly navigating the crowd, Maggie, the barwoman, appeared carrying two pies.

'Here you are, gents,' she announced, 'though goodness knows where you're going to eat them. There's not a spare inch in here.'

The two friends received the pies, which Lambourne noted, were neither burnt nor cold. They tried to find a space on the fireplace range, but after some shuffling gave up. Silus inclined his head at the door. Maggie turned to make her way back to the bar, but Lambourne put his hand on her arm. He tried to adopt the same conspiratorial tone he had with Silus, but the hubbub in the bar made this impossible.

'Have you had any problems with the Redshanks' account,' he shouted into Maggie's ear. Several faces turned toward the group.

Maggie looked perplexed. She took half a pace back toward the two men.

'No,' she was closer to them now, 'but I've been warned to be prompt with my bill for this month. Such a shame,' she said unhappily. 'Sir John's a lovely man and a good customer.'

'I'm only passing on what I've heard, but I wish I knew where these rumours were coming from,' Lambourne added. 'They don't make sense, not with what I see.'

'They never do,' said Silus, nodding. 'But there's no smoke without fire.'

'Well, I'll present my monthly account to Mr Jelf as usual,' Maggie was defiantly supportive. 'And then let's see what happens.' She disappeared back into the crowd.

The two men, balancing the pies on top of their pints, edged their way out of the public bar and found a seat outside, next to the pub entrance. A fine place to sit in the summer with a drink, thought Silus, but he felt chilly now. They set about their food in silence. The Thames ran parallel to the road across the fields a hundred yards away and he watched the mist from the river roll up towards them as the evening drew on. Lights from nearby houses began to glimmer as the darkness intensified and the shadows deepened. The minutes passed. Silus spoke.

'You think there's something in it then, this business about Sir John?' he asked.

Lambourne stretched out his legs. A large piece of pie was occupying him, and it took a while before he replied.

'All I'm saying,' he eventually announced, 'is that's the word and it's all over the village.'

'But why? What's gone wrong?'

'Who knows what goes on with those swells from the City. Trouble is, when you've got more money than you can shake a stick at, things come undone fast.' Lambourne spoke with an air of hollow wisdom and there was the smallest hint of satisfaction in his voice, 'I'm glad I've a simple life.'

Silus was concerned, not just for Sir John and the house, but also for one of his main sources of income. He decided they were both matters he would need to resolve.

'I'm due up at the house on Thursday. I'll see what I can find out.'

The mist had reached the two friends, and the seat was cold and damp. Finishing their drinks they made their way back to the doorway, leaving the glasses on a windowsill rather than battle back into the pub.

Lambourne had not meant to add to Sir John's problems, but the group standing nearby had picked up his shouted exchange with Maggie. Included in the circle was Harold Norwood, proprietor of 'Norwood's Grocers' who supplied the house. As Silus and Lambourne left the pub, Norwood finished his drink and walked back up the lane to his shop to check Redshanks' outstanding invoices.

9

A week passed, and Erskine had made no real headway. He decided to experience the streets around St Martin's at night, hoping by timing his enquiries to match with the disappearances themselves, he might find something. He started in the early evening as the gaslights came to life, visiting the City pubs and taverns with sketches of the missing three. Through the smoke of the snugs and public bars, he showed the pictures, laying them out on the sticky tables, but no clues were forthcoming. Now the pubs were empty, and he'd made his way back to the start of his trail.

For Erskine, walking London's financial district after midnight was a strange experience. He was alone, in a place full of shadows, utterly in contrast with its atmosphere in the day. From nine in the morning until around five, clerks and bankers mixed with stockbrokers and secretaries, each one intent on their day, making their fortune or meeting their friends. At night, it was different, thought Erskine; no one lived in the old City. The streets were empty, and the vast stone offices were left to themselves. The only remaining inhabitants, looking down on him from the top of the oldest, most imposing buildings, were the grotesque grinning stone gargoyles.

It was under one of these gargoyles that Erskine now stood. It leered down at him above the door of St Martin's Bank in Swan Lane, the departure point for Hubert Heath.

Fog had begun to rise from the Thames a hundred yards away. It filled the streets and alleyways one by one like an incoming tide. It condensed on the brim of Erskine's hat, collecting in the rim, and then dripped freezing, liquid misery down the inside of his jacket. Not for the first time that night he shivered. He checked the doorway and set off through the chill night air on the route to Liverpool Street station. The sound of his footsteps echoed off the pavement and disappeared into the fog, lost in the passages of the City. He paused for a moment, thinking he had heard something, but all was silent.

Erskine's sense of isolation grew as the fog closed in. He turned into Castle Court and passed the George & Vulture. He knew it was one of the oldest pubs in London and had featured in the works of Dickens and he stopped to take in his surroundings. The sign hung motionless above his head, a picture of St George high on horseback, challenging a gigantic vulture, flame red and talons arched. The fog dripped off the sign, pooling between the cobbles below. For the second time on his journey Erskine thought he heard a noise, a surreptitious, quickly masked soft scurrying sound. He waited outside the pub, peering out into the fog. There was nothing.

Erskine was about to continue when a startling thought, a shocking awareness of a change in his surroundings registered with him. Looking back, he took in the scene again. It came to him, this change. The vulture on the sign had disappeared; the flame-red bird was gone. St George was now alone, slumped over the saddle. He was dead.

Erskine's heart beat fast and hard. He forced himself to walk back down the passage and stand under the sign. The fog was still dripping off the brim of his hat and he reached up to straighten it. The droplets were tinged with red. He tried to think slowly, to stay rational.

From high above, invisible in the fog, something made a rasping, hissing sound. The noise was aggressive and there was no mistaking the hostile intent. Erskine flinched despite himself and ducked into the doorway of the pub. The rasping stopped. He stayed under the shelter of the doorway, expecting whatever was above to eventually drop into the street. Wedging himself into the entrance, he settled down to wait.

The hours passed and there was no reward for Erskine's vigil. Fog had penetrated every fibre of his clothing, and the damp was in his bones. He stretched his aching limbs and checked his watch. Dawn was just appearing over the East End and the silhouettes of the City churches on the skyline were becoming clearer. The fog was thinning, and the anonymous grey shapes that had been there before were gone. He moved cautiously out of his doorway.

Something on the cobbles caught his eye. He stooped and picked up an enormous, mottled feather, as big as anything he had ever seen. He stowed it in his jacket and then forced himself to look at the sign. To his astonishment, the picture of St George and the Vulture was restored. They were back in combat, caught in the moment of attack, St George rising to meet the vulture on his horse, rampant and fearless. The vulture blazed down, talons poised, and wings outstretched, casting a shadow over the knight. But as he looked, he saw there was a gap in the silhouette of the vulture's outstretched wings, and a shaft of light cut through the shadow down onto the chain mail.

A feather was missing.

10

Sir John was in a sombre mood again. He sat in the back of the taxi and reflected on a distressing morning taken up with his visits to the homes of George Stevens and Harriet Simpson. He had made every effort to assure the families that both the police and the bank were doing all they could, but the situation was full of uncertainty and there was no way to hide from this.

George Stevens' wife was worried, but stoic.

'It's very thoughtful of you to come and see us, Sir John. George is a good man,' she said. 'I know he wouldn't be mixed up in anything wrong. The bank sees my George more than I do, no offence. What do you think's happened?'

Sir John sipped his tea and looked at the small boy staring up at him from the hearth. He knew how vulnerable the family would be if they lost their breadwinner. Opposite him there was a small photo frame on the sideboard, it showed them together on a beach. These were good people he thought, and they deserved better than to lose their husband and father.

'I don't know yet. But the bank has appointed a special investigator to work with the police to find out what's happened.'

'The police?' Margaret Steven's paled. 'So, it's that serious?'

The boy looked from Sir John to his mother.

'Not necessarily, Mrs Stevens. But we want to do everything we can to find your husband. We know he hasn't done anything wrong, and we just want to get him home safely,' Sir John hoped he sounded optimistic.

Margaret Stevens cast around the room.

'He doesn't talk much about the bank, he says it's confidential work and he mustn't talk about the customers.'

Sir John felt a rush of pride in his man, and he hoped more than ever that they would find the missing husband. He finished his tea and stood up.

'Thank you for seeing me. I'll make sure you're told straight away if there's any news. I know it's a worrying time, but I promise the bank will help wherever it can.' Sir John had already decided to look after this family and made a mental note to follow up with the chairman.

Margaret Stevens followed Sir John back to the front door. The small boy looked out from behind his mother's skirt as they stood on the threshold.

'Thank you very much, Sir John.'

The chief executive walked back to the taxicab and turned to offer one more encouraging wave, but the door was already closing, and the family were out of sight.

On arrival at Harriet Simpson's home, he found her parents had prepared for his arrival. They had laid out a 'high tea' and the china was set on freshly ironed linen in the 'best room.' They fussed around anxiously while they showed him in.

'We're very proud of our Harriet at the bank,' Arthur, Harriet's father, said earnestly. 'I hope it's nothing to do with her work, she's very conscientious.'

'Not at all, Mr Simpson. We're pleased with Harriet; she's done very well.' Sir John made sure his smile took in Arthur's wife Jean. As with Margaret Stevens he felt the family's pain and hoped they would find the daughter. He was fearful of what might happen, but kept his tone as optimistic as he could manage.

The three of them continued talking. Then, having eaten a slice of exceptionally good fruitcake and offered as much encouragement as he dared, Sir John made his way back to the waiting taxi. Arthur Simpson followed him out, and as the cabbie opened the door, the father put a hand on Sir John's arm.

'I know it doesn't look good, sir,' he spoke quietly. 'If things go badly, will you let me know before Jean gets to hear of it? I need to look after her and she isn't the strongest.'

Sir John glanced at the father; he pretended not to notice the tears in the man's eyes.

The taxi arrived at Redshanks. Sir John, his mood a mixture of sorrow and anger, descended from the cab and marched wordlessly past his butler and into the study.

11

Roy Coetzee, associate partner of Owen & Joost, Accountants and Auditors, worked in the firm's office on the west side of Eloff Street, close to Park Station in Johannesburg's commercial district.

Coetzee was new to the practice and keen to make his mark. It was an established business with strong links to the commercial life of South Africa. Like other accountants, the corporate clients were wide-ranging in terms of scale, type, and age. Again, like their peers, they had 'strong suits' in which they specialised and for Owen & Joost this was heavy industry, and in particular, mining. Chief among these was Rand Mining, a long-standing and valuable client, whose annual audit, Coetzee knew, produced substantial fee income.

The firm had been around long enough to have lost the 'Owen' from the partnership, but the name remained, in deference to the family, which still lived on the outskirts of Johannesburg. Coetzee reported to Joost, the other half of the firm who supplied much of the commercial 'nous' behind the ongoing business.

The office in which Coetzee sat had no air conditioning, and in summer, it was an oven. The firm was on the second floor, close enough to ground level to suffer the extra discomfort of the noise and dust of the street outside. This made opening the windows of debatable value. Some of the staff preferred the clean baking updraft of the interior, while others opted for the hot, dusty breeze and the intrusive noise of the traffic outside.

A dripping Coetzee was in the former camp. He sat at his desk, staring at the papers in front of him. The heat felt as though someone had lit a fire on the floor below and the flames were now reaching his office. Again, he reviewed the rows and columns of numbers that marched across and down the report, a report he had struggled with all morning. Understanding it had been easier in the cool of the early morning, but as his office grew hotter, the intricacies of the analysis began to escape him. He tried again but still couldn't allow himself to accept his findings.

Coetzee ran his finger around the inside of his collar to release its sticky hold. Levering himself out of his chair, he edged around the desk and took a short walk along the corridor. He tapped on a door and heard the familiar 'kom binne' before entering. Oliver Joost, Senior Partner, looked up from his papers.

'Roy, my vriend, how are you today?'

Joost was a heavy-set man in his late fifties. His shirt was stuck to him in crumpled, sweaty folds, and his thick neck protruded over his collar in bulbous hoops. Like Coetzee, he suffered in the heat, but as Senior Partner, he had first choice of office. Not unreasonably, Joost picked a position that until late afternoon, had the benefit of the shade of the clock tower at Rissik Post Office across the road. As a result, Joost subscribed to the open window school of office use since the air outside was marginally cooler.

Coetzee stood in the centre of the room his arms folded, grateful for the small drop in temperature. The dust from the street mixed with the smell of hot rubber.

'Good, thanks; how was your bridge last night?'

'We came third, barely satisfactory.' Joost sighed. 'Why Mrs Tufnell played the ace on the third hand I've no idea, otherwise we would have won outright.'

Coetzee smiled; he knew how dedicated a bridge player Joost was.

'I've been going through the figures on the Rand Mining audit,' he began.

'Ah yes,' Joost noted, 'how's that coming along? Are we able to sign off the accounts yet?'

'That's just it,' said Coetzee, shifting in the heat. 'I think there are some issues.'

Joost tipped forward and rested his elbows on the desk. 'What kind?'

'In simple terms they may have overstretched themselves.'

'Borrowed or expanded too much you think?'

'Yes.' Coetzee frowned unhappily, 'I think they're going to struggle.'

Joost, this time, was more assertive. 'You *think* they *may* struggle.'

'Yes, of course. It depends on the next few months and how they get on. Under most scenarios though, unless all their exploration is successful, they're going to need a big tailwind. It's possible they may go under.'

'Well, they are a mining company,' Joost remarked drily. 'They also happen to generate our single largest fee, which is payable by them once we sign those sheets of paper.' He nodded at the report held by the sweating Coetzee.

There was a silence between the two men. Coetzee became aware of the noise from the street. The shade from the Post Office Tower had moved on, and the room was getting hotter.

'Why don't you leave the figures with me?' Joost suggested, stretching out his hand for the papers. 'Our report is only an opinion and there may be several interpretations. Let me see if perhaps you have taken too cautious a view.'

Relieved of his burden, Coetzee nodded at his senior colleague.

'Thanks for your help. Let me know what you think.'

Coetzee went back to his office, which now seemed a little less furnace like. He already knew what Joost's conclusion would be.

12

The other tables at the café had yet to receive their first customers and Erskine was on his own.

After the night's experiences he had awarded himself a decent breakfast. He placed the order and took a seat at his usual window table. He watched through the dripping glass; the street was already busy with determined figures on their way to work. A few scarfs were in evidence, wrapped below the usual homburgs and slouch hats, signals of the coming colder weather. The rattle and clang of the buses and trams making their way up Cheapside added a noisy background to the rush hour. The autumnal morning air, which entered behind Erskine as he opened the door, had a sulphurous quality to it.

The steam from the coffee machine erupted and the skillet sizzled. The café owner busied himself with the first duties of the day, dotting the condiments across the tables and noisily adjusting chairs. The routines of the scene were reassuring to Erskine after his extraordinary night and he relaxed into the morning, going over his encounter, trying to rationalise it. He'd been unnerved at the time, he conceded, although no harm had come to him. What, if anything, had he learned from his experience?

The breakfast arrived and he dedicated himself to it. The proprietor completed his duties and came over to the table.

'A bit early for you, sir.'

Erskine glanced at his watch.

'Night duties,' he smiled.

'I hope it was worth it.'

'Not sure yet,' said Erskine, 'we shall see.' He was a man grounded in logic and refused to believe that other forces were at work. There was no reason to assume the disappearances were in any way linked to the incident with the sign and he was determined to keep the focus of his attention on the missing people. How best to pursue the case though?

He had made no progress at all. His study of the routes home used by the unfortunate employees had yielded no clues, and his questioning of the bartenders and waiters at the public houses on the routes, no leads. He was sure the disappearances were connected by something; they had to be, but what was the link? His instinct was that either they were in a criminal gang of some sort or had unwittingly stumbled across something going on at the bank and been silenced for it. The first seemed much less likely given their endorsement from Sir John, although he couldn't be certain. After all, he thought, Sir John wouldn't be the only proprietor fooled into thinking his staff were above suspicion. If they were caught up in something, he knew the chance of recovering them alive was remote. If that were true, finding them at all was going to be difficult given the amount of development in London and the opportunities to hide a body or bodies. Then there was the river.

Erskine finished his breakfast. The next step, he decided, would be another meeting with Sir John. He needed to know more about the bank and its customers. Erskine left payment by the plate and with a wave to the proprietor, made for the door and pulled it open. At once the busy sounds of London and the acrid air from the east end assailed him. He tugged down his hat and set out into the traffic.

13

Erskine wasn't the only one in a reflective mood that morning. Across London and out to the West, past the busy streets and spires of the old City, in the breakfast room of a much grander property than the café, Sir John MacGregor was starting his day.

The house, almost as old as the bank itself, was set in grounds that ran down to the edge of the Thames. The property had a jetty, and Sir John sometimes took his boat down the river to St Katharine's dock. From there he could disembark and walk into the City and St Martin's head office branch. He was extremely troubled by the disappearances, but this morning something else was also causing him concern.

Redshanks had a loyal staff and included a butler, gardener, cook and several other servants. Sir John was a fair man and turnover was low. He was a widower, and since the death of his wife, several of the longest-serving employees, whilst not friends in the full sense, had become his companions and even, in some moments, his confidants. It was to one employee, Arthur Bridges, the butler, he now voiced his thoughts. The butler had served him for many years and was often a route to the broader group. For this reason, he valued the man's counsel.

'Bridges – is everything satisfactory?'

Sir John put down his paper as he spoke, folding it neatly. A long association with his employees and a relationship built on trust and affection had given him a sense of when all was not well. In recent days, he had noticed a brittleness in their behaviour. 'Corner conversations,' as he called them, were frequent and always broke off as he approached. No one was quite at ease. He appreciated this was to be expected, everyone was slightly 'on parade' when he was near them. This was more than that though, he thought.

Bridges paused and then placed the kedgeree in the middle of the shining cutlery. He straightened.

'By and large, yes, sir.'

'By and large?' Sir John, used to the butler's manner, noted the hesitation. 'Is there an issue? Is it related to anything in particular?'

The butler measured his reply.

'There has been some gossip, Sir John. In the village. Some of the staff are a bit anxious.'

'About what, Bridges?'

'The tradesmen in the high street,' Bridges hesitated, 'some of the shopkeepers have been asking questions.'

'What about?'

'About their account, Sir John, whether we'll be settling soon. It's very unusual for them to be quite so... forward. I wonder if they have heard something...'

The practice of ordering on account by a big house was well established. Sir John knew some landowners used this as a form of unlimited free credit, and it was not unheard of for shops to bankrupt themselves supplying goods for slow or non-paying estates. Being in finance, Sir John knew the predicament for the tradesmen, many of whom relied on the patronage of the grand houses, and he made a point of keeping Redshanks' account up to date. He recognised it took a lot for a shop owner to chase up settlement as it risked losing the account, and with his record of paying on time this made the questions even more unusual. He frowned, reflecting on the worried air of the staff in recent weeks. At least he'd found the cause of it.

Sir John trusted Bridges. The man was a senior member of the house staff and with the right information Sir John knew, could be relied upon to introduce some calm to proceedings. He steepled his fingers together and thought hard, staring out of the window down the lawns to the Thames. The water was grey and steely in the autumn morning light, nothing disturbed its surface as it slid by.

The grandfather clock in the hall chimed eight.

There were only two reasons tradesmen pursued their accounts, he thought. One was if they were too much 'up against it' to worry about keeping the customer's patronage. But then, according to Bridges, it sounded as though more than one shop had raised the question. The other was if they thought the customer's credit was in doubt. This was, to his certain knowledge, not the case. So, he wondered, what had caused the uncertainty? He could imagine the gossip in the high street. Like a run on a bank, a loss of confidence could be disastrous for the household. Gossip and speculation might damage the long-term prospects of anyone associated with it, services would dry up, and suppliers would avoid the account. He made up his mind.

'Bridges, there's no problem, I can assure you.' But that's what I would say he thought. 'Ask Jelf to come in would you.'

Bridges left the room and Sir John, for a few minutes, turned his attention to the kedgeree. Eventually the butler returned with the man responsible for keeping the house accounts. Jelf was a bespectacled, grey, dusty man, who, like Bridges, had been with the house for many years. Sir John entrusted him with routine financial matters, including the staff wages and the settlement of the tradesmen's bills.

Sir John smiled encouragingly at Jelf, who stood at the far end of the long breakfast table, hands folded behind his back. He addressed Jelf directly, knowing Bridges would take in every word and both men would pass on the exchange to the whole household.

'When was the last time we settled our accounts in the town?' he asked. He had the answer but wanted to underline his next action.

'The end of last month.' Jelf knew Sir John kept a close watch on finances. 'It was the end of the quarter, and we settled as we always do.' A trace of puzzlement escaped in his voice.

'Of course, yes excellent,' Sir John noted. 'I want to make a special settlement at the end of this month, just to help the suppliers fund their Christmas stock.' Jelf and Bridges did their best, but Sir John could see they were taken aback. 'Also,' he continued, 'I want to advance them a notional sum, say ten pounds, as a credit against our Christmas order.'

The two men eyed each other.

Sir John was warming to his task. 'And one more thing. I'm going to increase the staff Christmas bonus this year from one to two weeks extra wages. Make sure the arrangements are made please, Jelf.'

Sir John, amused to see Bridges and Jelf exchange glances, watched the men's faces. His actions, judging from their expressions, bordered on the reckless.

They left Sir John to his breakfast and made their way back into the main body of the house. A few paces down the corridor, they held an impromptu meeting.

'What on earth was that in aid of?' Jelf said animatedly, his sober grey persona shaken out of its normal state.

Bridges knew his master well. 'A military man would describe it as a show of strength,' he said. 'How many trade accounts have requested settlement already this month?'

'Around half a dozen, including two of the largest.'

'I assume Norwood's is one?'

'And Sampson's Coke and Coal,' said Jelf. 'Even the man who cleared the ditches, Tarbert, Knapp told me he'd been round too.'

'I've every faith in Sir John, but I admit I've been concerned, no smoke without fire,' Bridges looked at his shoes.

Jelf gestured in the direction of the breakfast room. 'It's unsettling. But what are we to make of all this?'

'I'd say the master is determined to put a stop to the gossip.'

'By showing such recklessness?' Jelf was still in shock. 'Well, it will stop *that* gossip, but you can be sure it will start a different sort altogether.'

'What sort?'

'Anything from the onset of senility to the discovery of a gold mine in the garden.'

'We'll have to see,' smiled Bridges.

They set off down the stairs and arrived together at the kitchen door. Bridges turned the handle,

'But first we should pass on the good news.'

Via Bridges and Jelf, the rest of the household received word of Sir John's generosity with varying degrees of astonishment. By the next morning word had travelled down into the village. From his shop window, Norwood saw first one, then another and then two more tradesmen walking past in animated conversation. He came out onto the street in time to waylay Ed Sampson the coal merchant.

'What's going on, Sampson?'

'Word is we're to report to the big house at our earliest convenience.' Sampson saw the expression on Norwood's face, it was clear he feared the worst.

'No, it's nothing like that. Our account's going to be settled today and,' he hesitated, 'there's some talk of payment in advance for Christmas stock. There's a bit of a rumour,' Sampson went on, 'that Sir John's come into money, but lord knows he's rich enough already, so heaven knows how much it is.'

Norwood turned back into his shop. 'Hang on,' he called, 'I'll get my book.' He reappeared clutching his ledger, and the two men walked up the hill together toward the house.

Over the next few days Richmond's tradesmen made their way up to Redshanks, where Jelf met them and settled their outstanding account. The bookkeeper also reviewed the money Redshanks spent the previous Christmas and made an advance in proportion to this expense. Strictly speaking, Jelf acknowledged to himself, this was not as Sir John instructed, but he couldn't quite bring himself to provide *every* business with the full ten pounds. This way, he reasoned, the shopkeepers were well set up, without the complete lunacy of using the full budget. Given time, he thought, Sir John would have seen the sense in this arrangement.

Sir John for his part, was sure the talk of the financial ruin of Redshanks would end. He was satisfied that the gossip would stop, but he was baffled why it had started at all.

14

Terence Knapp, Redshanks head gardener, leant on his fork. News of the increase in his Christmas bonus, as well as the settlement of the trade accounts, was puzzling him. Most employees had taken this at face value, but some tried to find a reason for it and Knapp was one of them. He was no fool and although an artisan, he had studied for his post, securing professional standards.

Sir John's actions had swept away the village's concerns about Redshanks. Talk in the high street now was of a secret source of Redshanks wealth, uncovered by the MacGregor family. Knapp was determined to find the real reason for the generosity, and he worried away at the issue, just like weeding, he thought.

Today though, Knapp's focus was on the gardens, damp and heavy from autumn rain. Frosts were only a week or two away and the pale yellow lights from the house formed halos in the early morning chill. Knapp was a consummate gardener and knew every part of the landscape. The vegetable garden where he stood, was the area closest to the rear of the house and abutted the kitchen, giving the cook easy access. A full crop of winter root vegetables was pushing up through the soil, and he could already see the tiny green shoots pricking through the surface.

The walled garden stood off to the right of the house. The summer blooms of the clematis were gone, and only their desiccated brown stems wound around its wrought iron gates. A narrow brick path led from the kitchen along the side of the vegetable plot, before turning down onto the lawns below. These shared the garden with Knapp's rose beds, and in summer the lawn and the roses offered a beautiful view offset against the backdrop of the river behind them. At present though, the roses were simply a tidy set of stark structures, with little to recommend them other than the skill he brought to bear on their preparation for spring.

Knapp's duties gave him flexibility and he saved time for himself. He took an interest in worldly events, which he followed by reading the newspapers that arrived in the greenhouse as liners for the garden pots. Sir John's broadsheet journals held little interest for most of the staff and other than Sir John's neat folds, they reached him unspoilt.

Knapp devoured them. Every story, every comment, the changes in tone and messaging of the papers approach to a storyline, he studied them all. But on this occasion, Knapp had worked out that there was a problem at the bank, not by following the news but by using his powers of observation. He was aware the issue, whatever it was, had been kept from the papers and house staff, but Knapp had seen enough to know there was trouble somewhere.

The first time Erskine visited Redshanks, Knapp recognised him from newspaper photographs and accounts of the Komberley accident and following enquiry. Knapp made sure he worked in the gardens at the front of the house for several hours after the visitor's arrival. This meant he was able to overhear Sir John and Erskine speaking on the drive at the end of their meeting. Leaning on his fork, Knapp reconstructed this now.

His master had said he would prefer to meet at the house rather than in the City, and Erskine agreed. There was a reference to some kind of problem, and Knapp assumed that something had happened at the bank. At the time, he linked this to the rumours from the town and the worries about the household's solvency. This now seemed impossible, given the apparent health of Redshanks' finances.

He had considered the alternatives, including potential health issues for Sir John, although to Knapp, this was unlikely. After all, he thought, Erskine was no doctor. From his newspaper reading, he knew the visitor was from a mining background. He wondered if Sir John had decided to back a venture, personally or with the bank as the investor. Knapp decided he would pay even closer attention to events at the house.

His thoughts returned to the job in hand, where he was preparing the garden for winter. A major pruning project was underway, and Knapp ran his eye approvingly down the geometric lines of the plants. Yes, he thought, there was more news to come from Redshanks.

15

Erskine remembered that evening in South Africa. He'd spoken well and felt the adrenaline of success. Through the fug of the cigarette smoke that hung heavy in the club, beyond the yellow footlights that picked out the tiny stage he was standing on, he could sense the miners, come to hear him. There was a hum of interest, of approval and he was excited.

He could see Amanda speaking to the men, spreading the message of mine safety. He watched her slim figure outlined against the lights, blocking and releasing their thin beams, as she crossed in front of them.

They had worked hard on the project, Erskine thought. At the beginning they had presented to mine owners and operators, who received them with a mixture of hard-boiled indifference and outright hostility. They changed tack and took their cause to the mines themselves, speaking with the miners and holding meetings. Their efforts had begun to receive attention, slowly gaining interest amongst the workforce. The next step was to revisit the owners and operators and try again to secure their support. They were convinced improved safety would ultimately lead to less 'downtime' and better production, but this had not translated into action on the part of the businesses themselves.

He remembered the assaults too, the one in the club especially.

A heavy hand descended on his shoulder, gripping his neck. The pressure of the thumbs turned his head to one side.

'A word my vriend if you will,' the voice in his ear was thick Afrikaans and the breath smelt stale and sour. Another hand pushed into the small of his back, and he felt himself propelled off the stage.

He tried to catch a view of Amanda, but the chance was gone. Erskine struggled for his footing, but the men forced him off the platform and pushed him through a door and out into the corridor. Three men other were waiting. His assailant pushed him face first into the wall opposite. His arms were pinned to his side, and he could taste the salt of his own blood.

'These gentlemen would like to speak to you.' The sour smell was there again, and the man turned him around. A square set, red necked man, in a tight-fitting shirt, spoke first.

'Mr Erskine. Your concern for the safety of your fellow miner does you credit,' the neck got even redder. 'But we think you need to look closer to home.'

A second man in a dirty brown jacket spoke up. He was breathing hard. 'That girlfriend of yours is a beautiful woman. You should be concerned with her safety, Vriend.'

'And worry less about those Neanderthals back there,' the stale smell came again.

'We can find you any time we like and as for her...' The brown jacket made an obscene gesture.

The third man spoke. His accent was lighter, and he held himself apart from the group ranged around Erskine.

'What's it to be, Mr Erskine? Will you be leaving your lovely girlfriend to the tender mercies of the... ah, night? Or can we rely on you giving up this, this money wasting crusade?'

The red necked man punched him in the stomach. There was a kick on the back of his leg, and he went down. He raised his arms in defence, but the boots kept coming. Darkness closed over him.

16

Erskine strode into the lobby of Le Homard. There was no place quite like it in London and supper this evening held a special attraction. The golden lighting and rich red upholstery of the restaurant beckoned him as he greeted George, the maître de.

After the meeting with Sir John, he had begun thinking again about his old life in South Africa. Where was Amanda, and how was her business doing? He spent his time outside of the investigation calling contacts and journalists who covered the mining industry. Eventually he discovered that Amanda was raising finance for a new venture, and astonishingly, this had brought her to London.

He had finally intercepted her schedule at the offices of Dammar Security, who supplied support and protection for senior industrialists. No doubt he thought, Amanda would explain why she was using such strict protection. She was a courageous woman, so there must be something afoot.

'Mr Erskine, so good to see you again,' beamed George. 'Your guest is already here - we've made her comfortable.'

Involuntarily Erskine glanced up and across to his usual table. Amanda was there, on time, business-like and beautiful. He crossed the room with George, and she rose, smiling and relaxed, as he approached. Amanda was a tall redhead, and Erskine thought, still dazzled. He was pleased to see that she had kept her penchant for low backed green dresses to set off her flaming hair, and her fiery green eyes danced as he approached. Erskine drank her in as he reached the table. She still wore the long necklace looped down her back, Wallace Simpson style. Despite her years in the blazing African sun, she had somehow kept her clear pale complexion, and for Erskine, the effect of this combination against the golden lighting and rich red backdrop of the restaurant made him catch his breath.

'Robert, this is fabulous.' Erskine remembered that low smoky voice, which still sounded to him like something from a jazz quartet. They kissed shyly but held each other close.

'Wonderful,' he took his seat as George stood behind it. 'Where are we going to start? It was a tough task tracking you down.'

'Well, you *are* an investigator, Robert.' Amanda smiled. 'I'm surprised it took you this long.'

Erskine looked at Amanda across the fresh white linen on the table. He could see she kept the professional deportment of a woman in business. Her angular features had been hardened slightly by the years, but there was no lessening of the energy and charm she'd had throughout their relationship. Amanda twisted her hair but held his gaze.

'I found you in the end.' Erskine pulled at his tie and straightened the cutlery. 'But what brings you to London?'

'The usual,' Amanda smiled. 'It's really terrific to see you again.'

The waiter arrived and they fell silent. It felt to Erskine as though they were catching their breath, taking in the years that had passed between them.

'You look good, Robert,' Amanda eventually said. 'Glad to see you're taking care of yourself. I hope things are going well for you?'

'Yes, not bad at all.' He added, 'Are you here in London on your own?' Then wished he hadn't.

Amanda looked at him, her eyes crinkled at the corners and there was a touch of something, sympathy or regret, Erskine couldn't tell.

'Yes, just me.' She looked down at the white tablecloth.

They placed their order and turned to each other again.

The restaurant was filling fast, but the table was a good one and Erskine knew they could speak without anyone overhearing them. 'There aren't many mines in London, so let's have it, what's the project?'

Amanda leant forward. 'True, but there are lots of investors here.'

Erskine nodded his understanding over the soup.

'Have you had much luck?'

'There's plenty of interest, the trick is to convert it into something solid,' Amanda went on. 'No one wants to be the first to put their money in. It's a kind of Indian rope trick. You must convince at least one investor that the others are already in or as good as, and then they will commit. Once you get the rope 'up' as it were, the rest will believe in the venture, and then you get the support you need.'

'And once the rope is up, what's the venture going to be?'

Amanda's voice lowered. 'Platinum. A lot of it. In the Transvaal.'

'Have you got positive samples then?' Erskine asked.

'Not yet but very soon. The geology is very promising and the mix with other deposits makes sense. I'm sure of it. I need to press on. My licence there won't last forever, but I have the unions with me, too, which is a big step forward.'

'Well done on the unions. So, what's next, backing money? I assume that's why you're here?'

The entrée arrived; they talked about the difficulty of securing investment for a mining project.

When they pushed their plates away, Amanda remarked:

'The problem is, as Mark Twain said, the definition of a mine is "a hole in the ground with a liar standing next to it." This doesn't help build confidence,' she hesitated. 'But how are you now?'

Erskine straightened and sat back in his chair.

'Pretty good,' he acknowledged.

'What does that mean?' Amanda regarded him steadily over the rim of her glass.

'I'm back in the swing of things,' Erskine said. 'Life's treating me well and there's plenty to keep me busy.'

'Well, that sounds like an improvement,' she put down the glass. 'We've done well for a couple of rookie engineers.'

'Not very rookie these days.' Erskine grimaced, but then he laughed. 'If only!'

'We were quite something back at the start,' Amanda said. 'Hard going but we made a difference.'

They certainly had.

Erskine remembered the evening of their first encounter at the firm's party. Amanda, a recent graduate, was a passionate, driven engineer and her commitment to the project they worked on was total. South Africa was a dangerous place, and at the beginning, he'd been worried for his new colleague. A few weeks with Amanda dispelled his concerns. She had a robust personality, and he quickly realised she wasn't intimidated by the grizzled Afrikaners who ran the mines.

Individual security and safety were critical areas for everyone at the installation, especially for a woman, but Erskine learned Amanda was risk conscious and was careful not to get herself into any tight spots. This awareness, borne out of a tremendous vein of common sense, had not just been for her own account, though.

'Do you remember all those long nights on research,' she said.

How could he forget?

'We were sure the new tunnel structures were better,' she continued.

'And we knew the costs were high,' rejoined Erskine.

Amanda stared into her glass.

'We had to fund the work somehow,' he continued, 'and it was for the long term good of the miners.'

'My God we were right.' Amanda's South African accent came on stronger as her passion for the subject increased.

'Even then we might never have convinced them,' said Erskine.

'But,' Amanda faltered.

'Yes,' Erskine said, 'but for the losses.'

'Which made it even more important, we had to finish that work, no matter what.' Amanda fell silent. A sigh escaped her.

'But you, you're alright now though?' she asked eventually. 'So, you say?'

'Pretty good,' Erskine repeated. 'Pretty good.'

For a while, both retreated into their own thoughts. The waiter returned with the plat principal.

'Who have you approached?' Erskine asked, 'or more to the point, who's interested?'

Amanda became the businesswoman again.

'There's a lot of interest. We have some strategic investors and some passive ones. Quite a few big fish are circling.'

'Strategic?'

'Some investors are passive and just give us seed money, they get us going in exchange for a small share of the profits. But some want part ownership and a say in the running of things, those are the strategic ones.'

'What about loans?' asked Erskine. 'Couldn't you help fund it using loans? That way, the mine is still owned by you?'

The businesswoman was in full flow, 'Yes agreed, and we are in contact with a few banks. We'll take out some borrowing, if we can get the right terms, but that's not always easy when it comes to funding exploration.'

'Which investors do you have?'

Amanda half closed her eyes. 'Mining Investment Ventures, Associated European Funding, CLM and Terra Nova Funding.' She folded her arms on the table.

'Who are CLM?' asked Erskine – 'I haven't heard of them before.'

'Consolidated London Mining. They want a strategic role,' explained Amanda. 'Bright lot, new firm, they asked some tough questions.'

'I hope they stump up,' observed Erskine. 'Do you do any research on the new investors?'

'Absolutely.' Amanda said emphatically. 'I haven't spent all these years trying to improve the mining industry,'

'Only to take dirty money,' Erskine finished.

Amanda leant forward, tapping the prongs of her fork on the table.

'I'm curious. What do you do with this research?' Erskine asked.

'We cover the mining side using our industry contacts. But for non-industry investors, where we haven't come across them before, we use a more covert approach.'

'Intriguing,' Erskine raised his eyebrows. 'Sounds as though you have it all covered. But if you need any help on the covert work let me know.'

Amanda folded her hands under her chin.

'So that's what you meant by keeping busy.' She opened her eyes wide in friendly mockery.

The evening continued with the two of them swapping experiences and personal history since they were last together, enjoying each other's company as they had always done. Dinner was over and they were close to calling their cabs when Amanda, for the third time, asked Erskine's for reassurance.

'Yes, I *promise* I'm ok, really.' He hesitated and then added, 'I'm on a strange case just now though.'

'Aha!' Amanda exclaimed. 'Now that does sound intriguing. Let's have a brandy; you can tell me about it.'

They relaxed back into their chairs. Erskine knew Amanda could be relied upon to keep things to herself, and he welcomed the chance to talk through the case with someone, especially as intelligent an operator as this beautiful woman, a woman now back in his world.

'I was contacted by a surgeon who worked on my knee after Komberley,' he began. 'Some people have gone missing here in London.' Erskine recounted the events of the bank employee disappearances, leaving out the identities of those involved, including St Martin's itself. He also missed out the episode of the George and Vulture but returned to it at the end. He expected Amanda to roll her eyes dismissively, but he was surprised to find she looked interested. If he was right, there was also a flicker of something else, misgiving perhaps.

'So, no trace of anyone at all,' Amanda said rhetorically. 'Seems like dirty work afoot. Is there anything that links them, other than the bank itself I mean?'

'Nothing yet, but I'll keep digging. Any thoughts?'

Amanda looked past Erskine's shoulder and into the middle distance. A habit Erskine remembered from their days together.

'If I were you,' she said slowly, 'I'd find out which customers they looked after and see if you can identify any transactions that might seem odd.'

'Like loans for example?'

'Yes, but not domestic stuff. Not big enough. Business loans and commercial arrangements, that's the kind of thing.'

'You think they might be mixed up in something?'

'Yes, but not *necessarily* on the dubious end. It might be they've stumbled across something, and it has gone badly for them.'

'I'm going to look at the bank's records anyway; I can include this in my review. Any other nuggets?'

Amanda laughed.

'Never far from the mining metaphor, Robert, I see.'

He chuckled too. The evening had gone well.

'I may need help on this stuff, are you around for a while?'

'Yes, I'll be here until I raise the money, or give up and go home,' Amanda said lightly. 'You know where I'm staying?'

Erskine didn't, but Amanda let him know it was White's, a well-appointed hotel in Mayfair.

'Very nice,' noted Erskine, 'and expensive too, no doubt.'

Amanda sighed.

'Yes, it is. Not in my budget normally, but on trips like this you need a smart address in case a backer wants to call. It's all part of the rope trick.'

Erskine smiled.

'Yes, I can see how that might be important. Just as long as I'm not *roped* into paying for any of it.'

Amanda grinned again.

'If you need help, my rates aren't cheap.'

They rose and made their way arm in arm to the foyer. The door attendant saw their approach and, at a signal from Erskine, moved to summon a cab, stepping out into the fog which had rolled into London once more. Amanda turned to Erskine.

'This, whatever you call it, apparition, you saw during your night research. What do you put that down to?'

'That's the biggest puzzle of all.' Erskine sighed. 'I know what I saw, and it's completely nonsensical.'

'You hadn't been on the sauce?' Amanda suggested without mischief.

'No, not at all.'

'Medication?' Amanda asked gently.

'No, not these days,' Erskine squeezed her hand. 'I really am ok now you know.'

'You mentioned the fog was very thick, could you have been fooled by that?'

'I don't think so. I might have missed something in the fog, but to see something that shouldn't have been there, that's altogether different. And then there's the feather.' He thought for a moment, 'No, no it doesn't work.'

'But you've seen nothing else, nothing that seemed, sort of, unearthly?'

'No, but I've felt, well I suppose you could call it unsettled, as if I'm being watched.' He couldn't bring himself to say anything stronger.

Amanda continued to look worried, Erskine thought. He tried to put her mind at rest.

'Listen, I'll follow up with the bank and let you know if there's anything you could help with. I promise I'll look out for, shall we say, the unusual. In the meantime, you press on with your rope trick.'

'Get straight back in touch if you have anything you'd like to talk through,' Amanda said. Erskine could feel her anxiety.

The cab arrived and they climbed in, moving off in the direction of White's hotel. The journey was a short one, but as they travelled along the south side of Grosvenor Square, Amanda smiled at Erskine. 'It would be nice to find a reason to work together.'

There was a warmth between them again, and Erskine felt better than for a long time.

'Yes, it would,' he said. 'We must make sure it happens. Don't go anywhere now...'

The cab reached White's. Erskine got out and made his way around to the curb. He opened the passenger door and Amanda stepped out. She kissed him on the cheek.

'Goodnight, Robbie.' Her husky voice was more in evidence than ever. 'Take care, promise me.'

He hadn't heard her use his name that way in years.

'Don't worry, and I'm not letting you get away from me after all this time,' he said.

Erskine watched her enter the hotel. What an evening it had been. He climbed into the taxi, which swept back into the traffic and home. Not he thought as smart as Whites, but it would do.

17

Du Carne Court was a block of apartments on the Balham High Road in South London. Erskine had moved there soon after the development was completed, and he enjoyed its closeness to the open spaces of Clapham Common. The heart of London, with all its hurly-burly was within easy reach, but it was distant enough to create a marked change of pace once the door closed behind him. It was here the cab took him at the end of the previous evening, and it was here that Erskine now stirred into life.

On waking he could see sunlight around the edges of the curtains. This meant the fog which had plagued London for several days, was, for the time being, in retreat. Erskine rose, stretched, and drew back the blinds. Thin autumn sunshine had found its way into the apartment courtyard. There was warmth where it landed, and the western corner of the quadrangle occupied by his flat felt like a sun trap. He opened the steel Crittall windows and inhaled the lukewarm dusty air.

The discussions of the previous evening crowded back in on him, and he thought about Amanda's suggestion. The idea of a common theme was an obvious one, but his efforts so far had focused on the bank's own staff, rather than the involvement of an outside group or gang. Erskine was due to call Sir John, and he decided to follow this up at the same time.

An hour later, breakfasted and ready, Erskine was about to pick up the telephone when there was a knock at the door. He opened it to reveal an earnest looking middle-aged man with a notebook and pen. The figure was faintly familiar.

'Mr Erskine, so glad I caught you in.'

Erskine examined his visitor, who clearly knew who he was, he tried to place him.

'Yes, thank you, won't you come through, Mr...'

'Oberdean's the name, yes I will.' The man eased past him in the doorway, there was the smell of carbolic soap. That was familiar too.

'I've been meaning to call in,' Oberdean continued, 'after our chat in the foyer the other day.'

Erskine remembered him now, but what was the chat about?

'So glad to bump into a fellow music lover, especially one who shares the same passion.'

'Passion?' Erskine was still unsure of his ground.

'Bandstands,' said his visitor brightly. Then with a nervous laugh added, 'Well, one bandstand, actually.'

Erskine was floundering. 'Remind me.'

'Clapham Common?'

Erskine could see Oberdean wasn't going to be put off his stride by his own failure to grasp the point.

'We both agreed the bandstand on the common needs repair. I think at the time,' Oberdean bobbed deferentially, 'at the time, you agreed to donate to the bandstand fund. I'm here on behalf of the fundraising committee.'

'Of course,' Erskine remembered. How had this come about? He'd been out walking and passed the bandstand. A brass band were playing. The tune continued in his head, and when he got back to Du Carne Court, he had been buttonholed by Oberdean who had overheard his whistling. He realised the man must have followed him in, he certainly didn't live in the flats. Somehow, they had got into a discussion about the bandstand, and he must have agreed that a refurbishment was due. And here was Mr Oberdean, come to collect. Well, he thought, hats off.

'What's the donation?' Erskine asked. He glanced at his watch; it really was time to be calling Sir John.

'Well, it's not for me to say,' Oberdean shuffled his feet.

'What are other people giving?'

'We have quite a lot of donations between one and two pounds.' Oberdean tried a winning smile.

Erskine cast around for his jacket and saw it hanging over the chair. He walked across and, removing his wallet, took out three one-pound notes.

'Would this be acceptable?' he asked.

'Thank you, that *is* excellent.' A thought seemed to strike the man. 'The Committee you know. It's always looking for new blood. I don't suppose you could be prevailed upon?'

Erskine was already manoeuvring Oberdean back through the door, he pretended not to hear. 'I shall look forward to seeing the new bandstand in all its splendour in the spring,' he added.

Oberdean tried to hold his ground, but Erskine outflanked him in the doorway and the fundraiser was soon retreating out onto the landing.

Erskine closed the door. Perhaps, he thought, he should have agreed to help. After all, raising money for a bandstand was nothing compared to funding campaigns for mining safety.

He picked up the telephone.

Miss Denby put Erskine through. Sir John greeted his investigator warmly.

'Good morning, Erskine, what news?'

'Nothing so far, no real progress yet. There's plenty to work on though. I think I mentioned to you I'd like to review things at the branches. Could someone arrange for me to see the setup, please?'

'Of course, Erskine, what sort of thing are you checking for?' Sir John sounded intrigued.

'To tell the truth, I don't know, but I want to get a feel for the workplace of the employees. I'd like to compare the branches with one where no one has gone missing.' Erskine knew it was a fishing trip, but getting a feel for operations would be helpful.

'Also,' he followed up with the more delicate matter, 'I want to take a look at the business they approved in the weeks leading up to their disappearance.' Erskine could sense the flinch at the other end of the telephone, and he squeezed his eyes shut, waiting for the rebuff.

To his surprise, after a few moments, Sir John replied,

'If you think that'll help, then of course you should see the files. I can't let them leave the bank, though.'

The two men reviewed the timetable for the investigation. They agreed Erskine should conduct the on-site visits at each branch first, before going back to inspect the transactions. He agreed to Sir John's request, rather extravagantly in his view, to use a disguise for the on-site trips so as not to spread any more alarm amongst the staff. They decided he should adopt the persona of an architect, a Mr Robert Newbone, whose firm had been appointed by St Martin's to carry out a refurbishment of each branch. The fictitious Newbone was visiting each location for the purpose of quoting for the work.

'Your engineering background will come in useful as part of your cover,' Sir John suggested.

The two men agreed this would at least allow him to appear genuine, even if he lacked the technical specifics.

Sir John also agreed the books and records of each missing employee be moved to the head office branch for review. Erskine noted he would have to change from architect to auditor for this purpose. Finance was not his strong suit, he knew, but he was working on an idea.

The disappearances had occurred at three branches: Swan Lane, Embankment, and Hope Street, Blackfriars. He planned to visit these locations after sampling one untouched by the recent events, so that he could establish the 'norm' for St Martin's operations. The bank bestrode London like few others and there were plenty to choose from. He selected two 'benchmarks', the Lombard Street City branch, and the branch in the Strand. The inestimable Miss Denby made the arrangements for him and dates were set for 'the architect' to visit each branch.

Two days later Erskine arrived at Lombard Street. The manager, John Tuff, came forward to greet him as Erskine gave the receptionist his name.

'Mr Newbone, good morning.' Tuff was wearing a morning coat with a white waistcoat and silver tie. He was bespectacled and his once black hair was now grey and retreating up his forehead. He shook Erskine's hand with enthusiasm. 'Welcome to our branch. I've received my instructions,' he smiled again. 'When Miss Denby calls, we are ready to spring into action at her command.' Tuff emphasised the word 'spring' with good humour.

Erskine guessed that Miss Denby, on her metal, would be a fearsome assistant to Sir John.

'Well, as long as I have a desk and access to the whole branch, that's all I need.' he said.

The manager showed Erskine to a part of the bank behind the teller's counter, where they had cleared a place for him.

The branch was a busy one, unsurprising Erskine thought, given its location at the heart of the financial district. The customers who came and went were almost all businessmen of a certain 'type', being well dressed and with an air of industry about them. They weren't disrespectful to the bank staff, Erskine thought, but they held them at a slight distance. Their exchanges were polite but lacked engagement, although it was clear they regularly dealt with the same people.

Erskine began measuring walls, spaces, doors, and windows in an effort to appear the architect he was supposed to be. He made notes, licked his pencil, and studied the customers.

Eventually, he found himself in the post room, where he met the bank's messenger boy, sorting through internal mail envelopes for other St Martin's branches. The messenger eyed him quizzically.

'Haven't seen you before sir,' he said. 'I'd better note your name.'

Erskine stared at the messenger.

'What for?' he asked, almost slipping out of character.

'In case I get any post for you. If there are any new people, I need to know.'

'Well,' said Erskine, 'my name's Newbone, but you won't get any post for me, I'm only visiting today.' He explained the arrangements. 'But now you have to tell me your name too.'

'James Bennett. I'm the messenger, I deliver letters and files to all the branches around here. And some beyond that when it's needed. I'm glad they're thinking of sprucing the place up, it's very grand but...' he tailed off, concerned he'd said too much.

'A bit dated?' suggested Erskine.

'Yes,' Bennett was relieved. 'Are you working on lots of branches?'

'Yes, quite a few.' Erskine had an idea. 'So, you get to see all the branches then. This seems like a nice place, are they friendly here?'

'Mostly,' Bennett said. 'They can get a bit uppity if things don't go to clockwork mind, but that's the same everywhere.'

'What about the other City branches? I'm going to be visiting them too this week.'

'They're alright I suppose. Not all the customers are as posh as they are here though,' he glanced at Erskine again. 'They have some right strange ones. Strange names too. I deliver to them sometimes, all parts of London, even out west.'

'Have you ever done anything unusual here?'

His new young friend furrowed his brow.

'What d'you mean?'

'Oh, I don't know, maybe an unusual parcel, an odd customer or a delivery at a strange time of day?' Erskine began to wonder if his architect cover was wearing a bit thin, but Bennett seemed to take his questions as simply gossip.

'You get all sorts of requests here,' he chuckled, 'nothing surprises you after a while.' He had completed his sorting of the mail and placed the buff envelopes into his carry bag.

'Nice to meet you, Mr Newbone.' Then over his shoulder as he left, he added, 'I'll look out for you at the other branches.'

Erskine continued through the afternoon, measuring spaces, and engaging in small talk. He checked most parts of the bank, although he drew a line at visiting the ladies' powder room. Theoretically he thought, it was within the brief of his cover, but it was unnecessary, and he didn't want to become the subject of bank gossip. By the end of the day, he'd decided there was nothing unusual about the place. There were the typical, and in this case, mild employee gripes, but it seemed life at the branch for St Martin's staff was well ordered if a little dull. Exactly as Sir John and the board would want it, he surmised.

The chat with Bennett had changed his plans. He decided to go straight to the three locations where employees were missing, starting with the Swan Lane branch. He telephoned Sir John and at the same time, congratulated his client on running a 'happy ship.' Sir John sounded pleased and confirmed he would ask Miss Denby to make the new arrangements.

18

I was Jacques Le Roux, Caprice club manager, and I remember that evening very vividly.

Life in the Transvaal was like the Wild West, or as near as you could get to it. The feeling that nothing could stop progress left the bleak war years only a shadow in our memory. Houses were more luxurious. Cars got bigger and faster. The clothes we wore became more colourful, more outrageous and for the ladies, more provocative. Makeup was brighter, rouge was redder, kisses sweeter, more readily dispensed, and let me acknowledge more eagerly received. There were rivers of alcohol and more. Music was loud, behaviour was brash, and the dancing never stopped.

Surplus and spontaneity, excess and excitement were everywhere. It felt as though we'd been uncorked, and within reason (and there wasn't much of that), anything went. There were other substances too, recreational, they were called, and our bodies had to deal with this wild new world.

At the heart of this madness, generating the wealth that paid for it all, was the mining business.

Into this delicious, dangerous confusion, eager to make their mark, walked those two. They arrived, each on their own, but by the time that evening was over, they were inseparable. I never saw them apart again in the whole time I knew them.

I welcomed him at the door. 'Erskine,' he shouted over the din. 'New recruit. Any tips?'

'Just watch and learn,' I said, checking the list. 'And by that, I mean learn what not to do.' He laughed and I waived him on in.

There were always plenty of girls at the parties; The Company made sure of that. They were either on hand or brought in for the evening. Hence the confusion.

'Hello,' I said, 'on your own?'

The girls normally arrived in groups. Sometimes they were bussed in.

'Yes, just me,' she tapped my guest-list. 'Ferreira, Amanda Ferreira.'

She must be new at this, I thought; the girls were never listed, it might cause problems at home. I smiled.

'That's ok, you don't need to be on my list to get in.'

'Perhaps,' she said, 'but better check just in case.'

Something in her manner made me look. There was an entry on the list - Mr A Ferreira. My face must've shown surprise because she laughed.

'Found me then. Happens all the time. Quite helpful mostly.'

I studied this new arrival. Yes, for sure there was more to her than entertainment value. The demeanour was much more purposeful, and more intelligent. A woman in a man's world, but one who could stand her ground.

'Don't worry,' she laughed, 'I won't tell.' There was the hint of a sigh, and then she was gone, into the throng, but not taken by it. No doubt having to explain herself to every man she met.

Robert Erskine was struggling, and he knew it. Faces came at him from every direction. The voices around him were all at full volume, competing with the music, and consonants flew like bullets around the room. 'Ts' rattled and 'Rs' reverberated as the men introduced themselves. This new Afrikaans accent, strange and aggressive, cut through the noise and assaulted him. It was impossible not to feel slightly intimidated by these swarthy muscular miners, but at the same time, Erskine was excited.

He was here at last.

An earnest, pugnacious Boer was shouting in his ear. The man was short, round, and hard baked by the sun. He looked like a walnut.

'And so, Mr Erskine, we have great need of your expertise. The mine shafts we're sinking now are into some bloody treacherous ground let me tell you.'

Erskine nodded. 'I can't wait to get started; I'm not sure I can make things much safer though.'

'It's not safe we're after,' shouted the Boer. 'We need better. If there's a collapse, even a small one, everything stops. Danger we can live with, unproductive mines we can't.'

'I hope we can manage both,' said Erskine.

'This TNMCA has been causing us a lot of problems,' continued the Boer, 'but it seems to be on the wane now.'

'What?'

'Transvaal Native Mine Clerks Association. They were stirring things up for a while, but they seem to have gone off the boil, thank Christ.' The man eyed Erskine, appearing

94

to sense his reluctance to join in on the point. 'It's difficult and dangerous work, we all know that. People get hurt, now and again they get killed. I lost three of my best diggers to a collapse at the beginning of the year. Put us back a week. But everyone knows the risks, that's what we sign up to and why we get paid well.'

'I guess the risks get greater as the seams extend,' Erskine ventured. 'But no doubt we learn too.'

'For sure,' the Boer poked him in the chest. 'Trouble is we dig faster than we learn,' he roared with laughter and slapped Erskine on the back.

Erskine's attention was beginning to wane. There was no doubt the party was moving up a gear. The chatter increased, and the band upped their volume to keep ahead. On arrival, he'd noticed only a few women at the party, each with a circle of male admirers standing in close attention, talking and listening, albeit with a little too much laughter. Now, the ambience had changed. There were a lot more women. The dancing was more intense, more syncopated. Erskine could only hear snatched, unintelligible sentences; he checked his drink.

He inverted his glass, pointed to the bar, and detached himself from the Boer.

Working his way through the crowd, a glittering woman with eyes like a bird of prey intercepted him. He managed to extract himself from her grasp and with a few final steps, he made it to the safety of the bar.

'Beer,' he leaned forward and shouted into the barman's ear. 'Quite a party.'

The man grinned, 'Just getting started.'

Erskine turned to the room again. If anything, the music was even more intense. The band were taking the whole evening onto another plane. The mining staff, away from the danger of their work seemed to have entered an alternative world. A youngish man, his white shirt soaked in sweat, passed him, wiping his nose. A woman wearing feathers grabbed the man by the arm and they whirled away, vanishing into the crowd.

He watched as the Boer he'd been talking to surfaced from the pulsing mass on the dance floor and was dragged under again by a dancer who appeared to have a snake wrapped around her torso. The trumpeter from the band, still playing, left the stage, and was doing a kind of limbo under the legs of a tall woman who stood astride his prone body. More dancers, leaping and screaming, joined the sweaty young man and the feathers on the floor.

Erskine heard a shout. A new guest and his entourage entered the room. The man was tall and dressed like an Arabian Prince; gold dripped from every stitch of his clothing. He pumped his arms in the air and waved his followers into the throng. More exotic-looking women appeared and worked their way amongst the crowd.

The drink arrived at his elbow. He watched the pulsating mass on the floor of the club and reminded himself that the people in front of him faced danger every working day and were entitled to 'take the cork out' occasionally. Of course, he thought, the girls here lived vastly different lives from the miners, but they shared the same sense of abandonment; they behaved like there was no tomorrow.

He felt a tap on his hip. A woman wearing a pink tutu and a badge with Julie on it held out a tray. On it were a choice of multicoloured drinks and several bowls. One held a white powder; the others had lozenges and pills of varying size and colour. Erskine shook his head, and the tray moved on.

A group at the far end of the bar caught his attention. He could see the woman was talking animatedly with two Afrikaans who were trying to appear interested in her point. When she focused on one of them, Erskine watched the other run his eye over her appraisingly. Erskine was intrigued. Why hadn't they been dancing? The woman wasn't provocatively dressed, and her demeanour was a world apart from the dancers. He moved slowly down the bar.

'Evening!' he shouted as he approached, 'what a party.'

One of the men turned. 'You're new, you'll get used to it.'

'Are you one of the new engineers?' asked the other. 'Jeez, do we need you.'

'Maybe you two can work together,' the first man inclined his head toward the woman. 'Two heads better than one.'

Erskine introduced himself to the men. The woman leaned in and shook hands too.

'Amanda Ferreira. Newly qualified, like you I suspect.'

Erskine tried to cover his surprise.

'Yes, we didn't believe it either,' said the man, who called himself Thompson. 'The first woman engineer we've ever had on site for sure.'

'Where did you study?' asked Erskine.

'Bloemfontein. You're English?'

'Imperial London. What were you talking about, you looked very fired up?'

Thompson spoke again.

'Miss Ferreira here is trying to persuade us that mining safety is an economic benefit.'

'Whereas we,' interjected the other man, 'want to get the stuff out of the ground as quickly as possible. The less time spent down there,' he pointed with his foot, 'the safer we are.'

'Too bloody right' Thompson said.

'Maybe we can manage both.' Erskine ventured.

'My point exactly. Shall we dance?' Amanda offered.

Erskine followed Amanda out into the throng, and it closed tight around them. The woman in the tutu with the tray of 'treats' reappeared, and they both grabbed a bright blue drink and demolished it.

'Another!' shouted Amanda. This time, they each took a red one and finished that, too. The music beat up in their veins, and they veered and shimmied around the dancefloor. Every time their movement brought them close, Amanda grinned insanely and then retreated again before circling back to Erskine.

'We're respectable highly skilled engineers,' Erskine shouted in Amanda's ear. He rotated away.

'Who have huge responsibilities,' she returned at the next pivot, swooping on another blue drink, 'but that can wait,' she continued, 'until tomorrow!'

They collapsed at the bar.

'Where are you staying?' asked Erskine.

'I've got a room at Vanya's, over near the ferry. I need something permanent, but it'll do for now. What about you?'

'Sambrook's Hotel. When do you start at the Company, or are you there already?'

'Not until next week, they thought it would be an idea for me to get to know the team and invited me tonight. What's Sambrook's like?'

'Not bad. No luxury but the plumbing works, the food's decent and the beds are clean.'

'Well then, shall we?' Amanda smiled, and he was lost.

They had met for the first time just hours ago. Two souls, finding their way in this strange African world, full of new voices, new tastes, new sounds. The party had thrown them together, but he knew they were inseparable now. In the taxi back to the hotel they talked with a suppressed excitement.

'What brought you to South Africa?' Amanda asked.

'A sense of adventure.'

'You've come to the right place. I hope you're ready for it.'

'What type of people are the Africans?'

'Impulsive, dangerous, exciting and brave.' Amanda laughed.

'Like you then?'

She slid across the bench seat. The taxi bumped and bounced its way along the dirt road. 'Well, I'll let you be the judge of that.'

He watched the night out of the taxi window. Yellow pools of light followed in front of the car, plotting their way around the ruts and bumps of the road. Taking them who knew where, he wondered. He gave her waist a squeeze and she leant against him.

All his senses felt alive and receptive to this new world. Even the air tasted of Africa, he thought. It had an intrusive, earthy quality to it.

The smell of Africa hung heavy in the hotel room, hot, dusty, and lightless. Erskine felt a kind of anonymity, a sense of detachment from everything else, of being invisible to the outside world, but sharing his vulnerability with the woman in his arms.

Amanda made no effort to find the light. Erskine felt her reach up and touch his face, gently tracing the contours of his nose and chin with her fingers. His hand held the small of her back, and her smooth, curved shape felt good under his touch.

Their breathing was ragged, and Erskine's blood beat up. He felt every fibre of his being was present in the moment, and his future, his whole life, was being decided for him in this small, hot, hotel room.

'I thought we were supposed to be professional people,' Amanda breathed as they pulled together.

'Not given to wanton acts of...' Erskine lost his words.

'Lust,' Amanda giggled.

He would grow to love that giggle. Amanda fell back, and they toppled across the bed, invisible in the dark, fabulous, and alive in a world where only they existed.

The heat of the room and his passion for her were almost too much to bear. Erskine ran his hand along her soft skin, it felt hot and sticky to his touch. All thoughts of the outside world were gone, and he was lost in a moment which would connect him with Amanda forever, however far apart life pushed them.

19

The great London flood of 1928 didn't begin in London at all, but in the Cotswolds, where the river Thames has its source. Heavy snow settled there during Christmas 1927 and with the New Year came an unusually rapid thaw, accompanied by heavy rain, which swelled the Thames to almost double its normal volume. The torrent coincided with a high tide and something the meteorologists call a storm surge. This raised water levels off the east coast of England, and as the melted snow flowed down through the estuary the surge pushed it back upriver.

The Thames in London burst its banks just after midnight on the seventh of January. Water poured over the Embankment, washing away much of the Chelsea section, and engulfing the capital. It inundated The Houses of Parliament and The Tate Gallery, and the moat at The Tower of London filled with water for the first time in a hundred years. The heart of the city was submerged by the river as it cascaded over London's meagre defences. Even the land at the foot of Big Ben was underwater.

The deluge claimed lives. Sadly, as is often the case, this was most marked in the poorest of neighbourhoods. In the East End, families were caught in crowded basement accommodation, with no time to escape. They drowned where they lay in bed. One father lost four daughters, Florence, Maude, Rosina, and Doris. The dreadful human cost of such an event left its mark upon everyone.

The damage to property and land in London was profound. In the following months, a reconstruction program began, and over time, the scars of the catastrophe faded from view.

But not everything that arrived that night left London as the waters receded. Something remained behind. It used the disaster to reach its destination, taking the opportunity of the flooded streets and lanes to inspect its new territory. And it was satisfied with what it found.

20

Erskine, in the guise of Robert Newbone, arrived at the Swan Lane branch of St Martin's, on the edge of the City. The manager, a thin man dressed in the usual morning suit, came forward.

'I'm afraid you've got me today, Newbone,' he said briskly. 'My assistant, Leonard Ash is on holiday.' Erskine caught the manager's tone, clearly intended to convey he wouldn't usually deal with the likes of an architect, even one sent by head office.

'Good of you to see me,' he said and explained his brief. 'I'll try not to get under your feet.' The manager was already turning away as he finished.

Erskine struck up conversation with the clerks and tellers. In general, as at the earlier branch, he found them to be an accommodating group, generally happy in their work. It was in mid-afternoon, while he was speaking to a man in his early thirties named Goode, that he encountered the disappearance of Hubert Heath.

'Of course,' whispered Goode, 'we're all in a bit of a tizzy about Hubert. What with him missing.'

'Missing?' asked Erskine, affecting an air of casual curiosity.

Goode adopted a more conspiratorial tone.

'Yes, completely missing. Here one day and phoof, gone the next!' He widened his eyes. 'Well thought of too. Goodness knows what's happened there. Of course, we're all under *strict* instructions not to talk of it, or perish the

104

thought, mention it to the customers, but it is, *unnerving.*' Goode rolled his eyes.

'When you say missing, you think he's been dismissed?'

'No, no, I mean properly missing, disappeared, no one knows. He just never came into work one day and hasn't been seen since.'

'Strange. Was he finding things difficult at the branch?'

'No,' said Goode, 'he was very popular, good at his job too.'

'Did he have any run-ins or issues with his customers?'

'No, at least I didn't see anything.'

Erskine smiled to himself; the idea Goode would miss anything like that seemed unlikely.

'We get a few odd ones though,' Goode added. 'I grant you.'

'What makes them unusual?'

'Well, there was the family who wanted to start a marmalade business, sugar beet too. They absolutely insisted it was possible to grow oranges here in the southern counties if the plants were well cared for. They wanted a loan to set up things up.'

Erskine was intrigued.

'Where was the site?'

Goode waived his hand.

'I don't know, somewhere in Surrey.'

'I take it that got declined.'

Goode nodded vigorously.

'Any others?' Erskine needn't have prompted; Goode was in full flow.

'Then there was the one with a funny accent. Not sure where he came from, but he wanted money for some sort of overseas business.'

'Where?'

'Somewhere in Africa, I think. It might have been an expedition, and they did get a loan, though goodness knows how.'

'Really?' Erskine was surprised.

'Yes, and quite a large one. The problem *is,*' the conspiratorial tone returned, 'the customers are usually well off and doing very nicely thank you. The bank won't turn down requests like that in case it loses the account.' Goode's voice got quieter as he went on, it was barely audible now. 'So, we do sometimes indulge in some very odd arrangements.'

'How interesting,' said Erskine, trying to sound vague.

'Then there's the customers themselves, they can be odd too. But that's the gentry for you, I suppose,' Goode added.

'You must have a few chuckles,' Erskine encouraged.

'Absolutely. Gents in all sorts of get ups, some look like they've just been shooting, some hardly dressed at all, we even had one come in wearing silk pyjamas,' he rolled his eyes again. 'Would you believe one came in with water weed stuck in his hair, I could see it. Goodness knows what he'd been doing. Mind you, he wasn't actually a customer.'

'How does everyone keep a straight face?'

'It's more than our lives are worth,' continued Goode. 'There was one teller who laughed when a gentleman brought in his pet owl, Horatio I think he called it. The teller asked who was the wiser and he got into a lot of trouble.'

'Never a dull moment,' observed Erskine.

'Oh, there are plenty of dull ones, it's just we remember the ones that liven up the day.' He paused. 'I must get on. Simply lovely to meet you,' he turned and disappeared back into the bowels of the bank.

Erskine reflected on his conversation. He could see there was more to the bank's business than might be expected. But was it so different from any bank that had affluent customers used to having things the way they wanted? He would follow this up with Sir John.

The day ended, and as Erskine left the branch, he took stock of his surroundings. Swan Lane ran down to the Thames, and he joined the towpath along the river. It was a pleasant evening, and he walked back towards London Bridge in the sunshine. He reached a set of steps on the bank of the river and followed them down to the point where he stood at the high tide mark. The vast body of water slipped powerfully past in front of him, and he felt part of the river, immersed in it.

He watched a passenger steamer as it pushed upstream, working hard against the current. He moved back up a few steps to avoid the wake as it washed ashore. Where had the three gone? Why had nothing turned up, not even a body? Perhaps the solution was in front of him, though even a body thrown into the Thames should wash up somewhere, and the chances of three not doing so were remote. He turned back up and onto London Bridge and home, still deep in thought.

21

It was on the Tuesday after his second meeting with Erskine that Sir John's telephone rang. Miss Denby announced the bank's stockbrokers, Saviour and Bell, were on the line. She put through Toby Saviour, the Senior Partner.

Pleasantries were despatched more rapidly than usual, then Saviour said,

'John, is everything in order at the bank?'

Sir John examined the chandelier hanging in the centre of the room. This was an unusual start to a call from his professional friend.

'Yes of course. Is this a routine enquiry, Toby, or is something wrong?'

There was an embarrassed hesitation at the other end of the line.

'There has been some talk at the Exchange this morning. Some gossip about the bank's loan portfolio. I'm sure it's nonsense but the shares have slipped a little.'

Sir John relaxed.

'Toby, I can promise you there are no concerns in that direction, we have an excellent portfolio. As you would expect, there are a few non-performing loans, but certainly none that threaten our solvency.'

'Thank you.' Toby sounded relieved, 'I knew it was all nonsense; I appreciate you taking the call.'

'Not at all. I must have you and Felicity over for dinner soon. Do let me know if there is any more gossip.'

The call ended.

***

St Martin's had been a member of the square mile for centuries. News of Napoleon's retreat from Moscow and the despatch from Lieutenant Lapenotiere announcing the victory at Trafalgar had been read out in the boardroom. The financing of wars, righteous or questionable and the lending of monies to build empires and estates; all were part of the fabric of the building. A visitor, without knowing quite what it was that surrounded him, would sense the institution's standing. St Martin's reputation was a cornerstone of City history, and following Toby Saviour's call, the spirits of the bank were left thinking hard.

***

A week later, Sir John received another call from Saviour. This time, the broker's voice had a definite crackle.

'The rumours have returned. The shares are down almost fifteen per cent this morning.'

'This is very irritating, Toby – I can promise you we're in excellent shape.'

'We need to clear this up,' Saviour said. 'I think it would best if we met with the shareholders, at least the major ones.'

Sir John studied the ceiling again. 'What if we make a statement noting the rumours and confirm there's nothing to report?'

Saviour knew the perils of a shareholders meeting, which, if it went badly, could add to concerns rather than allay them.

'I take your point, but I think it would be better to have the meeting and then put out the statement, just to make sure.'

Sir John sighed. He knew the territory, and the wisdom of the advice was undeniable. 'I'm sure you're right, Toby, we'd better get on with it.'

'I'll make the arrangements,' a relieved sounding Saviour confirmed. 'But could you call Almanack, you have the relationship there.'

Sir John agreed. He knew them well. Almanack were one of the bank's largest shareholders and the investment company for the Lanark family, whose wealth, like the bank's, had multiplied during the Industrial Revolution.

He also knew the Lanark's were not averse to adventure, or the financing of it. Along with St Martin's, they had funded The Marquis of Douglas and Clydesdale's successful expedition to mount a flight over Everest, the first man to do so. The project had brought Sir John and Sandy Lanark closer together and they were good friends.

The call ended and Sir John summoned Miss Denby. 'Can you get hold of Sandy Lanark, ask him if he's free for coffee this week.'

***

Over the next few days, the spirits at the bank were witness to a series of telephone calls between Sir John and Toby Saviour, each one covering arrangements for the shareholders meeting. Financial performance, key points, and potential areas of dispute were all discussed. All the while Toby Saviour reported the steady fall of St Martin's share price.

'What the devil's going on?' Sir John asked.

'Someone's got it in for you, John,' said Saviour. 'It's as well we're going ahead with this meeting.'

A few days before the meeting, Sandy Lanark visited St Martin's. The tellers watched their shareholder as he entered the building. A tall man with aquiline features and a shock of silver hair, Lanark cut an imposing figure as he strode past them through the foyer. His hands rested on the lobby counter, they were elegant, and his long fingers looked like they would be nimble.

'Lanark, for Sir John,' he said to the receptionist.

Sir John appeared from his office. As the two men greeted each other, he thought, not for the first time, his friend might be mistaken for a surgeon if it wasn't for his complexion, which was that of an outdoorsman. This legacy of Lanark's industrial heritage had been softened by years spent in the financial world, but thought Sir John, the appearance had never completely left him.

Sir John guided his visitor through to the boardroom. He avoided the head of the table and sat opposite his guest. The meeting pleasantries covered; he began.

'Sandy, I don't enjoy taking up your time, but we have an issue.'

Lanark nodded, 'Is there a problem?' he asked.

'The only problem,' Sir John remarked tersely, 'is someone, somewhere, thinks there's something wrong, when in fact we're in very good shape. The gossip's having an impact on our shares, I'm sure you've noticed.'

'Yes, I have.' Lanark paused.

'You could issue a statement.'

'Yes, we plan to, but we want to back it up with this shareholders meeting.'

Lanark was sympathetic. 'These things can do more harm than good. You never know quite what's going to come up, they can be hard to control.'

'I know,' Sir John sighed. 'That's why I wanted to talk to you. If I can use your support as the largest shareholder to help reassure the meeting, that will go a long way to keeping things on track.'

'Well, yes, that's certainly possible,' Lanark said, 'but I would need to see the books first.'

'Of course,' his host agreed. 'I can arrange that this afternoon.'

The two men went through the information needed.

'The loan portfolio seems to be the basis for the rumours,' Sir John offered.

'I'll send Chorley over; he'll do the work.' said Lanark.

Sir John crossed to a telephone in the corner of the room. 'You'll get an outside line from this,' he said, and offered the receiver.

Sandy Lanark dialled and stood waiting.

'Chorley's very thorough, commercial too. He will enjoy this.' Lanark said.

Sir John heard Almanack's reception answer. There was an audible jump in the voice once the caller identified himself. The woman put Lanark through, who told Chief Accountant Robin Chorley, that he would be despatched to St Martin's to conduct the review.

'Are you free for lunch?' Sir John asked.

'I'm afraid not,' Lanark shook his head. 'I'm going to a lecture today.'

'What's the subject?'

'Winston Churchill's presenting. He still has a lot to say even though he isn't in the Cabinet. He's lecturing on the rise of fascism and the rearming of Germany.' Lanark passed his hands through his thick silver hair.

Sir John sighed heavily. 'I hope we aren't going to go through all that again. Haven't we learned anything?'

By the time Chorley arrived, Sir John and his staff had covered the huge boardroom table with the bank's books and ledgers. Sir John made sure every aspect of the business was ready for review. In truth, he thought, eyeing the piles, it was more than one man could hope to cover in a week let alone a few hours. Today though, his intention was to underline the transparency of the bank's dealings and provide reassurance, just as much as it was to supply specifics.

Chorley, Sir John observed, contrasted with the often-held image of dry, dusty accountants. The elegantly suited man shook Sir John's hand, eying the mass of papers over his host's shoulder. 'I can't see any skeletons from here' he smiled, 'but perhaps they're hiding under the ledgers.'

'Let me know if you need anything. Over there may be of the most interest.' Sir John gestured at a tower of blue folders.

Chorley gazed at the pile. 'Is that the loan portfolio?' he asked.

Sir John nodded, 'the orange file at the top is a summary of the whole thing.'

Chorley draped his jacket across one of the chairs and pulled up a second one next to the blue pile. He secured his shirtsleeves with brass garters and began to examine the files.

Returning to his office Sir John was in better spirits. He was sure there were no issues. With the undertaking from his largest shareholder subject only to Chorley's verification, he was, if not pleased about the shareholders meeting, at least sure of his ground.

Chorley was enjoying his task. He had no issues with the bank and was hoping nothing would come up, but such an interesting exercise needed his concentration. Apart from the auditors, it was unheard of for any bank to open its books to a third party and the review gave him a chance to improve his understanding of the banking business. The historic nature of some of the accounts at St Martin's filled his afternoon with interest and his curiosity deepened with each turn of the page.

***

High above him, cloistered in the soaring ceiling of the bank's ramparts, the spirits watched, aghast. The bank, founded in 1672, had never allowed anyone other than its auditors and staff access to its records. They shuddered and groaned, and something of their disquiet vibrated in the walls and corridors of St Martin's.

***

By evening Chorley had finished his work, and although he had made some notes, he was satisfied the bank's loan portfolio was sound. He had found a small number outside St Martin's typical arrangements but was confident that even collectively these wouldn't cause any damage. He had reached his conclusions and was indulging his own interests. He took his time, studying a section of the records dealing with loans the bank had written off due to Napoleon's Russian campaign before it came to its disastrous frozen end.

He was about to close the files when he felt a touch on his shoulder. Turning, he expected to find Sir John, but to his surprise there was no one there. Disconcerted he scanned the room, but he was the only person present.

He stretched himself to shake off the cramp which had settled on his frame.

A soft but agitated whisper echoed over his head, and he paused again. The vaulted ceiling was invisible beyond the chandeliers, but he was aware of the void above him. He pulled across the last of the files and had begun to copy down some figures, when the sharp snap of a ledger hitting the floor startled him. He bent down to collect the file. As he ducked below the eye-line of the table he became aware that a brooding presence had joined him. Straightening abruptly, his eye ranged down the length of the room, but he sensed rather than saw something.

Sir John checked the clock. It was about to chime 6:30, and he decided to see if Chorley was near the end of his task. Leaving his office, he walked along the corridor and was approaching the boardroom when the accountant appeared. He was holding a sheaf of papers, gathered carelessly under his arm, and he seemed flustered.

'All done I trust,' said Sir John.

Chorley smiled weakly at him. 'Yes, all in order. I'll give Mr Lanark my report in the morning, but everything seems fine.'

'I'm sure the shareholders will be pleased to hear it,' Sir John said. Then, because he always valued an independent view he asked, 'Out of interest, I know we're in good shape, but was there anything out of the ordinary?'

Chorley dropped his papers. He knelt and began to gather them up. 'On the books you mean?'

Sir John put the accountant's clumsiness down to the nerves people sometimes showed when visiting St Martin's, after all, he thought, it was an imposing place. He began walking towards the doors, shepherding Chorley with him.

'A couple of the industrial loans might be a bit speculative, or rather the businesses themselves could be,' said the accountant. 'But they weren't material in the scheme of things.'

They reached the doors. Chorley turned and surveyed the grand marble lobby. The customers and employees had long since gone home and the bank was silent.

'This is a special building, those ledgers, you have quite a history here.'

Sir John was proud of the bank and its achievements over the centuries. 'Yes, there are some stories I could tell that would surprise you.'

'Perhaps it has a few ghosts too,' Chorley said.

Sir John smiled. 'Certainly, there are, but they keep themselves to themselves.'

Chorley regarded his host thoughtfully. 'Maybe not all the time.' He swung the door open.

The pavement was busy with people intent on their commute. The bank was halfway between the two mainline stations that took their patrons home, one to Essex and one to Kent. Outside St Martin's, these two currents of humanity were at their most chaotic. Commuters jostled for position and stepped around each other as they found the stream towards their station. Chorley, still wondering about his encounter, looked for the Kentish current and, after some negotiation with the Essex contingent found the slipstream. His route took him past his employer's office, and on impulse, he decided to drop in, finish his report and leave it on Sandy Lanark's desk. He knew the chairman would appreciate his quick work in the morning.

Turning into the building he took the two flights of stairs to his own office, spread his notes out on the table and began to write. The report was a straightforward task and Chorley completed it easily. Satisfied with his day's work and pleased there were no issues, he left the office. Stepping into the calm of the post rush hour streets, he set off for the station.

The following morning, Sandy Lanark's car dropped him at his office. He was surprised not to have heard from his accountant, but he assumed, correctly as it turned out, that Chorley's review had found nothing serious.

Dropping his coat over the stand he saw the report on the teak desk that filled this bay window. Settling himself in his chair he began reading. As his accountant had done, Lanark was pleased to see that other than a handful of 'outliers', there were no material matters to report. Lanark drained his coffee and made ready for the rest of his day.

Miss Denby kept an eye on reception as the shareholders of St Martin's began to arrive. She briefed Sir John regularly as she watched them go through. The institutions and investment managers with the largest interests arrived last.

There were a few other holders too, most of them long-standing customers of the bank, the biggest of these being Almanack.

The attendees acknowledged each other but arrived with the pensive, conspiratorial air of those anxious for news but not sure who to talk to. Edwards, the senior cashier, met each one and offered them a small glass of sherry before directing the shareholder to the boardroom with a respectful 'Sir John will be along shortly.'

One of the last to arrive was Sandy Lanark. Miss Denby relayed his arrival to Sir John. He waived away the sherry and strode into the meeting room, nodding his acknowledgements and taking a seat in the front row. The other attendees, seeing him, tried to decide whether his attendance was an omen for good or ill.

Sir John looked at Toby Saviour and the company secretary, a man called Bartholomew. 'Ready Gentlemen?' He pushed open the mahogany door of the boardroom. The secretary was clutching a sheaf of papers along with a notebook and pen, Bartholomew looked pale, he thought. Sir John took a position at the front and centre of the room. Saviour and Bartholomew, as agreed, sat either side of him.

'Gentlemen,' he began, 'thank you for taking the time to come today. Before we begin, I would like to introduce our broker, Toby Saviour of Saviour and Bell. Toby is here to keep us on the straight and narrow.' The majority of those in the room knew Saviour and briefly acknowledged him.

'The reason for the meeting needs little guesswork,' continued the host, 'and relates to the reduction in the price of St Martin's shares in recent weeks.'

There was no comment from the floor of the meeting. Sir John could see he had their full attention. 'Our investigation suggests this stems from rumours about our loan portfolio.'

This time, apart from Sandy Lanark, the heads in the room inched forward. 'Before we go on to the substance of the meeting, I can assure you the bank's loan portfolio is sound and there is nothing of any concern.'

There was a snort from somewhere within the room. Sir John searched the faces, looking for the source, but then an insistent nasal voice spoke up,

'Well, you would say that wouldn't you.'

Sir John and Saviour glanced at each other. Before they could continue, the voice came again.

'My sources suggest some of your largest loans are subject to default, what have you to say to that?'

They had the man in their sights now. Sir John could see the rotund figure in the middle of a row. He was wearing a voluminous olive suit with a tie slumped unsuccessfully around his neck. His hair was a mop of rusty brown curls, and to Sir John, there was something of the old-fashioned scribe about him. Sir John shot a glance at Toby Saviour – it was clear his broker didn't recognise the shareholder either.

'Just one moment, Mr...' Sir John hesitated.

'What evidence can you show this meeting,' the man continued, ignoring the invitation to give his name, 'to give us confidence in the bank?'

The rest of the meeting homed in on the man too. The questioner had voiced their own concerns, fed by the recent gossip. Toby Saviour sensed their courage increase, and he could see their support for the scribe grow as they nodded and muttered at each other.

'We are going to make a formal statement to the Exchange after this meeting,' Sir John continued, 'which will be countersigned by our broker,' he indicated Saviour. 'The statement will confirm everything at the bank is in good order.'

Sir John heard more rumblings and a voice from the back of the room shouted, 'Not enough!'

Sir John played his first card, 'Before that though, we have some information for you.' He motioned to the company secretary, who rose to his feet.

'Bartholomew, would you circulate the schedules.'

The secretary, looking even paler than when he'd entered the room, shuffled down the lines of chairs, handing out the information. Sir John was reminded of a churchwarden giving out hymn sheets at the end of the pews.

Once everyone had a copy, Saviour stood and addressed the meeting.

'Gentlemen,' he began, 'these papers set out the bank's loan arrangements for the last two years.' He continued through the analysis, explaining each line item and column, which showed the loans, assets, and associated information, although with customer names removed. After a few minutes of technical explanation Saviour concluded,

'And so, you can see that there are no material matters of concern, and St Martin's financial position is extremely strong.'

The olive suit made another attempt.

'How do we know this information is genuine or even complete?' he demanded.

Sir John was ready with his *'coup de gras.'* 'I acknowledge the point sir,' he raised his voice slightly, 'perhaps a word from our largest shareholder would be appropriate.'

Sandy Lanark stood. His tall frame dominated the rows of shareholders. He took them all in as he spoke, scanning up and down each line of seats, before fixing his gaze on the olive suit.

'It may be helpful to know,' Lanark's modulated Edinburgh brogue was like a soothing balm, 'that my chief accountant has conducted a detailed review of the loan portfolio. He's drawn up a report,' Lanark lifted the document above his head, 'which you're welcome to study at leisure. I will leave it with Sir John. This comprehensively confirms the chief executive's statement and Almanack will be increasing its shareholding in the days ahead.'

After the meeting broke up, Sir John and Toby Saviour compared notes. At the same time, Bartholomew walked round to the Stock Exchange and delivered the formal statement, giving the bank's assurances.

'I can't place that accent,' said Saviour, 'it has me stumped.'

'You mean our dissenter?' said Sir John, 'how about you, Sandy?'

The tall man shook his head.

'We must find out which shareholder he is or who he represents,' said Saviour. 'You would have thought his intention was to damage the bank, not invest in it.'

'Can we check the share price, Toby?' asked Sir John.

The broker went to the corner of the room and lifted the telephone. He spoke into the receiver and waited. After a pause he returned, satisfied. 'The announcement went out a few minutes ago and the price is already tracking up.'

Sandy Lanark excused himself, shaking hands with both men before leaving.

Saviour was visibly relieved. 'I hadn't expected Lanark to go quite that far and buy more shares.'

Sir John spoke warmly. 'Sandy is a great ally, especially when things are bumpy, but I wouldn't want to get on his wrong side. Do you think that's the end of the problem?'

The broker hesitated. 'Unless someone has it in for you, then yes. Is there a rival that might be trying to buy the bank?'

Sir John paused. 'Very unlikely,' he said after some thought.

'Then we are done.' Saviour wished his friend a good day and went to collect his coat.

***

Although unsettled, the spirits at the bank were past the worst now that the meeting was out of the way. Over the next few days, life returned to normal, and to the onlooker, at least, all was well.

22

In his guise as Robert Newbone the architect, Erskine continued with his plans to visit the branches. These were on the Embankment near Whitehall and on the south side of the Thames, near Blackfriars Bridge in Hope Street.

He found things were much as on his other visits. There was no equivalent of Goode, brimming with gossip and eager to pass comment, but with the themes in his head, Erskine could now prompt the exchanges. There was the same pattern of broadly satisfied employees concerned for their missing colleagues and, as before, a few tales of idiosyncratic customers. No one had any idea of the reason for the disappearances, although, of course, there were theories, most of them of the extramarital nature. Individually this might be possible, Erskine thought, but to have three within such a short space of time was next to impossible.

Erskine telephoned Sir John from time to time, but these calls only underlined the lack of progress. The two men agreed to meet at Sir John's house and conduct a review of the 'case' to date.

The next evening Erskine arrived at Richmond station and hailed a taxi. The driver seemed impressed with his passenger's destination and spoke up over the growl of the cab.

'You know Sir John MacGregor then?'

'Hardly at all,' Erskine said briskly, not wanting to be drawn on the reason for his visit.

'He's a bigwig in the City you know, runs St Martin's Bank. A toff, but quite a decent bloke by most counts.'

'I've heard that.'

'You're well in if you've been invited to the house.' The cabbie was intrigued. 'Especially at this time of day. It must be unusual to see customers this late, and at the house as well.'

The taxi was growling past The Slow Pony. Erskine watched the lights of the pub pass his window. He glanced up into the cab's rearview mirror and met the driver's polite but inquisitive gaze.

'That's an interesting accent you have there.'

'Good spot, have a guess.' Erskine was relieved to move the conversation onto another tack.

'Well, it's not that strong but there's something there, Dutch?' asked the cabbie.

'Nearly.'

The driver flicked his eyes from the road back into the mirror and took another glance at his passenger.

'South African?'

'Well done. I spent a lot of time out there. I've been back in England a while, but the twang is still there I suppose.'

They swung into Redshanks and the driver lost his chance for further questions. Sir John himself appeared from the house and stood on the drive. The cabbie saw the host and checked back up into the mirror. Clearly his fare was a man of importance. Erskine paid the driver and left the stale warmth of the cab; he could feel the dampness of the evening. The diesel engine ticked over noisily in a cloud of fumes.

'Evening Erskine, have you eaten?'

'Now you mention it, I am a bit peckish.'

'Then we'll talk over supper,' said his host and took him into the house.

Sir John guided Erskine into the study and having confirmed supper with Bridges, the two men settled into heavy armchairs in front of the fire. The coals were glowing in the grate, and to Erskine, Redshanks felt as though it was preparing for winter. The house was quiet, although somewhere, he could hear a clock ticking, measuring the evening in steady, even paces.

'Brandy?' suggested Sir John. Erskine began talking while his host busied himself with the decanter.

'I don't have much to report,' Erskine took the proffered glass. 'I understand things better now though, and if you don't mind, I have some questions.'

'Of course. I wasn't expecting some great solution at this stage. Tell me what you've found and what you want to know. I'll help if I can.'

Erskine leant forward; the heat from the coals warmed his face, although his back felt a chill as it left the chair.

'The customers,' Erskine continued, 'they're quite a varied group, aren't they?'

Sir John smiled, 'It takes all sorts.'

'Yes, of course. But the business they do with the bank isn't always what I expected, not in all cases anyway. I know most of it's routine, but some seem quite speculative to me. And the customers themselves, a few of them, have, shall we say, unusual characteristics.'

Again, his host smiled.

'Yes, that's true, but they aren't the core of the bank's affairs, not the bread and butter as you might say. Our business is managing the assets and affairs of families that have been with us, in some cases, for generations. I know it's a cliché, but it really is a case of cradle to grave.'

'I think I said before, the staff are a pleasant group to deal with, and I didn't pick up on any issues with them, or anything that might link the disappearances.'

'No internal plot that you could find then?' asked Sir John, relieved.

'None,' Erskine continued. 'What did interest me though, was whether there might be any third-party scheming, something like a fraud which they might be involved in because they were recruited for it...' Sir John stiffened.

'Or...' continued Erskine, 'because they had unwittingly stumbled into it. They might not even realise they'd found anything.'

'And how would that show itself?'

'Well, there might be a pattern of unusual business, or the customers themselves might stand out in some way. They might even be disguised, so it wouldn't necessarily show up in their appearance. Their behaviour at the branch, the way they conducted themselves, even their speech or accent might be a clue.'

'And has there been anything like that?'

'There have been a few comments from staff.' Erskine was mindful of the gossip relayed by Goode, but knew he must protect his source.

'I hope you weren't given any customers names?'

'No, just descriptions. But for example, if a customer comes to the branch for a loan, say for something unusual, are there rules which help the bank make its decision?'

'Yes of course, but there are levels of judgement applicable to these things too.'

'And who exercises that judgement?'

'Up to a certain loan amount it's the manager, for larger loans, he refers the matter to me. The referral limit varies by branch and depends upon the customer's relationship with the bank, as well as the manager's experience.'

'Is it always the manager, or could our missing employees have the authority to agree to larger loans?'

'The two men, at their level, they would have the same or at least similar authority to the branch manager.'

'When you say customer relationship with the bank, what do you mean?'

'Some of our customers have very large portfolios with us, property, investments, commercial loans and so on. In quite a few cases there are several members of the same family banking with us. Some are even based abroad but keep an account here in London.' Sir John raked the coals. Smoke spiralled up from the fire and briefly filled the space between them. He continued.

'Where these relationships are long-standing, we may sometimes lend on a speculative basis, simply because the family is important to the bank. I'm sure you can understand the commercial logic.'

'Of course,' Erskine said, 'What about simple indulgence?'

'For example?'

'An application for,' Erskine remembered the conversation with Goode, 'an expedition for example.'

Sir John looked surprised. 'That would be turned down,' he said, but then he added, 'actually, there are two or three families where we might consider it. But we've never had one.'

This time it was Erskine's turn to be surprised.

'Oh, but you have,' he rejoined, 'although I haven't the details, other than it was possibly to somewhere in Africa.'

Sir John was astonished.

'Well, something like that would have to come to me and I can tell you, no such application has landed on my desk.'

Erskine moved on. If it turned out to be important, he would have to double-check.

'We agreed I should look in more detail at the business approved by the missing staff.'

'Yes.' Sir John nodded. 'I'd rather do that in the Head Office though. We're going to need to explain what's going on. It's an unusual request, and the books will have to be brought up here.'

Erskine said, 'I can think of someone who might help. I met him on one of my visits to the branches; his name's James Bennett.'

Bridges arrived with supper and Sir John and Erskine ate in silence for a few minutes. Erskine had been turning something over in his mind and now put it to his host.

'Do you remember when we first met, I talked about my mining friend from South Africa? At the time you suggested I should try and get in touch.'

'Yes, I do.'

'Well, I've found her, and she's currently in London.'

'How interesting. On business?'

'Raising money for a new mining project.'

'Well, if she wants to come and...'

'That isn't the reason for mentioning her. I was wondering, though, if she might help me with the investigation. Amanda's a very bright woman, she could add some insight.'

Sir John was concerned. By his count, this would mean five people would be involved in something that was intended to be confidential. He and Erskine, James Bennett, Miss Denby and now a new addition. But he liked Erskine and followed his rule of, 'good people know good people.'

'If you think it would help,' he agreed. 'But really, that must be the limit.'

'I'll bring her along to our meeting.' Erskine smiled. 'And I'll tell her not to pester you about investing in new mining projects.'

Sir John laughed.

23

With his outdoor duties over for the day, Terence Knapp had been cleaning and oiling the garden tools ranged along the wall of Redshanks' Victorian greenhouse. The space, warmed by the heat from the pipes that ran through it from the main boiler into the house, was a pleasant place to spend a late autumn afternoon. The greenhouse was next to the kitchen, and he was talking with Mary, the cook, when they heard a taxi.

'That'll be Sir John's guest,' Mary announced. 'I've been told to arrange supper for two this evening. Sounds like it's time to get things ready.'

'I wonder who it is?' prompted Knapp.

'Don't ask me, but Bridges thinks he's a foreign gentleman.'

Knapp made his excuses and left the kitchen, turning up toward the house rather than back down towards the gardens. He stood in the shadows on the edge of the drive, away from the pool of light cast by the lamps on the porch.

Knapp recognised the visitor as soon as Erskine got out of the taxi. Sir John and his guest went inside. He decided to delay his journey home and walked back to the greenhouse, visiting the kitchen again on the way.

'Mary, let me know when they ask for coffee,' he called, 'I want a word with Sir John before he turns in.' Cook was busy with supper, but a summary wave let him know she had heard.

Knapp was beginning to think of abandoning his plan when Mary arrived at the greenhouse door. She was wiping her hands on her pinafore and had the air of someone who had completed a good evening's work.

'Almost done, but I doubt you will catch Sir John at this hour,' she called.

Knapp put down his oilcloth and followed her back out of the greenhouse. He turned onto the drive and stayed back in the shadows. The evening was still, and in the distance he could hear the chug of boats on the Thames. Knapp, used to the chill of autumn near the river, waited comfortably for the two men. A few minutes passed, and then he heard the familiar growl as a taxi made its way up the drive. The driver brought the cab to a halt outside the house and waited, engine running.

Redshanks' front door opened. Sir John and Erskine were still in conversation, and Knapp could see the meeting had gone well. They looked animated, but to his frustration the noise of the taxi made it difficult to hear what they were saying. He inched forward and stood at the edge of the pool of light, taking advantage of the headlights of the cab, which defined the two men's vision. He caught snatches of their exchange.

'I... call Bennett over to see us together... the need for discretion... the ledgers... we shall have to see.'

Knapp was puzzled; who was Bennett? He hadn't seen any other visitors to the house, had he misheard? Knapp guessed he was another involved in whatever it was. If a mining plan was underway, then maybe Bennett was part of the team or lending his expertise?

Erskine closed the cab door behind him. He wound the window down for a final word and shouted over the rattle of the taxi engine. This time, Knapp heard him.

'There's a good chance we'll find something in the files. We'll be back in on Friday around ten; we can speak to Bennett and get things moving.'

Knapp stepped away as the taxi disappeared down the drive. He was careful not to kick up the gravel, but Sir John turned away from the headlights just long enough to pick up his shadow.

'Hello, who's there?'

Knapp saw there was nothing for it. 'It's me, Sir John,' he came forward.

'You're working late,' observed his master.

'Just looking out for rabbits, they've been making a mess of the lawns.'

'Very good, but you should be home with Mrs Knapp.' Sir John sighed. 'You need to be careful, Knapp. There are some strange things going on just now, and it wouldn't do for me to lose the best gardener in London.'

'What sort of things?'

Sir John came over.

'I'd rather not say too much but just be on your guard.'

'I'll do that sir, thank you.' Knapp took a chance, 'Are these things why the gentleman called tonight?'

His master studied Knapp.

'Yes, in a way. You saw him then.'

'Just for a minute, sir, but I know him from the papers. His name's Erskine, I think.'

Sir John was taken aback. He knew Knapp was brighter than others would assume of a gardener, but he wasn't prepared for this level of insight.

'Goodness, Knapp, you *are* very well informed. I must ask you to keep this to yourself though, it's most important. Lives could depend upon it, really, they might.'

Knapp, his reputation enhanced, was content to have turned a potentially embarrassing encounter into a profitable one. He was loyal to Sir John but always welcomed the chance to remind his master he was no fool. 'Of course, sir, you can rely on me.'

The two men parted, Sir John turning back into the main entrance. Knapp walked down to lock the greenhouse. He put his head in at the kitchen, but Mary had left. Good, he thought, no explaining to do.

Knapp strode out across the drive and over the lawns to the gate in the garden wall. He walked down the lane towards the lights of The Slow Pony. Just time for a half, he thought, and checked his pockets.

***

Sir John, Erskine and Knapp weren't the only ones party to events on the drive. From a distance and unobserved at the bottom of the garden, another pair of eyes watched the proceedings. The owner was tall and muscular, and moved silently through the evening mist. Unlike the others, the watcher had four feet.

24

I still thought the world of Amanda, even though I hadn't seen her for years. Being with her in London again was special. We were close back in the South African days, and what happened to us there had shaped the rest of our lives. There was a time when marriage was on the cards, I suppose, but we were both very driven then, Amanda especially so. My being caught up in Komberley hadn't helped either.

Our careers had taken over, and the events of those times carried us with them. Occasionally we'd found a quieter pool, but always we moved back out into the torrent. We never found the right time.

It was typical of Amanda to ask about my health, even after all these years. I manage pretty well these days, and it takes something grim to trigger those thoughts. I know I can never go back to that world, but I decided to use the skills I learned then, and to build a life for myself. That is what I've done, with some success, I think.

The idea of bringing Amanda into the investigation was obvious. Very smart, courageous, and undoubtedly an asset, I hoped Sir John would think so too. I made Amanda promise not to mention her project, but I was sure Sir John would be impressed by her and might eventually ask anyway.

We met for tea at White's hotel and picked up where we left off at Le Homard. This time I was able to explain the whole case to her, and I think we both enjoyed the *feeling of working together again. We talked about her role, and she suggested that with her understanding of financial matters, she should focus on reviewing the transactions, while I checked for patterns or unusual features in the business or the customers. She also mentioned she could 'butter up' anyone who needed it. I said I found that hard to imagine, but she reminded me of our early months together, that put me right.*

And I wasn't surprised that Amanda was an instant success with Sir John. I don't think a man of his calibre is ever exactly smitten, but I could see he was taken with her.

The one drawback of being with Amanda is it reminds me of the events I've mentioned already. When she asked me how I'd been, it was thoughtful of her, but to have to face those demons again was asking a lot. Those feelings, the near certainty of death, I'll never completely forget them, but I hope the fault lines won't reopen, we shall see. I feel good at the moment, a natural state when I'm with Amanda, whatever the circumstances.

So here we are, sitting in the boardroom of St Martin's Bank, waiting for my contact, James Bennett, to appear. Poor chap, he must be wondering what all this is about. I only met him briefly, but my instinct is he'll be very useful. Amanda's talking to Sir John, I wonder what he thinks. We haven't made any great progress, but I'm beginning to feel our 'prep' is adding to the picture.

I recognise those footsteps, Miss Denby approaches.

25

James Bennett, messenger 'boy' to St Martin's Bank, was terrified. He had received instructions from the clerk at the Embankment branch he was to attend St Martin's Head Office the next morning at 10:30. He visited the bank almost every day as part of his duties, but this was different. It was made clear to him there were no packages to collect and no messages to deliver, it was just he, James Bennett, who was required. In person. The clerk had told him not to speak of it to anyone, but as he'd confessed to his girl Violet that evening,

'I had to tell someone. To be going to the head office branch on a special errand. There was even talk I might meet Sir John. What the heck's going on?'

'You can't be getting the sack,' Violet assured him. 'Sir John wouldn't bother with you if that's what's going to happen. It might be a promotion?'

'More like a dressing down,' James remembered the architect. He'd said a few things, but the man, what was his name? Newbone? He seemed a decent sort. Hardly the type to rat on him. What if he was a spy, sent to check on the branches? But, he thought, the way Sir John treated his employees made that unlikely too.

And so here he was in Lombard Street, reporting in, as instructed. Suit pressed, shoes licked to a shine and stomach churning. He checked his tie again and pushed through the familiar swing doors.

'Hello, James,' smiled the receptionist. 'No mail for you today. Take a seat over there; Miss Denby will be out soon.'

For James, the circumstances of the meeting were strange enough, but the idea of being allowed to sit in reception was just too much. Bennett stood and waited. Ordinarily, he would have no time to look around, but today was different. He let his gaze wander, and his eye followed the black veins that ran through the marble pillars in the huge hall, they divided and ran on each one...

'Hello, James.'

James Bennett practically stood to attention. He tried to speak but nothing came out, so he nodded at Miss Denby instead. She turned and walked briskly back into the interior of the bank, her heels sounding a percussive tattoo on the marble. Bennett followed in her wake, keeping his hands out of his pockets, and trying to think of something to say.

They arrived at a set of double doors Bennett had never been through before. Miss Denby tapped smartly and opened them without waiting for a reply. 'James Bennett,' she announced.

There were two men and a woman looking at him. They were sitting at a huge table; it disappeared into the distance and the lights above it seemed to run on forever. It felt like he was in St Pancras station. But now the men were standing, and the older one was speaking. James paid attention.

'Good morning, Bennett. We haven't met but I'm Sir John MacGregor.'

So, it was true, he had met the head of the bank. He wasn't being fired then...

'This is Miss Ferreira, and you've already met this gentleman.' James Bennett recognised the architect he'd spoken to a few days earlier. The woman smiled.

Bennett found his voice again.

'Good morning, ma'am, Sir John, nice to see you again, Mr Newbone.' The man smiled. Sir John motioned Bennett to a seat. He sat bolt upright, making sure his elbows weren't touching the table. After some adjustment, he folded his hands into his lap. He glanced from one man to the other. Sir John spoke.

'I expect you're wondering why you're here this morning.'

That was an understatement.

'I'm afraid we have used some harmless subterfuge to get you here; I hope it hasn't made things difficult for you. The fact is we need your help on a most confidential matter.'

So, no dismissal but no promotion he thought, what came next? Maybe he was to deliver a special package for the architect, or did the woman need a secret message taken to someone? Don't be stupid. This was serious. Newbone cleared his throat.

'I introduced myself to you as Mr Newbone, an architect, when we met,' the man said. 'But my real name's Robert Erskine. I'm conducting some confidential work for the bank and needed to visit a few branches without attracting attention.'

Bennett decided to say nothing.

Sir John broke in. 'We're trying to find out what's happened to those unfortunate people. Miss Ferreira and Mr Erskine are helping us.'

'Having met you, I recommended to Sir John you could be trusted to act as a kind of assistant to Miss Ferreira and me,' Erskine added.

James Bennett's head was spinning. Wait until he told Violet. No, hang on, he wasn't allowed to. What could he say? It felt like he was in the middle of one of those stories in the Evening Standard.

'Can I call you James?' the woman asked. He turned to answer, she spoke with an accent too, what was it?

'Yes, ma'am,' he managed.

'James, we need someone who can come and go at the branches without causing comment, someone who can collect things and run messages at short notice.'

'Well, that's – that's what I do,' she made him feel a bit giddy.

Sir John continued. 'I have to tell you there may be some unusual situations and hours to keep too, perhaps even some ah, danger, we don't yet know the full picture.'

James Bennett felt a stab of excitement. He could see Mr Newbone, who was now calling himself Erskine, had come to a decision. The man leant forward on the table.

'You must tell no one.' He spoke calmly, and, Bennett thought, with the same accent as the woman, but not as strong. 'We'll be working from here as a base, and if you need any of us, you can speak to Miss Denby.'

'Yes, Mr Erskine.'

'Better call me Robert, that *is* my first name. If I may say so, anyone who overhears may think you're being familiar. But if you need to remember to call me Newbone in one place and Erskine in another we'll both get confused.'

'In that case I'll call you Mr Robert,' said James Bennett. 'It covers everything, and I usually add Mr to first names when I'm speaking to City gentlemen.'

The woman chuckled.

Sir John was earnest. 'Bennett, we need you to collect the notes and records of the missing people. Any customer files, correspondence, their diaries, anything that gives us a better understanding of their dealings, say over the last three months.'

Miss Denby was still in the room. 'I think the police will have taken the diaries, Sir John,' she said.

'Yes of course, quite so. Well then, anything that seems relevant. The point is, we must do this discreetly. The best solution might be to gather up lots of records and make sure the ones we want are included among them. Hide in plain sight as it were.'

'What would be the reason for collecting them?' asked Bennett.

'I've thought about that. The bank has just bought one of those Checkograph machines, it takes little pictures of used cheques and the like, as a way of storing information but saving space. We can say we are recording all the old business on the new film process, and we want Bennett to test it.' The others in the room regarded their host with admiration.

'Brilliant!' exclaimed Amanda, 'that's it then, when can we start?'

'As soon as we've had some tea,' said Sir John, 'do you take tea, Bennett?'

Under the table James Bennett pinched himself.

Through the afternoon Amanda worked with Miss Denby to draw up a list of the files, including some random ones as a form of misdirection. Sir John and Erskine talked to Bennett about the kind of questions that might come up. Towards the end of the day, they were ready.

James Bennett left and headed back to his normal duties, armed with the cover story for his visits. As he put it to Violet that evening:

'I'm going to be trained in how to use the new Checkograph machine, and they wanted to see if I was up to it. Might be a promotion for me at the end. It's going to be lots of extra work and funny hours, but I can't turn down a chance like this.'

'See I told you there was nothing to worry about. I'm so proud of you,' Violet squeezed his arm and kissed him. 'My James, at St Martin's Head Office. Well, I never.'

If only I could tell her the whole thing, he thought.

26

Amanda could see James Bennett had been hard at work. The boardroom at St Martin's Bank looked like a book bazaar. Boxes, papers, and documents were everywhere. Most of them were untouched, piled in groups, their contents still clipped together, though Bennett had left a small number open for her review.

Bringing all the research together were several large sheets of paper. Each loan agreed by the missing employees was set out, with columns for information covering purpose of loan, amount, the company that had borrowed the money, and the date of the arrangement. As Amanda explained,

'We need to be able to see if there are any common features. Once we have everything set out it will be much easier to see if there are any patterns.'

Over the following days, Erskine and Amanda taped the sheets together and filled them with more information from the files.

The staff had questioned Bennett a few times on his mission, but never seriously challenged him. A call from Miss Denby to the branch before his arrival, coupled with his cover story, made sure of this. He was back on his regular beat, but with a promise from Erskine that he would recall him once they had put the information together.

By the end of the week, the team had recorded all the transactions and begun to go through the information.

They hadn't found any clear themes, and at Amanda's suggestion they agreed to start again on the Monday, refreshed after a weekend's rest. Sir John offered to move the papers to his house.

'That way, we can continue our work at Redshanks without worrying about all this attracting attention,' he gestured at the chaotic boardroom.

'What about James?' asked Amanda. 'How will he feel about coming to your house?'

'I'm sure he'll be delighted,' chuckled Sir John. 'This will feel like an extra stripe on his arm. There aren't many bank employees who've been to Redshanks, and we can say it's an urgent errand.'

'There are a lot of files, Sir John,' said Amanda. 'Why don't we give you a hand back to Redshanks in the taxi?'

'Well, this is exciting,' whispered Amanda as they waited for Sir John in the lobby. 'A grand house in Richmond. Are there any wildebeest heads stuck on the wall?'

Erskine grinned, 'No, only defaulting borrowers. Thank you.'

'For what?'

'For not asking Sir John to invest in the new project.'

Amanda chuckled, 'I think he might be persuaded though, don't you?'

Their host arrived in reception. Gathering up the papers, they went out to the waiting cab.

Amanda sat next to Sir John, with Erskine in the fold down seat opposite her. They piled the papers between them and braced against the stops and starts of the journey.

'So, Amanda, what brings you to London?' asked Sir John.

'Mining, as always.'

'Well, there aren't many mines in London.'

Erskine, recalling their evening at Le Homard, shot Amanda a glance.

'Yes, that's what Robert says, but there's more than one kind of mining.'

Sir John looked amused.

The taxi neared the house. Miss Denby had called ahead to tell the cook supper would be for three. Mary was excited.

'First one foreign visitor and now two,' she said. 'I wonder what to make of it all.'

Knapp wondered, too. He was conscious he'd got away with one eavesdropping but couldn't take any further liberties. Sir John was a trusting employer, but he was no fool. He decided to content himself with a stroll along the drive to coincide with the arrival of the group and to see what he could glean, but to leave it at that.

Knapp busied himself in the front gardens and waited. Eventually, he heard the growl of a diesel and walked across as the taxi drew up. His master got out along with the now familiar Erskine, but the third member of the party, the one Mary had mentioned, was not at all as Knapp expected. A tall, glamorous woman stepped out onto the drive. She took in the house and garden.

'This is wonderful, Sir John. Everything is so lush and green. What a garden...'

Knapp's professional pride got the better of him and he coughed gently from a distance.

'And here is the very man responsible,' announced Sir John. 'Knapp, come and be introduced and while you're at it, you can help us.'

Knapp shook hands with Amanda and Erskine.

Amanda looked across the grounds. 'This must be beautiful in the summer.'

'You must come back and see the garden when it's at its best,' enthused Sir John. 'Knapp is too modest, but it is superb.'

'Be careful I don't steal him and take him back to Johannesburg,' Amanda laughed, 'we have some fabulous gardens there.'

Knapp held open the door and the others carried files and papers past him into the house. So that was it, South African. What was she doing here? What was all this stuff? He tried to appear uninterested in the material as it went past him; the fronts of the files were irritatingly nondescript and where he did see a few names, they meant nothing.

Sir John made one final trip to the cab, this time for a roll of paper that he took care not to crimp as he eased through the door. 'Thank you, Knapp, we mustn't detain you further.'

Knapp walked back down toward the greenhouse. He was no further forward. He hoped he could persuade Sir John to bring him into whatever was going on. First though, he would have to prove his value. And how was he to manage that? Knapp thought hard as he returned to his duties.

For the investigators, the task of laying out the papers for analysis began. At the start the plan had been to set these out in the library, but Sir John suggested they place everything on the billiard table. This meant they could spread everything out and make sure nothing drifted off the top. Sir John unrolled the taped sheets and weighted the ends down with billiard balls. After a quick check, all three adjourned to the lounge for supper, leaving their work for Monday morning.

Their discussion of the case went back and forth, and they had nearly finished eating when Erskine said,

'There has to be a common denominator, I'm sure we'll find something next week.'

'Could there be any personal possessions left at the branches?' Amanda asked.

'I doubt it,' Sir John said. 'It's not the sort of thing people do, leave personal effects at work. A desk is hardly a private place.'

'When James comes in on Monday, ask him to double check,' suggested Amanda, 'just in case.'

'I doubt we'll find anything worthwhile, but we should do it,' Erskine agreed.

Sir John raised his glass. 'Here's to detection.' All three sank back in their chairs, staring into the fire which danced in the grate.

Time drifted by. The fire, warm and seductive, built a comfortable cocoon around the three in the room and they dozed in its glow. No one spoke. Eventually the coals began to lose their heat. Sir John stirred himself, 'Well you two, I'm going to call it a night.'

Erskine levered himself up in his chair, 'We should be going, can someone call a cab?'

They summoned Bridges, and the investigators, still talking, made their halting way toward the door.

'We meet again on Monday?' Amanda said.

'Indeed, as agreed. And we'll get Bennett to check your possessions idea,' Sir John raised his finger. 'A long shot, but worth a try.'

The two engineers climbed into the taxi and set off back down the drive.

'He's a good man, I hope we can help him,' Amanda said. 'There's a thread in all this. If we can pick it up, the whole knotty problem may unravel.' She paused,

'Isn't it great to be working together again?'

Erskine was stretched out, his legs extended into the footwell of the cab. He smiled up at her.

'It's tremendous, and all the better for being so unexpected.' He drew his legs in and sat up. 'How long can you be in London? This might take a while, if we ever solve it at all.'

'I'll have to see how things go. I should call the team to let them know it may take longer than expected.'

'The team in South Africa you mean?'

'They'll begin to think there's a problem if I don't call. I can say things are going well but they need to give me more time. That should stop them from getting too concerned. They might start to get twitchy, and I don't want them looking for other backers.'

The taxi continued east into the heart of London. When they arrived at White's, Amanda gave Erskine's arm a squeeze.

'See you nine-thirty Monday,' she whispered.

The driver continued towards Balham and Du Carne Court. After a few minutes in the cab Erskine decided to give himself some extra thinking time.

'Just drop me here please,' he called.

His walk back to the flat took him along the periphery of Clapham Common. He took stock of the team's limited progress to date. He was sure their idea of checking the transactions was a good one. He went over what they'd found in recent days. All three were involved in agreeing loans, and their focus had been on loans to businesses, not individuals. This backed up the comments Goode had made during Erskine's visit to the Swan Lane branch.

There were all sorts of industries involved in the loans, Erskine thought: chemical, manufacturing, shops, even mines. He noted this latter group wryly, given Amanda's reason for coming to London. There were smaller businesses too, grocers, butchers, and others. Did one of these hold the key to the disappearances? But how could three different people in three separate branches be associated with the same venture?

It was late, and Erskine left Clapham Common behind him and turned closer to home. The fog of the autumn night had descended, but he knew his route. He passed Holmside Road on his right and had just reached Old Park Avenue when he thought he heard a sound on the curb.

'Hello,' he called, and peered into the gloom. There was no answer, and he could see nothing. He pressed on, his steps brisker.

There it was again he thought, an unmistakable step. He called out, but then he reasoned, why would the walker reply? Erskine's presence would be just as sinister to his companion. He slowed his walk deliberately so the man would catch up with him, but there was no contact, and the sound of the anonymous steps dissolved into the fog.

The dripping steel structure of a railway bridge appeared out of the night and Erskine picked up his pace. He knew Du Carne Court was close. His heart beat faster, but he reminded himself there was no threat, other than that summoned up by his imagination.

On impulse, Erskine stepped into Elmfield Crescent, a left turn just before the access road to Du Carne Court. He stood hard against a lamppost and waited. For a minute there was nothing. Then, out of the fog, came the sound of the steps he'd heard earlier. They were not the 'tick tock' of a walker, but neither were they the stealthy tread of a footpad. His instinct was to make a bolt for Du Carne Court and the safety of his flat. Not this time he told himself; this was just too much. Footsteps in the fog might be unnerving, but they were no cause for this. He waited, straining his senses.

The steps were closer now. He could feel their vibration through his shoes, they beat hard on the road, something of colossal weight and power was coming... and then, no more than six feet from him, passing so close he could have stepped forward and touched it, dripping with fog, great clouds of steam rising from its nostrils, was an enormous black horse.

Erskine felt ridiculous. The mystery, the strange steps, the whole thing, made indecipherable by the fog and his overworked imagination, was explained. His pulse rate was racing. What on earth was a horse doing wandering the streets of Clapham? Perhaps it had come from the common or escaped from some nearby coal merchants? Whatever had happened, it wasn't his problem. The sound of the hooves receded, and he walked the few foggy, relieved yards to Du Carne Court and home.

27

The investigators met at Redshanks on the Monday as arranged. Sir John travelled into the City in the same taxi, agreeing to return mid-afternoon. He also asked Miss Denby to track down James Bennett and tell him to call the house for instructions.

Erskine and Amanda sat together in the taxi. The journey out to the house and the jostles and turns of the cab reminded Erskine of that first trip back to the hotel in South Africa. He made no attempt to avoid contact with Amanda and it seemed to Erskine she was happy to be with him.

Once at Redshanks they got to work on the analysis. Erskine felt there was a breathless quality in their conversation, and it seemed to him that Amanda welcomed their time together. It was as though they were conspiratorial, separate from the investigation itself.

'It feels like old times,' Amanda said.

Erskine smiled. 'Who'd have thought it?'

'Just like the evenings on the safety project, and there are lives at stake here too. We must get this right.'

Erskine had been looking at the papers on the billiard table.

'We need some symbols or marks to pick out things of interest on the sheets. This all just melts into one if you stare at it long enough.'

'Let's ask if there is anything we could use.' Amanda was about to open the billiard room door when Erskine pointed at the bell pull. 'Just give that a tug.'

Amanda laughed. 'Amazing! English country houses have everything.'

Bridges appeared. Amanda explained the problem and he thought for a moment.

'There are some coloured pencils in the study,' he offered. 'Sir John bought them on his sketching holiday in the Lake District. Would they do?'

'Just the ticket,' agreed Erskine.

Bridges left, returning with a decorated cardboard box bearing the name Derwent Colour Pencils. Amanda slid open the box.

'These are excellent. And we should have separate colours for the different types of loan and industry.'

They began to highlight the entries on the sheets.

Bridges reappeared. 'There's a call for Miss Ferreira.'

Amanda followed the butler out of the room. Taking the receiver, she found James Bennett on the line.

'Hello James, we have another task for you, I hope you don't mind.'

'Standing by,' Bennett said enthusiastically. He'd tell Violet, he thought, but all in good time.

'James, we need you to revisit the branches, to see if there are any personal possessions left at the bank, you know, of the missing people.'

'Of course, Miss Ferreira. I'll need an explanation though, to go to their desks. I mean it's not something a messenger would normally do.'

'How about checking if they've left anything their families or the police might want?'

'I'll give it a try,' agreed Bennett, 'but I'm not sure there will be much anyway.'

'Well done,' Amanda enthused. 'When you've got everything, such as it is, call again, and we can agree on what to do.'

An excited Bennett hung up, filled with his new mission.

Amanda went back to the billiard room. Erskine had been busy, and the papers were a mass of colour. Circles and boxes were everywhere, and lines and arrows flowed across the pages.

'Very pretty,' she teased. 'You should design wallpaper.'

'Highly amusing.' Erskine straightened and surveyed his handiwork. 'Gets results though.'

'Oh really. What've you found?'

'The range of businesses is huge, but the branches seem to have what you might call strong suits.'

'Go on.'

'So, Blackfriars has a lot of shop loans, in fact more than the other two combined. But Embankment seems to specialise in property and finance. Swan Lane has a lot more overseas business.'

'Perhaps the staff have expertise in some areas more than others, and the customers gravitate to them?' suggested Amanda.

'Good thought. That's something Sir John will know.'

28

James Bennett was excited; he was back on the team. He had spent the last hour practising his request, trying to keep it sounding light and unimportant.

'Just popped in to check their desk in case there were any belongings,' he said to the Embankment branch receptionist. 'Only be a minute.'

'On whose say so?' challenged reception, not used to the messenger boy being so familiar.

James Bennett played his trump card. 'Miss Denby, call her if you want to check.' This was more than reception could muster, and he was waived through. He approached a clerk who regarded him with curiosity.

'What do you want, Bennett?'

James repeated his request. The clerk gestured at a small brown bag in the corner of the hall.

'Over there. We kept Stevens' stuff separate in case anyone wanted to check it.' The clerk took another look at Bennett, evidently decided there was nothing to be gained by conversation with a messenger and returned to his papers.

Bennett checked the bag. The contents were almost all bank related. There were rubber stamps, a pen, some pencils, a blotter, and a jotting pad. The only personal items Bennett could see were a matchbook and some raffle tickets. Being an expert on Evening Standard detective stories, he checked the matchbook for secret codes or messages, but there were none.

'Cheerio,' he called as he made his way back past reception, 'I'll just take these.'

Back out on the pavement, he felt disappointed; Sir John had said it was a long shot. Bennett admitted though, he had hoped to find at least a clue. Still, he reasoned, two more branches to go.

The Swan Lane branch produced the same result. The receptionist was less concerned than at Embankment and waived him through, barely breaking off from her work. There was more stationary and a small tin of mints but nothing else. Bennett opened the tin. He hesitated, weighing up whether they might be laced with deadly poison, but then took one. At first, he moved it around his mouth cautiously, but having decided it was safe, he crunched it and set off for the branch south of the river.

He crossed Blackfriars Bridge and arrived at Hope Street, a branch Bennett visited less often, where he sensed a different atmosphere. To him, the slightly stuffy, stiff feel of the other two was missing, and the branch was busier and had a market feel. He put this down to the customers who were tradesmen or ran small businesses. Jenny, the receptionist, gave him a smile. She eyed Bennett from top to toe and back again.

'Hello James, I haven't seen you for a while; you're looking important today.'

'Nice to see you too, Jenny. Just popping in about Miss Simpson, the missing lady.' Bennett replayed his now well-rehearsed lines.

'Yes, Miss Denby called. I've collected her things, they're under here.'

Jenny reached under the reception desk, brought out a canvas bag and put it on the desk. She watched Bennett as he checked through the contents.

'Are you trying to find anything in particular?'

'No just collecting everything. I need to make an inventory, that's all.'

'Of everything?'

'Yes, all of it.'

Jenny reached to the other side of the reception desk and pulled open a drawer. 'You'll need these then.' She produced a tin of mints, the same make as the one Bennett had crunched earlier in Swan Lane. 'I've had a few but I don't suppose it matters.' Jenny regarded him apprehensively.

Bennett felt a surge of excitement, but he kept his voice calm. 'Not at all, Jenny, just so long as you've left some for me.'

Jenny laughed. 'Always nice to see you, James, and don't leave it so long next time.' She smiled again and Bennett could feel himself blush. Not the conduct of an investigator he thought. Whatever would the others say?

Those mints, he thought, they might be something. Could they be a link? Were they evidence? If they were, then he'd been important to the investigation. He stretched back his shoulders.

'A clue,' he said aloud as he walked back over Blackfriars Bridge, 'a flipping clue.' Passers-by within earshot looked twice at the young man. If only they knew, he thought.

29

Erskine and Amanda studied the charts.

'Brilliant,' Erskine said. 'The colours and symbols, they help a lot. You can see the differences by bank branch much better now.'

Amanda chewed her lip. 'Nothing jumps out at me.'

Erskine frowned and pushed his hands into his pockets. 'I know we're getting somewhere; I can feel it.' He took a few steps back from the billiard table as if to achieve a better perspective. 'Now, what is it we've identified?'

'We have, type of loan, coded in blue for business and pink for family, size of loan in green, orange, and red by scale, industry in dots, circles, boxes and triangles, length of loan in blue shades by duration and...'

'Most impressive,' Sir John's voice interrupted Amanda as he entered the room.

Erskine swung around and caught a globe resting on the edge of a bookcase, it crashed to the floor, breaking into a dozen pieces.

'I'm sorry, very clumsy of me.' Covered in confusion, he collected the pieces, cupping them in his hand.

'Not to worry,' Sir John said, 'nothing important. Let me ring for Bridges.'

Erskine placed the pieces in an awkward pile back on the bookcase. They slid off each other and some fell back to the floor. Embarrassed, he bent down to gather them again. He stared at the pieces as he rose.

'I tell you one thing we haven't done. We need to code them by country, especially the ones that aren't based here.'

Amanda frowned. 'That's not on the files,' she said gloomily.

Sir John spoke up. 'No. But I can help you there, at least with most of them.' He circled the billiard table, eying the rows and columns, talking to himself.

'Yes, that's the Fabien family, from Toronto.' He peered a little closer at one entry. 'Hmm, must be the Androssini's, from Rome, I think.' On he went, mentally cataloguing each one.

Amanda and Erskine began following him around the table, marking each entry using the colours.

After twenty minutes, Sir John straightened and massaged his back. The investigators surveyed their work.

'That's most of them,' said Sir John. 'But I'm not sure about those,' he waived a hand at some blanks on the charts.

'Well done,' Amanda congratulated. 'You have a pretty encyclopaedic knowledge of your customers I must say.'

Sir John was pleased too. 'Not bad, though I say so myself. Sorry about the gaps though, they're beyond me. You'll have to ask at the branches.'

Erskine, his face lit up, almost shouted at the others. He pointed at the charts. 'Can't you see – the gaps, those ones, they were all done in the same week.'

The three stared at the dates on the chart for the unidentified loans. Amanda saw at once that they were all arranged within a few days of each other.

In the hall, the telephone rang. They heard Bridges answer it.

'Yes. One moment.'

There was a pause and then the door opened.

'Mr Bennett's on the telephone. He wants to know if he can come over.' The butler coughed gently, 'he sounds excited.'

The taxi growled back down the drive. James Bennett stood in the billiard room, his collection spread out on the table.

'As you see not much in the way of clues to work on,' he said breathlessly, 'until I came to these.' He reached into his coat pocket and, with the air of a magician, produced two tins of mints, placing them with a flourish on the green baize. The others looked on nonplussed.

'What do they mean?' Amanda asked.

'It's a link see. They're the same tins. I mean they were at different branches.'

Erskine was interested. 'At different branches and in the possessions of the missing people?'

'Employees aren't allowed sweets at work, it makes the notes sticky if you're not careful, I know that.' Bennett glanced at Sir John.

'Which means they were given to them by a customer.'

'And what are the chances of two different customers giving the same sweets to two of our missing people,' Amanda said slowly.

'So, it was probably the same customer,' Erskine said.

'Exactly.' Bennett let out a low whistle but then added resignedly, 'but to two, not all three.'

'Well, the other tin may have been finished,' Amanda encouraged.

'Excellent, young man,' Sir John beamed. 'Let's collect all our clues together.'

Erskine explained the discovery of the 'missing country' link and the close timing of the loans to the attentive Bennett. As he spoke, he placed the two tins of mints on the chart and moved them around like chess pieces, trying to find some vague way of linking the clues.

'They're nice mints too.' Bennett stopped in mid-sentence, red in the face.

'Have you been eating the evidence?' asked Erskine sternly, then chuckled. 'Are they good? Let's try one.'

Erskine prised open the lid. There were plenty of mints in the first tin and he offered them around. There was silence.

'They are good,' said Sir John. 'I wonder where you can buy them?' he bent over and studied the upturned lid. 'Yaram Mints. Never heard of them.'

'Yaram?' Amanda was curious. 'That's an Afrikaans brand.'

Erskine snapped the lid closed and checked the base of the tin.

'Made in South Africa,' he read out. 'Yes, you'll be out of luck here.'

'Well, it means something for sure,' said Amanda. 'Let's hold on to that for now and check these mystery loan cases.'

Erskine and Sir John busied themselves with the papers, pulling out the files and confirming as they went that the dates were all close to each other.

Erskine led the charge. 'We've found five files, let's spread them out and go through the papers in detail.'

The minutes went by as Erskine, Amanda, and Sir John inspected each file. When they'd reached the end of the exercise, Erskine felt a thrill. 'They're all from companies based in South Africa.'

'Are they now? Just like the mints.' Sir John also seemed to sense a shift in the investigation. 'What else can we find?'

'They're all industrial. Chemicals, mining, steel...' Erskine was thinking hard.

'I took some papers to a mining company a few weeks ago,' Bennett said.

'What was it called, James?' Amanda asked.

'I'm not sure. Something mining...' he looked sheepish.

Amanda was flicking through one of the files. 'Was it Rand Mining?' she asked. Bennett brightened.

'Yes, that's it.'

'I know them, one of the biggest we compete with,' she studied the file afresh. 'And a large loan too. In fact,' she continued, scanning across each file, 'all the loans on these files are in our red category... That's interesting.'

30

The creature was far from home. The journey had begun hundreds of miles north, but it had reached its destination some time ago and was standing by the river, watching the house on the far bank. A man was working on the gardens that ran down to the water's edge; he had been there since dawn, and the two had been aware of each other for several hours.

Knapp had seen the watcher but paid it no attention. He was conscious the horse seemed to be studying him, but he was busy, today was a day for the roses.

Knapp untied the climbers from the garden wall and laid them out ready for pruning. As he prepared the garden, he went over the events at the house again. He was no clearer, but the addition of the South African woman added to the intrigue, and then there was the question of how to involve himself in the venture.

The promising whistle of a kettle intruded on his thoughts. He broke off from his work and walked around to the kitchen doorway.

'I thought you'd hear that kettle boiling,' Mary said good-naturedly. Knapp watched as she busied herself with the pot, running hot water through it before brewing the tea. 'All happening in the house today, goodness me it's busy up there, lots of comings and goings.' Mary arranged two cups and then turned back to her table. She was kneading a large roll of pastry and the smells in the kitchen were warm and wonderful. Knapp helped himself to tea and leant against the wall. Mary, without turning away from the table, inclined her head in the direction of a pile of biscuits resting on the griddle.

'Over there if you're hungry, I'm not watching. Mind it's just the one though.'

'And be sure you take a lumpy one,' Mary warned. Knapp took two lumpy ones, slipping the second into his pocket.

'Mary, what's going on with all these visitors?' he managed through a mouthful of crumbs.

Cook, still not looking up, continued.

'Sir John's in a better mood from what I hear. There are some foreign folks working in the billiard room on something too, but no one seems to be able to get to the bottom of it, even Bridges. They're using charts and all sorts. They even have the masters drawing pencils out.'

'It could be a map?' suggested Knapp.

'Ah, buried treasure, I've no doubt,' chuckled cook. 'But where? And I haven't seen Long John Silver yet, or his parrot.'

'Who are the visitors I wonder?' Knapp persisted.

'Well, the foreign lady has a very strange accent, Bridges says, not one he has heard before, and he has worked in some very grand houses. They've been here on and off for a few days now. Sir John seems keen on all of them, whoever they are. And then that lad arrived, he seems to be in on it too.'

Knapp stopped chewing. 'What lad?'

'Apparently, he's a messenger from the bank. Too familiar with the lot of them if you ask me.' She sniffed. 'He should be taking his meals in here, not in the dining room.'

Knapp received this news with some shock.

Mary stopped and wiped her brow. 'Whatever it is, it must be quite something. A messenger boy eating with Sir John and the foreign guests, it makes you think.' She straightened her back and turned, pointing a floury finger at Knapp. 'Why bring them here, that's what I ask. Why not do all this at the bank?' She hesitated, 'Mind you I'm not saying it's wrong and it is the master's house and all.'

'Well, we'll know more soon. If messengers are being summoned and charts drawn, the story will come out, you can be sure of that.' Knapp hoped he sounded confident.

Mary turned back to her duties and Knapp made his exit, leaving the empty mug behind. On his way out he lifted another biscuit.

'I saw you. You'll swing for that next time,' she called after him.

Knapp walked round to his garden workshop. Whatever the affair was in the house it had lost none of its interest. It occurred to him that if he could track down the messenger, he might find him better informed than the cook. He needed to arrange a chance meeting. Picking up his secateurs he gave them a final rub with the whetstone and turned back down into the garden and the roses.

Stepping across the laid-out branches, Knapp began to tidy the plants. As he completed each one, he climbed the ladder to tie the top spurs back into the wall, using the nails driven into the brickwork. On the third rose, Knapp paused at the top of the ladder and surveyed the garden. It was late autumn and most of the warmth and colour was fading, but Knapp took a lot of pleasure in its structures and planting. The ladder gave him a much wider view of the estate and Knapp saw the horse that had watched him from the far bank was gone. His gaze ran along the river, and he picked out barges and boats anchored along the towpath. Most were working vessels, but there were pleasure craft too. He could see a few horses tethered in the fields next to the path. Knapp knew the animals were used to pull boats of holidaymakers in the summer and for towing the working barges off-season. He fancied he saw his four-legged observer in the distance.

Mary appeared from the kitchen. 'Be careful up there, you must be heavy with that pocket full of biscuits,' she called.

Knapp raised a hand, 'You shouldn't tempt me, Mary.' He began to descend the ladder. Cook watched him climb down the rungs; she didn't speak until he reached the ground.

'You've got a hole in your fence.'

Knapp was eyeing the next climbing rose. 'No holes in my fence,' he said firmly, still studying the plant.

'Then how did he get in?'

Knapp looked at cook, but she was pointing back over his shoulder in the direction of the river. He turned and followed her arm. At the bottom of the garden, now standing on the house side of the riverbank, even from this distance visibly dripping wet, stood a black horse.

31

Erskine looked around the billiard room.

'Customers common to at least two of the branches, a series of transactions that have taken place in a short timeframe across all three banks, and what appears to be a South African link. Quite a haul.'

'Indeed,' agreed Sir John. 'What's next?'

'We need to make some visits,' Amanda said. 'We need to see what's behind these loans. Robert, you and I should do some due diligence.'

'Which cases will you start with?' asked Bennett.

'With customers from the branches where your mint tins were found, James.' Amanda smiled.

'We need a thorough inspection of everything you have collected, James. The smallest matter may be important,' Erskine said.

'I can spread everything out here and go through the lot,' said Bennett. His eyes ranged across the table.

Sir John said he had some matters to attend and left the others to their work.

'You keep at it, James,' said Amanda. 'Robert and I are going for a walk in the gardens, to talk tactics for the customer visits.'

Amanda and Erskine summoned Bridges. He walked them down a long hall that opened into a large Victorian orangery. The autumn sunshine beamed through the glass, and the air around them was warm. Lush Mediterranean plants soaked up the heat in the space. Erskine felt good.

Amanda slipped her arm through his. 'What do we have so far?'

'Well, we have three missing employees. Then there are a series of large loans, all to industrial businesses based in South Africa, although some have London offices. All arranged by the same individual but at different branches.' Erskine ticked off the points, emphasising each one with a little nod of his head.

'But only two mint tins not three,' Amanda cautioned. 'Maybe we should check the branch without the tin for a mint fiend.'

'Or someone with bad teeth,' Erskine chuckled. 'In a sense, we have two cases although one may be perfectly innocent. We have the missing people, and we have the mystery loans. The second of these could be legitimate.'

'But why go to different branches?' Amanda urged. 'That has to be suspicious.'

'I agree. It could be to hide an accumulation of loans to one place or region. In aggregate they could be unusual but spread through the branches they wouldn't cause concern or be turned down.'

'They *are* to different firms,' Amanda said, 'but the loans were all arranged at branches where people have gone missing.'

'We need to pay a visit to a few of the loanees,' Erskine said resignedly. 'We won't make any progress without some face-to-face questioning.'

Amanda withdrew her arm, and turned, stopping directly in front of Erskine. 'It's good to be working together again, Robbie,' she kissed him.

The two turned to make their way into the main body of the house. Just before they left the Orangery, Erskine looked back down the long garden towards the Thames. 'This is a superb place.'

Amanda followed his gaze. They could see two figures down near the river, they were pointing at something that wasn't visible from the Orangery.

'It's Knapp,' Amanda said. 'Do you remember, we met him on the drive? He seemed nice.'

'Yes.' Erskine collected his thoughts. 'Who's that with him I wonder?'

Amanda, in her best investigator tone remarked, 'I'd say that's the cook, judging by her outfit.'

'Well, they're heading our way. Let's say hello. We can check your analysis of the mystery figure.'

'Shall we say a shilling?' Amanda added.

Erskine grinned. The two figures were on their way up the gravel path back to the house and had seen the investigators. The man increased his pace, and the woman hurried with him, bobbing as she went. Erskine and Amanda waved. Knapp and the woman turned in toward the Orangery.

'Hello again, Knapp,' Erskine said as they approached.

'Mr Erskine, how nice to see you again, sir.' The gardener moved to tap his cap, then stopped himself. His companion studied her shoes.

'This is Mary, our cook,' said Knapp. Amanda coughed. Mary raised her eyes level with Erskine's chest.

'This is Miss Ferreira. Mary, I must say if the kitchen is as well run as the garden, Sir John is a lucky man,' Erskine encouraged.

'Thank you, sir.' Mary avoided meeting Erskine's gaze.

'Sir John's a very fair employer,' said Knapp, 'most of us have been with him for a long time.'

'I can see that,' Erskine said warmly.

'What were you looking at?' asked Amanda. 'I saw you pointing.'

Mary turned and smiled at Knapp.

'Terence here runs a beautiful garden as you can see ma'am. But he's upset at the idea there's a gap in the fence. Animals might get in and spoil the roses.' Cook gave Knapp a teasing smile then went pink.

'Surely that's easily fixed though,' said Amanda.

'Yes, ma'am,' Knapp said. 'But I can't understand it. There are no holes in my fences. I'd swear to it.'

'Well, that horse got in somehow,' Mary said. 'I doubt he swam the Thames, even if he was dripping wet.'

Amanda felt the jump in the crook of Erskine's arm.

'Have you seen it before, Knapp?' he asked.

'No sir, and you wouldn't miss it, being that big. Probably one of those towing horses from the field, got in somehow.'

'Maybe he came by boat.' Mary went even pinker.

'Beats me,' said Knapp flatly.

Erskine was thinking fast. 'I saw a horse the other night, it was wet-through. He was just off Clapham Common walking the street on its own, very strange.'

'That horse would have done well to get up here, sir,' said Knapp. 'That's a long way. As I say, I think it's one of the horses used to tow the barges. They're tethered in the field down by the river. With respect, the one you saw must've been a different beast.'

Erskine decided to leave it there. Both beasts had appeared in unusual circumstances, but there was nothing more to say for now.

'I'm sure it's not my business, but if I can help with anything I'd be pleased to,' Knapp said to no one in particular. He inclined his head back towards the interior of the house and crunched the gravel with his foot. He eyed the disturbed stones with irritation.

'Thank you, Knapp. We'll be sure to ask for your help if anything occurs,' Erskine said.

'I imagine the work must be quite... challenging. If there's any help needed, particularly outdoors then...'

'Absolutely,' emphasised Amanda. 'We'll let you know; you can depend on that.' She smiled at the gardener.

Knapp had to be content.

Mary bobbed once more and then detached herself from the group announcing that,

'Lunch won't cook itself.'

Knapp turned out of the Orangery and Amanda and Erskine at last made their way back into the house.

32

Amanda and Erskine found James Bennett still working in the billiard room. There was no sign of Sir John.

'These loans are all the same type, and they're spread over just these branches.' Bennett said, straightening up from his studies.

'Make a note of the company addresses,' said Erskine. 'We should visit them.'

'Most of them are in South Africa from what I can see,' said Bennett. 'But there are a couple in London, including the one I went to before.'

'Rand Mining you mean,' Amanda said. 'Give me the other details, the South African based ones. I'll see if I can find out anything. I'm going to call the office anyway; to let them know how things are going on the fundraising.'

'And how is it going?' asked Erskine wryly.

Amanda grinned. 'Well. Where is Sir John?'

'Gone to the bank,' said Bennett.

Erskine organised his thoughts. 'Amanda, you take the South African company names and check those on your call. Bennett, you keep going through the stuff here. I'll get Miss Denby to arrange some visits.'

James Bennett cleared his throat. 'How do you call South Africa?'

'You ask an international operator to set it up,' Amanda explained. 'It can take a while. Imagine my voice travelling all those miles, some of it under the sea.' She was slightly wondrous, but that was nothing to James Bennett's incredulity.

'I bet that's expensive,' was all he could muster. Calling South Africa, that would be another story to tell Violet; at the proper time he reminded himself.

'I'll call from the hotel,' Amanda said. 'I don't want to take advantage of Sir John. But, Robbie, I must come with you on the visits, two heads are better than one.'

'Understood,' Erskine agreed, 'but let's set them up first.'

Bennett found only two addresses in London. One was Rand Mining, and the second was a firm called Tragopan Exploratory. The others were all based in South Africa. Erskine called Miss Denby and asked her to arrange the London meetings using, 'getting to know our best customers,' which they all agreed was a reasonable cover.

The three investigators agreed to stop for the day. This time, the taxi dropped both James Bennett and Amanda before continuing to Du Carne Court. As the cab reached his flat, Erskine thought about the incident with the horse. It was a strange tale, especially if you tried to link the two appearances. He put it to the back of his mind as he entered the block.

It was supper time when his phone rang, Amanda's voice had a crackle in it.

'Robbie – I've had an unusual afternoon. It's sort of no news, but even that's interesting.' Erskine waited.

'You know the three South African based firms we added to that list. Well, there's nothing to find. No one at home has heard of them.'

'That can't be,' began Erskine. 'No one loses two steel manufacturers and a chemical works, even in South Africa.'

'I know. I spoke to Jonty who does our finances, but he didn't know them. So, I got him to do some checking, and he called back. No one in the firm, or our contacts, have ever come across them. We could have missed one, but three?'

'It doesn't make sense,' said Erskine, 'let's stir that into the mix when we meet at Sir John's.'

'There's something else too. Jonty said there's a rumour Rand Mining is in financial difficulty. Nothing solid but no smoke without fire and all that.'

'Remind me,' said Erskine with a chuckle, 'you said they were one of your biggest rivals.'

'Yes, I know, it's always the other lot that are the rogues. But Jonty is one of those cool objective types. For him to mention it, there must be something.'

'Let's hope Miss Denby's set up the meetings,' said Erskine. 'I'll pick you up on the way to Sir John's tomorrow. And thanks for the detective work.'

33

The next day saw a return of the autumnal mist in London. The investigation team, including James Bennett and Sir John, had installed themselves in the billiard room.

'At least this time we have something to report,' said Erskine.

James Bennett completed his inspection of the files. To his disappointment, there were no more clues; Amanda, however, reassured him.

'Your finds have been extremely helpful, James. Those tins of mints give us a definite link between the missing people. We now know, well believe anyway, that there's a plan to get around the bank's loan limits by arranging finance across more than one branch. Whoever it was needed a lot of money for something and quickly.'

'We haven't tied in the reason for the missing staff or the third branch where there was no mint tin,' Erskine acknowledged, 'but there's bound to be something.'

'What makes you so sure?' asked Sir John.

Amanda explained the mystery of the missing companies. 'They could be a front for something else,' she said.

'It's possible, but what?' puzzled Sir John.

The phone in the hall interrupted their thoughts.

'That'll be Miss Denby,' said Sir John. 'Erskine, you'd better take it. If she's her usual efficient self, she'll have arranged the visits to Rand and Tragopan.'

Erskine went out into the hall and lifted the receiver to find Miss Denby waiting.

'I have arranged your appointment with Rand Mining.'

Erskine noted the details. 'What of Tragopan?'

There was a pause. 'I'm afraid I've had no luck so far. There's no answer.'

Erskine frowned. 'Let's check the number, what did you call?'

'I called the number you gave me, Chelsea 1571,' said Miss Denby crisply.

'Amanda,' Erskine called out from the hall, 'what was the Tragopan number?'

'Chelsea 1571,' Amanda shouted.

'That's the right number, Miss Denby. Let's leave it for now.'

Erskine returned to the billiard room.

'Well, we now have a missing firm in London to add to the three in South Africa.' Erskine announced.

'So, of the five firms in these files,' Amanda gestured at the table, 'so far, we've found only one that actually exists.'

'Rand Mining,' noted Sir John. 'That was the one you delivered a package to wasn't it, Bennett?' Sir John and the others turned to James, but the messenger was transfixed, staring at a blotter on the table, it was the one he had recovered from the Embankment branch.

'The number you called out, Miss Amanda.'

'What of it?'

'It's here,' James Bennett's pressed his finger on the corner of George Stevens' blotter. His voice was triumphant. 'Mints or not, we have all three branches now.'

Erskine looked over the messenger's shoulder. Above Bennett's finger, written on the margin of the thick white paper was a note: Chelsea 1571.

34

'What do we hope to discover from a visit to Rand Mining?' asked Sir John.

Amanda was briefing the others over lunch at Whites.

'They are an old successful mining operation, based in the Transvaal area. They have other offices too, including the one here in London. The offices are used to market the mined minerals, or to raise development funds from investors, a sort of exploration starter capital.'

Amanda continued. 'The unusual thing is they've gone to a bank for loans, not tried to find investors; it isn't the normal way of operating; you normally do the loans at the end as a top-up.'

'So, they're trying to borrow money rather than get an investment partner,' Erskine noted.

'Yes, and what are they borrowing against?' Amanda frowned. 'It's hard to borrow money against assets which are in another country. Especially when that country is thousands of miles away, it makes the assets hard to verify. They must have been looked on very favourably by someone in the bank.'

'We'll have to see what we can turn up when we visit,' said Erskine.

'I'll come too,' Amanda said, 'but I won't be able to go into the office, they might recognise me.'

'Then what's the point of your attending?'

'I can wait outside and make sure you come out afterwards. If you unearth anything illegal, they might not let you out.'

'Very melodramatic.' Erskine laughed.

'May I remind you, Robbie, three people are missing.' Amanda said tightly.

Erskine sighed and pursed his lips. 'You're right,' he nodded. 'I'll collect you tomorrow morning. I'm due there at eleven. Now that we have all three branches in our sights, there could be other links. It might help us find a common factor in the disappearances.'

'There has to be something,' Amanda said. 'The idea that the same three branches share two things, one of missing people and a second of non-existent businesses, is just too much of a coincidence.'

35

Rand Mining's London offices were on the edge of Mayfair in Aldford Street, a well-appointed commercial thoroughfare that ran east towards Carnaby Street. Erskine and Amanda found the building easily. Unlike the neighbouring properties, it wore a dark façade; the stonework was stained with years of London grime, and the doors were heavy, uncompromising oak. Erskine eyed them anxiously.

Amanda looked at him. 'It's not very encouraging, is it? Our offices are much nicer. Now I'm going to have to leave you here. Do you promise you're going to be alright?'

Erskine grimaced, 'I can't say I'm looking forward to it, but it'll be fine.'

Amanda gave his arm a final squeeze and detached herself, walking off in the direction of a coffee shop. Erskine gathered his thoughts.

He entered the building and the door behind him closed, extinguishing the daylight. The pale lamps on the corridor walls cast thin shadows on the dark mahogany panelling. The interior reminded him of the shuttering of the mine props in the Transvaal basin, and despite everything he'd promised himself, he broke out in a sweat. He was thrust back into the heat and dust of the shafts. The creaking and shuddering of the rudimentary tunnel supports were there with him. He was deep underground, in Africa again.

A longer groan, more sonorous than the others, shook the structure and lifted his body off the ground. A roar followed, dreadful in its implication. All around him he could hear the screams of men and the cracking of timber. He was in darkness but surrounded by the faces of long-dead colleagues, victims of the mine's collapse. They rose in front of him, beseeching. Their cries spiralled louder around him, rising in pitch until they made thought impossible. Erskine tried to explain, to tell them he was trapped too, but the words wouldn't come.

He reached for them, and they disappeared, he covered his face with his hands, and they returned. He tried to breathe more slowly, to quell the rising terror in his chest, but a second roar more terrible than the first came, and he was lost. The faces piled one onto another and tightened around him. The apparitions pushed and jostled. He could feel their hot weight bumping up against his back. He staggered forward in the subterranean darkness, feeling his way down the shaft.

A sulphurous burning air filled his chest. He tripped and collapsed onto the body of another man, motionless beneath him. The contorted shape, grim and without hope, betrayed the owner's fate. Erskine lifted himself again and stared into the mine's abyss.

'Mr Erskine, Mr Erskine, are you alright?' a voice, feminine, sweet, and concerned, echoed back to him down the shaft. From somewhere down in the gloom a light appeared. The horrors of the mine began to retreat, and a woman's face appeared, pale and bloom like out of the darkness.

Erskine felt limp; he was soaked in sweat. His surroundings began to resolve around him. As his focus returned, he realised he was sitting up on the floor, his back against a large iron radiator. He could feel its ridges hard against his spine and the heat of the pipes stung his back. The voice came again. He peered around.

'Mr Erskine, would you like a hand?'

He levered himself up on the radiator. 'Thank you,' he managed, 'sorry about that.'

'You were a little faint that's all.' The woman gestured down the corridor. The parquet floor flowed away from him along the passage and turned right into some offices. 'Rand Mining Pty' arched across the frosted glass in a neat black crescent.

'Mr De Fries is ready for you.'

Erskine followed the woman.

Pausing above the crescent, she ushered Erskine in and motioned him to take a seat. The woman eased behind a desk, and having composed herself she spoke again.

'Mr De Fries will be out directly.'

Still shaking, Erskine looked around the office. There were complicated looking maps hanging on the wall. Some of them were close, and he could pick out the details. They were technical, with coloured cross sections set into small grids drawn into the general landscape. Erskine recognised these as excavations. His gaze ran further around the room. In a glass cabinet to his right, there were small, highly polished machinery parts. He recognised the exhibits as drill bits and locking pins from the mining industry.

Coming full circle, the figure of a stuffed cheetah sitting on its haunches caught his attention. It seemed to be studying him. The door behind the cheetah opened and a figure in a sharply pressed blue suit appeared.

'Mr Erskine,' the blue suit said, 'good to meet you, Pieter De Fries.'

Erskine surveyed the man. He was tall and tanned with a shock of thick hair slicked back in a silver and blond wave. His well cut suit was matched by a crisp white opened necked shirt, buttoned down at the collar. Double cuffs reached out an inch on each side beyond his jacket sleeves.

De Fries' grey eyes responded to Erskine's examination with the same curiosity. The man's features were angular, and his cheekbones were set high in his face. When added to the grey eyes sitting above them, they lent him an impression of sophistication. He came forward and extended his hand. The cufflinks shimmered.

Rising from the chair, Erskine felt his sweat-soaked clothes holding fast, stuck where they touched his back. His crumpled appearance must contrast with De Fries, he thought, but he was determined not to be intimidated. They shook hands.

'Thank you for sparing the time,' Erskine said.

'Would you like some coffee?' De Fries gestured. 'Judith, would you be kind enough?'

The woman smiled from behind the desk. 'Mr Erskine, how do you like it?'

De Fries took him into another office. Erskine noticed his gait as they crossed the floor. The man had a slight but discernible limp in his left leg. It was not enough to cause him physical pain, Erskine thought, but over time it would lead to issues. A past mining accident, he assumed.

The second office was in two sections. In the heart of the room the layout was business-like. There was a large mahogany desk inlaid with dark green leather and studded with brass pins. Behind it sat a formal chair, with a high back and heavy-set arms. In front of the desk to the right and left were two smaller, lower chairs. These were without the same grandeur as their central opponent. A useful layout for tough talking negotiations, Erskine surmised.

They walked through to the second part of the office, which was a more relaxed affair. It reminded Erskine of a gentlemen's club. There were several individual chairs, along with a leather settee and a free-standing table. All the furniture was red and had the same brass pins. A signed photograph sat in a frame on the sideboard. Erskine noted with surprise that the figure in the picture was Oswald Mosley.

They eased themselves into the sumptuous club chairs. Erskine tried to appear relaxed.

'I hear you have a mining background.' De Fries' Afrikaans accent was more obvious now they were in conversation.

'That's right,' confirmed Erskine. I spent several years in the Transvaal after I graduated from Imperial.

'Boy, that was tough,' De Fries widened his eyes. 'There were a lot of losses in those early years.' He studied Erskine. 'You weren't in the Komberley collapse, were you?'

'Yes, I was, just about got out, thank God.'

De Fries let out a low whistle. 'You were one of the lucky ones.'

Erskine grimaced. 'For sure.' He noted with surprise that he was almost back in the Afrikaans dialect himself. 'We got a lot changed after that.'

There was a knock, and the secretary came in with a tray. Her perfume, combined with the aroma of the coffee, was a heady mixture.

De Fries leant forward over the tray but stopped suddenly mid reach. 'Wait. Are you *that* Erskine?' His Afrikaans twang became especially pronounced.

'Yes, that's me.'

'*Now* I get it, well it's good to meet the man who made such a difference.' De Fries poured the coffee, 'I can promise you we stick with all the protocols.'

Erskine nodded, 'I hope things improve even further in time.'

'Don't squeeze out all our profit,' De Fries observed drily. There was a moment's hesitation and then the two men moved on.

'So how can I help you?' asked De Fries, folding his hands together.

Erskine adopted the tone of a reluctant questioner.

'I'm doing some basic due diligence.' He leant back in his chair, keeping his tone light. 'St Martin's Bank is the client. They've asked me to review their loan portfolio. I'm calling on some of their larger customers to catch up on their business. Just to see how things are, you know - the usual stuff.'

'Interesting.' The blue suit held Erskine's gaze and then nodded sagely. 'Very sensible in these straightened times.' He flicked an imaginary piece of dust from his knee. 'Well, we're in great shape. The Fansc and Jongfontein mines are running at full capacity and the results of the test drilling for Volgersmine are promising.'

Erskine pursued the point. 'Do you see any challenges on the horizon – say financial or political?'

The suit studied him closely again. 'No, I don't.'

'How about your loan exposure? Are you comfortable with all that?'

'You'd have to ask Charlie Malan for the details, he's our finance director. But we have plenty of surplus, and lots of room to pay back when the time comes; I can ask him for more details when he gets back.'

'When's that?' Erskine asked. 'It would be useful to see the books. I can wait if that helps.'

De Fries shook his head. 'You'd be here a long time, he's in Joburg this week.'

'How about the headline figures?' Erskine persisted. 'Could I review them? Just to keep my client happy.'

'Charlie's getting them ready for the quarter end,' said De Fries brightly. 'I can send you a set though, as soon as they're done.'

'Yes please. Who are Rand's auditors?'

'Owen and Joost in Joburg, but they don't get involved in our quarterly accounts.'

'Of course, but they will be reviewing the full-year figures I assume?'

The blue suited man nodded.

The two men continued talking. After an hour's discussion of the South African mining industry, Erskine decided to finish the meeting. It was clear to him De Fries was a quick thinker, and any further sparring on Rand Mining's financials was unlikely to reveal anything.

He took in the room again. Everything was calm. His host showed no sign of stress, and the secretary had seemed genuinely concerned for him earlier. The visit hadn't revealed anything unusual. What would the accounts tell him? If there were trouble here, they would be false anyway. He needed to speak to Malan, though; the man might give something away, and he needed an excuse to meet him.

'Was there anything else?' De Fries was saying.

'If it's ok with you, I'll make an appointment to come back next week,' Erskine said. 'I can review the accounts with your finance man.'

'Sure, but make it the end of the week, he'll need a day or two to recover from the trip.'

They got up.

'So, I have met the great Erskine,' De Fries said indulgently, 'wait until I tell Charlie.'

Erskine paused at the woman's desk. 'Judy, isn't it? Can I make another appointment for next Friday? I'd like to see Mr Malan when he gets back from South Africa.'

Erskine saw the woman check over his shoulder at De Fries. She seemed about to add something but then stopped and reached for her leather-bound desk diary. The perfume rose to meet Erskine again.

'Would 10:30 suit?' she asked, without lifting her eyes from the pages.

'Thank you.' Erskine shook hands with De Fries.

The Afrikaans stood under the black crescent. 'You know your way out I think,' he said, glancing down the corridor.

The door at the far end of the passage opened, and a man came in. The light from outside shone past the arrival, casting him in heavy silhouette. Erskine could see the street beyond the figure, and he thought of Amanda in the coffee shop, waiting for him. He made for the exit, passing the man on the way. Reaching the entrance door, he stepped out into the lukewarm sunshine.

The figure who had passed Erskine continued his way along the corridor and walked under the Rand Mining crescent. De Fries saw the man arrive and beckoned him past the cheetah. Inside his office De Fries folded his hands together and lifted them behind his head, pushing back hard into his cupped palms.

'Charlie,' he said, 'we may have a problem.'

36

Amanda drained her coffee. She had just seen a familiar figure outside the window of the café, and was ready to pass on her information, but she put all thoughts of this aside.

'Robbie, you look dreadful. What happened in there?'

'Let's get a taxi back, I can tell you on the way,' he said.

In the cab, Erskine recounted the meeting to Amanda. 'I had a bit of a flashback to the mine; I can't say it was pleasant.'

'Was it the same as the old ones?' Amanda asked.

'Pretty much. They don't happen as often now, but I suppose when they do come along it catches me out a bit.'

Amanda squeezed his arm. 'Poor you. That explains why you look so awful; do you want to go home?'

'No, let's go to Redshanks and report in. There isn't a lot to say, but I'm going back to Rand Mining next week, which may unearth some more.'

'Really?' Amanda asked. 'Well don't forget what Jonty said about their finances, something might show up. Why do you have to go back? Couldn't you have done whatever it was today?'

'Their finance man, he's away until next week.'

'You mean Charlie Malan?'

'You know him?' Amanda was part of the industry, so it was unsurprising, Erskine supposed.

'Yes, I know Malan.' Amanda adopted a conspiratorial air, 'and he walked past the coffee shop five minutes ago. Where did they say he was?'

'In Johannesburg,' mused Erskine. 'Well, well, perhaps we're making progress after all.'

37

Bennett turned as Erskine and Amanda entered.

'How did you get on?' he asked.

Erskine could see the billiard room was much tidier than when they left. The messenger had collected all the papers, put the files back together, and laid them out in a neat row on the green baize.

The two investigators sat down.

'My word, Erskine,' Sir John said, 'you don't look good.'

'I wouldn't mind a brandy; I do feel a bit rough.' Sir John summoned Bridges, then Erskine, prompted here and there by Amanda, retold the story of the morning. When they got to the mystery of the missing Charlie Malan and the excuses for not meeting him, Sir John rumbled.

'Fishy. I wonder what you're going to find next week?'

'That we will have to see,' Erskine agreed. He finished his brandy.

Bridges had set out lunch in the dining room, and the whole group fell silent while they ate, turning over this latest information in their minds. You could almost hear the cogs, thought James Bennett.

Erskine broke off from his meal.

'Most of the things we've found suggest a fraud on St Martin's. There are links between the branches, the loans for what seem to be fictitious companies, and then there are the mints. But it's a big leap, putting this together with the disappearances. If we're right, there must be something else out there, you can't make three people vanish without leaving some kind of trail.'

Sir John, Erskine, Amanda, and James Bennett walked over to a map of London they had pinned up over the billiard table scoreboard. The bank branches where a person had gone missing were ringed in red. They studied the map for a few minutes, half-heartedly pointing out road names and features.

'It may be nothing, Sir John,' Erskine eventually said, 'but there is one thing. The branches, by my reckoning anyway, they're all ones close to the river. They must be almost on the waterline, at least at high tide.'

There was a pause.

'You know you're absolutely right, Erskine, well done,' said Sir John.

'If you had a boat, it would be easier to get away unnoticed,' added Amanda.

'Either as the employee, or with a body,' Erskine said. 'But if you needed to access a boat unnoticed, you'd have to do that at high tide, otherwise you'd have to carry a body across the shoreline to reach the water.'

'Wait a minute,' Sir John left the room. The others could hear him calling, 'Bridges, Bridges, where are my tide tables?'

They heard a distant answer, and all went quiet. Sir John reappeared clutching a well-thumbed booklet.

'I have this for my sailing. This part of the Thames isn't tidal, but once you get down toward the City, you need to know about the tides if you want to moor against the jetty.

Bennett, call over the dates of the disappearances.' James Bennett checked the charts and then gave the first date.

'High tide in London was at 6:47 pm.' announced Sir John. Bennett called the next date.

'High tide was at 7:20 pm.'

'And the last one?' Sir John asked. Bennett checked and Sir John confirmed high tide had been at 7:51 pm.

'All high tides at convenient times in terms of being after hours for the disappearances,' observed Sir John. 'This might be it.'

'Next stop Rand Mining,' said James Bennett.

38

'Our visitor this morning,' De Fries began.

Malan dropped into a chair and cracked his knuckles.

'What of him?'

'He could be trouble. Thank Christ you were out, at least we have time to get things straight.'

'We already have. No one will ever get through the dummy companies. Who is this guy anyway?'

'His name's Erskine, ring any bells?'

Malan stopped cracking - 'Robert Erskine? That's a name from the past. What's he doing here? I thought he'd given up mining after Komberley.'

'He has it would seem; he was here on bank business. A kind of check up on their major customers, he said.'

Malan boomed out a laugh. 'If only they knew how major.'

'Well, he's coming back next Friday, and he wants to talk to you.'

Malan stretched and opened his huge shovel hands. 'I'd love a chat, always glad to meet an industry legend. Maybe I'll ask him how he funded his early research while I'm at it.'

'Make sure you have all the numbers ready.'

'Which numbers shall I give him? The ones we showed the cartel or the other ones?'

De Fries ignored the question. 'Thank God they're off our back. I don't like having to check over my shoulder every time I leave this place.'

'Your right there my vriend,' Malan agreed. 'At least the banks play by the rules.'

'Which is their problem not ours,' said De Fries. 'By the way, our man on the inside has gone silent.'

'Our men,' Malan corrected him.

'I was thinking of Ash,' said De Fries. 'But since you mention it, what of Crawley? I was expecting news on St Martin's by now. There hasn't been any kind of problem at the bank, unless I'm missing something?'

'My information is the run was just beginning, but they called a shareholder meeting and stopped the gossip,' Malan rumbled.

'Well then, try again,' said De Fries. 'We need to keep the confusion going, it makes sure the lines stay blurred.'

Malan gave a qualified nod. 'The extra insurance would be useful, but it's not vital.'

'No doubt, but I'd be much happier if those cards fell our way. Are all the funds transferred to Kempez?'

'Yes, we're in the clear with them now.' Malan cracked his knuckles again.

De Fries was thoughtful. 'Which means we're ready to negotiate for a new supply. I'm thinking we should close this office for now and start somewhere new, say Paris.'

Malan cursed. 'Just when I was enjoying London,' he sighed. 'But you're right my vriend, there are too many skeletons around here, much better to leave while we're ahead.'

De Fries nodded.

'Talking of skeletons...' De Fries added.

'No, nothing in the papers,' Malan was upbeat.

'Something will turn up eventually.'

'By which time we'll be long gone,' said Malan. 'Leave it, Pieter, I know what I'm doing.'

The financier levered himself out of the chair. 'What are we going to do about Erskine?'

De Fries stood up. 'You do some tidying up on the ledgers and make sure there isn't anything for him to find. Then follow up with Crawley and see if we can muddy the waters around St Martin's again. We should aim to be out of here by the end of the month, no later.'

'Ok,' said Malan. As he left the office he turned. 'And think about Erskine,' he glowered, 'he might need sorting out.'

39

The following Friday morning, Erskine walked the long corridor leading to Rand Mining's office. As before, Amanda held back at the coffee shop. She was to keep track of time as well as all the comings and goings.

'Good luck, Robbie,' she said as they left the taxi.

Now here he was again. The light from the street behind him died away as he entered the building. This time he was determined there would be no repeat of his panic. He walked past the radiator and in under the black crescent sign. The secretary was there waiting.

'Mr Erskine, how nice to see you again. Mr Malan is expecting you.'

Erskine took a seat. He chose a position that gave him a line of sight into De Fries' office. But there was no sign of the expensive suit, and a different door opened. A large heavily set man in a grey jacket came forward.

'Mr Erskine, Charlie Malan, pleased to meet you.' The host had none of De Fries' cut-glass manners, Erskine thought. His Afrikaans accent was thick, and to Erskine, carried the hint of a bully.

Erskine noted the man's hands, they were huge. His own almost disappeared into them. Malan was wearing a crumpled shirt under his jacket but no tie. It crossed his mind that De Fries and Malan were the wrong way around. He would have assumed the urbane De Fries was the financier and Malan the engineer.

Erskine followed Malan into a small boardroom. There were some brown ledgers laid out on a table. They sat down on opposite sides of the paperwork. The financier spoke first.

'You wanted to see our accounts, well here they are.' Malan waived a muscular arm across the table. He thumbed at the ledger in front of him, the pages released one after another like a pack of cards. 'I haven't had a bank show this much interest in us for a long time.'

Erskine made a depreciative gesture. 'Yes, I'm sorry to be a nuisance. St Martin's has asked me to look at some of their larger customer accounts, just to get a better understanding of their business. Routine stuff.'

Malan nodded. 'So where are we on the list?' He adopted a mock surreptitious tone in his thick Afrikaans. 'And what have you found?'

'Oh, you would have been quite a way down the list, but the customers we tried before you have been harder to contact,' Erskine said evenly. He tried a speculative prod, 'I don't suppose you know anyone at Tragopan Exploratory, do you?' Erskine fancied Malan twitched for a fraction of a second, but he couldn't be sure.

'No sorry my vriend, I don't,' Malan said coolly. 'Let's show you what we have here though.'

Did Malan move on a little too fast, Erskine asked himself, or was he looking for something that wasn't there?

Over the next hour Malan and Erskine reviewed Rand Mining's finances. Erskine was in no doubt they would look solid given the time available to prepare them, and so it proved. The meeting was a chance to question the financier, and he pressed on with his plan.

'You must have a busy time of it,' Erskine suggested, turning over the ledger pages. 'Last week Johannesburg, this week London.'

'Quite right my vriend. I sometimes have to check out of the window just to see where I am!' Malan was affable but, on his guard, Erskine thought.

'Speaking of South Africa, have you ever heard of Pargen Smelting, or Banfo Chemicals?' again, perhaps, the tiniest twitch he thought.

'They vaguely ring a bell,' Malan said, 'I think we may've done business with them in the past.'

'Thanks, might be helpful. Have you been in London long?'

'A couple of years,' Malan said. 'It's a great city. How about you? Last time I heard, you were in South Africa. You were quite a campaigner in those days, you and, who was the woman?'

'Amanda Ferreira.'

'That's her. A formidable team.'

Malan had a smile like the radiator in the corridor, Erskine thought.

'I assume you arrange the finance for Rand in London?'

'For sure, I do all that,' said Malan. 'There's no one else at this end I'd trust to get it right. Mining business is tough enough without having to deal with the backers.'

'How do you keep them all happy?' Erskine asked.

'Work with people who understand the industry,' Malan went on. 'They have a lot more patience than speculative investors.'

'Have you ever been in a tight spot?'

Malan frowned. 'Now and again for sure, but nothing we couldn't deal with, that's part of my job.'

Coffee arrived. Erskine made a display of shuffling his notes and then cursed softly but loud enough for Malan to hear. 'Which branch of St Martin's did you arrange the loans with – I'm afraid I've left some of my notes behind.'

'The one by the river.' Malan paused. 'I think it's called Swan Lane. All our business is done there.'

'Nothing in any other branch?' Erskine asked.

'No need,' Malan said airily. He let his gaze wander up to the boardroom clock. 'How much longer will you need?'

'I'm pretty much done.' Erskine sat back from the ledgers. 'Thanks for the time.'

'Have we passed?' Malan asked drily.

Erskine and Malan rose, and the two men walked back to reception. The secretary was sitting at her typewriter.

Erskine tried again, this time watching the woman as he spoke. 'You mentioned you might have done business with Pargen Smelting or Banfo Chemicals,' he said as lightly as he could. 'Would you mind checking back on your records? Could you let me know if you find anything?'

'For sure,' Malan confirmed. 'Happy to help an industry legend if I can.'

Erskine watched the secretary over Malan's shoulder. There was no doubt this time, the typewriter stopped abruptly but then restarted. The woman coughed to hide her movement, but the cough took hold, and she couldn't shake it.

'Apologies... gentlemen,' she managed between fits.

Malan reached into his pocket. 'Take one of these,' he said. He turned to Erskine, 'How about you my vriend, would you like one?'

Erskine glimpsed the top of a lid in the man's enormous hand. 'Yes, why not.'

Malan proffered the tin. 'Yaram Mints. A South African delicacy,' he smiled, 'try one.'

Erskine took a mint. 'Well, it seems to do the trick.' He smiled at Miss Brand, who had recovered her poise.

The glazed entrance door opened, and De Fries entered.

'Ah, Erskine, I hope you got the information you needed?'

'Thank you. Yes, Mr Malan has been extremely helpful.'

De Fries flicked an involuntary glance at Malan who appeared unmoved. 'Excellent. Well don't hesitate to come back if you need anything else.' He stepped to one side and left the door open for Erskine, who took his cue and made his way out down the corridor.

Back in De Fries' office, Malan dropped into a huge leather chair. He examined the carpet and dragged his heels against the grain, making jagged blue scars in the pile.

'What d'you think?' De Fries asked. 'How close are they?'

'Given time they might get there,' Malan said slowly, 'it's possible. But they still haven't pieced together the loans to the shell companies, and there's nothing to link us to those.'

'But what about the staff?'

'They haven't got a clue. It didn't come up in my meeting or yours. At least as far as you explained it to me.'

'So, we keep to our plan for an end of month departure,' De Fries said.

40

Erskine and Amanda had given James Bennett the evening off. He'd protested but was secretly pleased with the chance to see Violet. Detective work was exciting, he thought, but he hadn't seen his girl for a few days, and she might begin to wonder. As a treat he had decided to take her to the pictures. They agreed to watch the new epic film Cleopatra, as Violet wanted to see Claudette Colbert. They paused outside to look at the posters.

'You look a bit like her,' James said. Violet smiled and gave James' arm an extra squeeze.

They bought popcorn and sat excitedly in the darkness of the stalls.

At Redshanks, Erskine was speaking.

'The mints are careless. They give us a link to the other branches. Malan was adamant he'd never visited them. I'm surprised.'

'Perhaps Malan didn't realise you can't get them here,' Sir John said.

'Good point,' Amanda said, 'but he's been here for a while, and you'd think he would know if they were a favourite of his.'

'Which does make it a mistake, I'm sure of that.'

'And why mention Rand may have done business with Pargen Smelting and Banfo Chemicals if they don't exist?' Sir John asked.

'Confusion, in a word,' Erskine said. 'Don't forget he denied any recollection of Tragopan, which is supposed to be in London but said Pargen Smelting and Banfo Chemicals might be familiar. He was hoping our overseas information would be unreliable but wouldn't take a chance at this end.'

'He remembered Amanda,' Sir John chuckled. 'You certainly make an impression my dear.'

Amanda grimaced. 'They're up to their necks in this for sure.'

Erskine nodded. 'I'm worried though. If this fraud is as big as it seems they might stop at nothing.'

'Including removing anyone who got in their way.' Sir John sat down heavily in one of the large chairs. He rubbed his hands across his eyes. 'Really this is too dreadful.'

'It's all about the reason for the disappearances; to get to that, we need to set a trap. If we can expose them, we may find a way to trace the missing people,' Erskine said.

The others were silent.

'We need Bennett and Knapp. If we can get them here tomorrow, we can make a start.'

The telephone in the hallway rang.

A grim-faced Sir John MacGregor returned to the study.

'That was Miss Denby. Someone else has gone missing. A chap called Ash, at Swan Lane, one of our best men, that's two from the same branch.'

'That name's familiar,' said Erskine. 'He's the assistant manager, isn't he? Do we know anything else?'

'Apparently he took some holiday but hasn't returned.' Sir John sighed.

'So, it could be he has got held up or something?' offered Amanda.

'Possibly, but St Martin's has only just introduced paid holiday, and I doubt anyone would blot their copybook so soon, especially Ash, he's one of our brightest stars.' Sir John's hands were behind his back and Amanda saw the knuckles were white. 'We need that trap, Erskine.'

Erskine and Amanda stared at each other.

'I'll telephone Miss Denby and ask for Bennett.' Erskine said. 'Sir John, can you ask Knapp to attend first thing tomorrow?'

41

Up to now, the spirits at the bank had been content to leave the current human guardians to themselves, but the disappearance of Leonard Ash alerted them to a much greater level of menace. They were restless, and their unease filled the bank. To some of the staff, the veined marble walls seemed to shudder slightly. There was a background whisper high in the vaulted ceilings of St Martin's, and in the Swan Lane branch, Goode and his colleagues were anxious. The fourth disappearance and the second at the same branch ruled out any kind of domestic theories and their talk now was of who the next victim would be.

James Bennett was back on his messenger duties. His evening at the pictures with Violet had been just what he hoped. His girl was keen to hear how the work with the Checkograph machine had gone, and he was ready with his cover story, knowing that Violet was not in the least bit mechanical. He'd come up with lots of technical-sounding terms, which she listened to in wonder.

It was mid-morning when he pushed open the door of the Swan Lane branch. Bennett saw Goode as soon as he walked into the lobby.

'One disappearance is mysterious,' he told Bennett. 'But this, this is just awful.'

'What's happened?'

'Leonard, Leonard Ash. He's gone missing too. Should have been back from holiday by now. Another one.' James could see Goode was close to tears.

Bennett left the branch with his mailbag full. He knew this latest disappearance would put more pressure on the team. There would be another call soon he thought. Best be ready for anything.

42

The next morning, Terence Knapp joined Bennett, Amanda, Erskine, and Sir John in the study at Redshanks. Bennett and Knapp stood. Amanda sat with Sir John. Erskine planted his feet in the centre of the room and began to speak, rocking slightly as he delivered each point.

'We're pretty certain the three branches with the missing employees have all been involved innocently or otherwise, in a fraud.' He looked at the others, but nobody interrupted. 'They made loans to what look like fictitious companies. The loans were all taken out based on fictional business plans approved by senior people at those branches. In fact, it's likely the monies from all of them have ended up somewhere in the coffers of Rand Mining. The reasons for all this aren't clear yet, although there are a few possibilities.'

'Why not just borrow the money directly?' asked Bennett.

'Because the total amount borrowed would be way beyond what the bank would loan to one firm.' Sir John explained. 'So, by inventing extra companies that appeared unrelated, they were able to borrow a much larger amount, spread across lots of companies.'

'But why would they need such an enormous amount of money?' Knapp asked.

'We don't know yet,' Amanda said. 'But it might be they are in difficulty money wise, or with a big project to fund.'

'So great it was necessary to kill anyone who found out about the fraud. There must be a lot at stake.' Erskine was grim.

'Or maybe the staff were in on it and needed removing,' Knapp offered.

'Be quite clear,' Erskine said, 'these aren't just fraudsters, they'll murder to protect their interests. If we're going to trap them, we will need to be brave as well as clever.'

'And careful,' Sir John added.

43

Over the next few days, observers of the Rand Mining offices would have noted a change in tempo. The telephone rang more often, Miss Brand typed more than usual, Malan and De Fries conducted conversations in English, Afrikaans, and French; boxes appeared, were filled, and disappeared.

Terence Knapp had left his garden and was now on watch in the Stamboul coffee shop in Aldford Street. Most of the time he sat by the window in the seat Amanda had used a few weeks before. The first day Amanda came with him, it was she who pointed out the Afrikaans. But now Knapp, on his own, made notes, sucked his pencil, drank coffee, and wished he had some of Mary's biscuits.

It was on the fourth day, out of sight of Knapp's surveillance, that De Fries' phone rang at Rand Mining. A voice at the other end announced,

'This is the long-distance operator. Will you accept a telephone call from South Africa?'

After a few moments, a familiar voice came on the line, although it belonged to a caller he hadn't expected to hear from again.

'Mr Pieter De Fries, how are you today?'

The voice brought back memories for the engineer. They were good ones, profitable ones, memories that recalled the early days of his time at Rand Mining.

'Jacobus Koss, well I must say it's been a long time. How's business?'

'Can't complain, can't complain.'

De Fries remembered the man's habit of saying things twice. 'Where are you telephoning from?' He was intrigued, the Koss he remembered wasn't in the habit of making social calls.

'Joburg of course. Where else?'

'And to what do I owe the honour after all this time?'

'It's in the way of a business opportunity. A business opportunity.'

'Well now, you had better tell me all, but I warn you, it will need to be something special.'

There was a chortle down the line. 'You'd better prepare yourself. You could say it's a once in a lifetime chance. Once in a lifetime.'

The call continued. De Fries eventually put down the phone and let out a low whistle. He left his office and found Malan, who was packing boxes.

'I've just had a call... from Jacobus Koss of all people.'

Malan kept packing. 'That's a voice from the past. What did he want?'

'He has an opportunity for us, but we're going to have to move fast.'

'And find a way to print our own money no doubt.' Malan growled.

'Yes, I know,' De Fries acknowledged. 'But let me explain it to you.' De Fries outlined the contents of the call. 'And no one else knows about the find yet, only Koss, a few of his men, and now us.'

'How do we know it's genuine?'

'Koss has a man here in London, he has the charts and test results. He's going to drop them off here tomorrow.'

'That doesn't prove anything,' Malan peered into a box and grunted. 'We've both seen plenty of fakes in our time, we even...'

'Yes, I know.' De Fries said curtly. 'I can make some calls though, to see if the site location is correct. I'll put some feelers out, as a start anyway.'

'And where do we get the money?' Malan was still going through the box. 'We've only just solved our problem with Kempez. I thought we agreed to wait until we were in Paris?'

De Fries grinned. 'If this is as good as Koss says it is, that will be the next step. Don't worry I have a plan.'

'Do the research and let's see those samples when they get here, but don't get your hopes up.' Malan said.

Activity in the Rand offices increased further. De Fries made some long-distance calls to South Africa and Malan visited his favourite London bars. A farewell tour he told himself.

Terence Knapp leaned on his elbows and sighed. He'd called in his reports regularly from the phone box near the coffee shop, but after a while one became like another. There were only so many ways he could confirm that De Fries and Malan remained 'on site' and that 'it looks like they're doing a lot of packing.'

'They're moving out,' said Amanda. 'There must be something going on behind the scenes. Keep watching Terence.'

A short while after Knapp's latest call to Amanda, a figure arrived at Rand's offices he hadn't seen before. The man was carrying a small rucksack with some papers sticking out of the top. The figure disappeared behind the main building door and down the corridor to Rand's offices. He checked the time and noted it in his book.

44

Charlie Malan knew the wisdom of De Fries' plan to leave London. He was disappointed, but had to admit it was the sensible thing to do. With the Chileans paid off and St Martin's none the wiser, he accepted the best thing was to find another place to operate from, and preferably before any bodies turned up.

But departure was some days away, and there were still his favourite haunts to visit, especially this one. He stood under the blue and white sign above the club door. The painted wooden figure of a blond woman draped across the lettering, *Scaramouche*, it read. By Malan's reckoning, it meant the club should have been Italian, and indeed, he knew the proprietor was from Naples. The girls, though, he thought emphatically, were not.

Malan shared a joke with the two doormen and eased down the stairs into the club. The lights were low, and shadows stretched conspiratorially into the corners. He looked around but she hadn't arrived yet.

The barman knew Malan's drink and poured a large one. 'Charlie, how are you this evening? You're early, Loretta isn't due here until eleven.'

'That's fine, Frank, I can wait. I plan a full evening here.' Malan winked and the man gave a brief smile.

'Talking of my favourite people, has Crawley been in recently?' asked Malan.

Frank broke off from cleaning glasses. 'What is it with you two? You've been as thick as thieves since you got together.'

'That's our business.'

The barman rubbed his chin. 'I haven't seen him for a few days, but he was in fine form last time he was here.'

Malan frowned. 'Fine form as in good spirits, or more than that?'

Frank looked at Malan and grinned. 'More than that.'

'I'd love to know where he gets his fuel from,' said Malan.

Frank leaned across the bar. 'See the corner table opposite the stage? There's a guy sits there, comes in every week. He gets quite a few visitors; your man is one of them.'

'What does he look like?'

'Hard to tell. He doesn't buy drinks at the bar and that table is one of the darker spots in here. He wears a hat though, a fedora.'

'If he's doing business in the club, he must pay a retainer. I assume that goes straight to Cellini?' Malan said.

'Certainly.'

'But doesn't he look after you too?' Malan was surprised.

'No.'

Frank wasn't telling, even if he did take a cut, thought Malan, sensible guy.

'I tell you who might help,' Frank said, 'Deborah, the guy's keen on her. She makes sure to drop by his table when he's in.'

Malan looked around.

'Due in soon,' said Frank. 'I'll introduce you.' He grinned again.

The club was still quiet. Only a few girls were working across the tables. Malan sat at the bar and ordered another drink. He was going to miss his evenings here he thought. He planned on a big send-off tonight though.

A pianist was playing at the edge of the stage. He'd begun on his own, but one by one the other musicians came in, adding to the scale of the sound. Malan ordered another drink and walked across to the band.

'Do you do requests?' he asked the trumpet player. The man nodded.

'How about sophisticated lady?'

The piano player smirked. 'Not many of them around here,' he said.

Malan returned to his stool. The Ellington classic began as he sat down. He checked his watch. Less than an hour before Loretta would show.

A girl he hadn't seen before appeared from behind the stage. She seemed tall by Scaramouche standards and moved confidently between the tables. Frank looked up.

'Deborah, my friend wants to see you.' The barman nodded at Charlie Malan.

'Sure, I'll have a bourbon,' the girl said. She walked along the edge of the bar, running her hand along the top as she approached. She reached Malan and stood looking at him. 'What can I do for you?'

Malan found himself comparing the girl with Loretta. Not much in it, he thought.

'Just information,' he said.

'And what would that be?' Deborah was almost insolent. Maybe her men liked that he thought.

The girl waited.

'Your gentleman friend, the one who sits at that table.' Malan pointed to the corner. 'What d'you know about him?'

'I have a few friends who sit there. You'll need to be more specific.'

Frank was on the other side of the bar, he leant in. 'He mostly comes here on a Tuesday,' he said. 'Sometimes wears a fedora.'

'Ah that's Jerry,' said Deborah. 'Jerry's a classy gent.'

'By which you mean he spends a lot on you,' Malan said.

'He knows a good thing when he sees it.'

'I bet he has a lot of friends. Does he ever have problems with any of them?' Malan asked.

'Not that I've noticed,' Deborah said.

'Have you seen him recently?'

Frank eased another drink in Malan's direction.

'He was in last Tuesday, might be in again this week, depends on who wants to see him.'

Malan had an idea. 'Can you contact him?'

'Maybe.'

'Tell him there's someone who wants to meet up.'

Deborah adjusted her stance. 'I might be able to help,' she said.

Malan reached into his jacket and examined his wallet. The girl eased her arm off the bar and Malan placed a note where it had been. Her eyes widened slightly but she gave little else away.

'Back in a bit,' she said.

The club had begun to fill, and the band were moving through their repertoire. Malan, several drinks into the evening, was enjoying himself. He wasn't quite sure what a meeting with Jerry might yield but he had it in mind to check if Crawley was likely to leak their plans for the bank. Was he loose tongued? It was possible. He also wondered whether to ask the dealer to dilute his supply to Crawley, at least until they finished with him. A less potent product might help keep their man focused.

All the time, he kept a watch on the space next to the stage where the girls came out.

At around eleven, Malan saw Loretta arrive. She favoured him with a huge smile. Walking along the edge of the counter, she reached Malan and draped her arms around his neck.

'Charlie, what a lovely surprise! I hope I haven't kept you waiting long.'

'Always too long,' Malan smirked.

'Martini,' said Loretta, over her shoulder. Frank obliged.

After a few minutes, Loretta led Malan away from the bar to a table in one of the corners. They sat talking and touching. Lorretta's head nuzzled against Malan's, but she stayed in the barman's eye-line, signalling for more drinks from time to time. Malan sank further into his alcohol-fuelled evening, and his animated speech became disjointed.

'And London is great, and you're here, and when we're gone it's not going to be the same.'

'You, not here?' The girl picked up the point at once. 'What's happening?'

Malan scrambled. 'Not leaving, no... just for a bit... things to do.'

'When?'

'Soon.' Malan tried to pull himself straight, 'But not tonight!' He thumped the table and almost fell off his chair.

'Back in a minute, Charlie.' Loretta left the table and walked back to the bar. She signalled to Frank and spoke earnestly to him, before sauntering back to Malan.

Scaramouche was busy, and the air in the club was full of sweat and smoke. Loretta and Malan were deep in their evening when Frank leant in between them.

'Jerry's here,' he said.

Malan raised his head and, with an effort, directed his gaze away from Loretta. He tried to focus on Frank.

'Jerry?'

Frank grinned at Loretta. 'You remember Charlie, you asked me to tell you if he came in. He's over there.' Frank pointed across the club. A man with a fedora was taking his seat.

Malan gathered himself.

'Good. Get me introduced.'

'He's expecting you,' Frank said with a smile.

Malan levered himself up and made his way across the club. The man in the fedora watched the Afrikaans unsteady approach between the tables.

'Charlie Malan,' the Afrikaans slurred and sat down.

'Jerry Dansen,' replied the man at the table. 'Good to meet you. Drink?'

Frank arrived with another round.

Dansen eyed Malan thoughtfully. 'How can I help you?'

'You have a customer... a client... a man called Crawley?'

'Rupert, he's a regular.'

'Regular what?'

'A regular friend,' Dansen said indulgently.

Malan leaned into the man's face, breathing heavily. 'I have an interest in his... his behaviour.'

Dansen laughed. 'How unusual. What would you want with Rupert?'

'Is he...' Malan struggled for the word, then leaned even closer, 'Discreet... Does he say much about... anything?'

Dansen frowned. 'What is it you want, Malan? Are you buying or fishing?' He picked his fedora off the table and upended the hat in his hand. 'I was asked to see you, so here I am, but unless there is something specific?'

'Hold on, hold on,' Malan said. 'So, Crawley hasn't said anything about, for example, a bank?'

'What?'

Malan could see Dansen was genuinely at a loss. He eyed the hat. 'Good,' he said. 'That's good.'

Dansen rose.

Malan squinted blearily up into the man's face. 'And your product line, for Crawley, is it... first class?'

'What takes place between Mr Crawley, and I is a private matter,' said Dansen, easing around his chair and looking across the club.

'Yes, but are you able to,' Malan tried to explain his idea, but the words wouldn't form in his head.

Loretta, who had been watching from the bar, saw Dansen get up, she moved across to the table.

'Tell Frank I'm done here,' he said to the girl. He nodded at Malan, 'It's on his tab.'

Malan watched the man leave. He wanted to pursue his idea of adulterating Crawley's supply, but it was beyond him. He sat at the table and tried to focus on Loretta, now back at the bar. He saw her turn to look at him and then begin her way across.

'Just you and me again, baby,' Malan slurred as she approached.

'That's nice.' Loretta stood next to the table looking down at Malan. She folded her arms. 'Frank would like a word.'

'Well, he should come over,' Malan said. 'The more the merrier.'

'No, he wants to see you at the bar.'

Malan looked across the room. 'Ok. I want you to know Charlie Malan doesn't usually agree to barman's requests, but as I'm a good guy...' Malan, with the help of Loretta, left the table and, after some effort, deposited himself at the bar.

'Frank, Frank, how can I help you?' Malan eyed the bottles with enthusiasm.

'Charlie, I need you to settle your tab.' Malan tried to refocus on the barman, who looked edgy.

The Afrikaans' befuddled stare met Frank's. 'What's the rush?' I usually settle at the end of the month?'

'We need it done tonight.' Frank said definitively.

Loretta inched herself away from Malan and circled round behind the bar. Malan saw her glance over his shoulder, and he turned instinctively. The two doormen were standing just a few feet from him.

'Boys, you look nervous.' Malan said. The men exchanged glances. They knew he was an expert brawler and no less dangerous when drunk.

Loretta, wide-eyed, leaned across the bar. 'Come on, Charlie, everyone has to make a living.'

'The end of the month. What's changed?' But even as he spoke, through the haze, Malan got it.

They wanted payment now, before it ended, before he left.

Loretta must have told them.

'Well, you'd better come and get it.' He swept the glasses off the bar and hurled a bottle at the head of one of the doormen. His target ducked and the missile disappeared into the darkness of the club. A woman screamed. A man's voice raised in alarm and there was the sound of chairs falling over.

'Christ!' Frank peered anxiously into the gloom.

The doormen took half a pace forward. Malan was angry now. Angry they had to leave London. Angry Loretta would be someone else's. Angry his big evening should finish like this.

With a bellow he charged at the men, smashing them apart. He careered across the dance floor, lunged at the trumpeter, and ripped the instrument from his fingers. Taking a step across to the pianist he smashed the horn down on the piano keys. The man leapt away from his stool as the doormen arrived. Malan tried to crash through them, but they had him this time and kicked his legs from under him. He fell back against the piano, and they pinned his arms. Bumping and growling, breathing heavily, the three progressed haltingly across the floor to the foot of the stairs. As they inched their way up, Malan, dragged backwards, could see the scene at the bar retreating below him. Loretta and Frank watched impassively as he made his exit.

The chill of the evening greeted them.

'Charlie, this is business.' The doormen grabbed their breath. 'Settle the tab and you're back on the list.'

But Malan looked at them with something like respect. 'Good effort guys,' he said. 'Don't write me off yet though, I'll be back.'

Malan's efforts had sobered him up enough to realise the last thing he needed was an arrest for fighting in the club, and besides, he thought, he hadn't paid the tab, so it was one up to him. He would be back someday, and when he did it would be as the owner, for sure. For now, there were other clubs to visit. Malan took a pace away from the entrance and the doormen lowered their hands.

Halfway down the street he turned back to shout at the men. They were opening the doors for two guests. One wore a fedora; the other was Rupert Crawley.

45

Scaramouche was just off the Strand and the incline of the roads that ran south of the club led the muzzy-headed Malan down onto the Embankment. His uncertain steps took him to the edge of the Thames, and he leant against the low stone parapet that ran up to Blackfriars. The cool of the late evening was sobering and he began to recover his senses. Just a few yards along from him a couple entwined wordlessly on a bench, partly hidden in the moonlit shadows of a plane tree. Further along the wall a drunk was serenading someone or something, singing breathlessly at the opposite bank, arms outstretched. Across the river he could just make out a tug appearing from beneath Waterloo Bridge. There were distant sounds downriver, muted, and conspiratorial.

Malan rubbed his knuckles and grinned. He'd have bruises in the morning, but he was no stranger to that. Honours even, he thought.

A movement beyond the couple on the bench caught his eye. The darkness was heavy under the trees, and it was difficult to make anything out, but then something detached itself from their shadows and began moving along the Embankment toward him. The figure was huge but indistinct and it took Malan a moment to recognise its shape. A horse, bigger than any he'd seen in South Africa walked silently past him. He watched the animal go by, no more than a few feet away. There wasn't a sound.

The drunk had stopped his aria and was also eying the horse. Malan watched as it approached the man, who threw his arms around its neck and began singing again. After a while, the songs started to lose their energy, and the drunk gradually subsided against the animal's neck. The singing faded into the occasional desperate word. Finally, there was silence.

Malan shook himself and focused on his journey home. He would need a cab, and he stepped out onto the edge of the road and waited, arm raised. It was late though, and traffic was almost non-existent. The minutes passed, and he could feel his tiredness and irritation grow. Then, from behind him, he heard a cry and a loud splash. He turned to look in the direction of the river. Probably, he thought, the drunk had fallen in, the splash was big enough. He returned his attention to the road in time to see a taxi moving down the Embankment in his direction.

The courting couple detached themselves and looked out over the river. Edward peered at the dark surface of the Thames.

'What did you think you heard, June?' he asked.

'It sounded like someone falling in the river,' his girlfriend sounded anxious.

'I can't see anything.'

The young man strained his neck over the stone parapet. 'Wait, what's that?'

A few yards away from the wall, moving out into the river, a large black shape was visible, its wake glittering in the moonlight. As Edward watched, the shape began to accelerate, and a bow wave spread out in front of it. With a final surge the shadow pushed hard into the water and disappeared under the surface.

46

'My God, Charlie, look at this.' De Fries stood in Malan's office holding a chart and a small tube. He shook the tube, which made a promising rattle. Malan was quiet; he had a splitting headache and was already three aspirins into the day. He raised his head slowly.

'OK, let's see it.' Malan sighed and moved his glass of Alka-Seltzer to make room for the charts.

De Fries unrolled the papers. He opened the tube and spilled the contents out over the charts. 'The layers of chromite are so thick, some of the broadest I've ever seen. There must be massive amounts of platinum.'

There was no doubt. The gleam of the rare metal, lustrous and beguiling, winked up at the two men. De Fries stood over the financier expectantly.

Malan's tongue kept sticking to the roof of his mouth. 'This could still be a trick,' he said. 'What else do we have?'

'I've called Mac. He's going to do some checking. He won't be able to get onto the site, but he can make sure there's a test drilling going on. He knows some of the guys on the inside, which'll help.'

'When's he going to get back to us?'

'It'll take him a day to get there, but he's already left. We should get a call tomorrow.'

'OK – just supposing this is all true, how the hell d'you think we're going to fund it?'

'Through Tragopan and courtesy of St Martin's Bank.' De Fries was triumphant.

Malan's head still hurt.

'No. They know me as a Rand director. I can't go back in.'

'But they don't know me.'

'Really?' Malan was unimpressed. 'How's that going to work? Suppose Erskine sees you.'

'Easy.' De Fries was into his stride. 'You make up a reason to see Erskine, but not here,' his eyes roamed over the packing crates, 'and we time that with my trip to the bank. That means he's out of the way when I visit and no one's the wiser.'

Malan was too hungover to argue, and besides, he thought, De Fries was right; no one at the bank had ever seen the engineer. 'We should do this through Ash.'

'If we can find him,' agreed De Fries. 'If not, we'll have to come up with another story. There won't be time to set up a new company, we'll have to use Tragopan.'

'Timing?'

'Yes, I know. Koss said he needs the stake with him by next Thursday, no later or it's off.'

'That fits in with our leaving date, but why the rush?' Malan's head was thumping.

'He said the investment was to take it to the next stage. He doesn't have the capital, so was giving us a chance before he has to offer it to the local guys. He can't leave it long; they'll be putting pressure on – you know how these things leak out.'

'But why us, we haven't done business for years?'

'He heard we were flush and got in touch. Also, I bet he'll have to give up more of his slice if he has to deal with the guys on the ground.'

'Now where did he get that nugget from?' Malan was wary, even through the fog of his hangover.

'You know what this industry's like. Paying off the Chileans was newsworthy, even if it was a different product.' De Fries grinned. 'Don't forget, at least there's an actual mine with an actual mineral in it. The bank may get some money back.'

This time, Malan grinned too.

47

Miss Denby delivered the news. Sir John, Erskine, and Amanda were back at the head branch of St Martin's.

'A Mr Hunter of Tragopan Exploratory has made an appointment. He wants to discuss a loan. He asked for Leonard Ash, but as he isn't available, I've suggested Nigel Stone. Stone doesn't have to know the background; we can just tell him it's important. He can treat it as a normal meeting.'

'Stone,' Sir John said. 'Good choice. He's a stickler for the rules, we can rely on him to follow instructions.'

'How did you explain away Ash?' asked Amanda.

'I simply told Mr Hunter that Ash was unavailable,' Miss Denby replied.

'Interesting that he asked for Ash, given he's missing. Maybe Ash is involved in their plot. I wonder what that means?' Amanda added.

'Is only one of them coming though?' asked Sir John.

'Just Mr Hunter.'

'When's the appointment?'

Miss Denby checked her notes. 'Eleven on Monday morning, Sir John.'

'We need both men to sign if the police are going to bring them in,' Erskine pointed out. 'There needs to be a reason why Stone needs both signatures.'

'I'll deal with that and speak to Stone. You can brief young Bennett.' The light of battle was in Sir John's eyes. He strode back into his office and picked up the telephone.

Nigel Stone had never received a phone call directly from his employer, and he put down the receiver in a daze. The instructions were specific.

'Stone, extend all courtesy to Mr Hunter. And if he asks for a business loan, make sure it receives the best possible consideration. Both directors of Tragopan need to sign the loan agreement, of course, but then I hardly need to remind you of that; I hear your knowledge of the procedure is quite something.' This was all pretty much instruction, as was the rest of the message, which made his job easier.

His wife, Daphne, was pleased too.

'You know what they say, Nigel,' she told him that night over supper. 'As one door closes, another opens. If Leonard Ash has run off with some floozie, then it's your big chance. Mind you take it.'

James Bennett, though, needed no prompting. Erskine had briefed him on his role, and he was ready.

'Follow him when he leaves the bank,' Erskine explained. 'But stay well back, you've been to their offices before, and he might recognise you.' Erskine paused.

'Why don't you wear a hat? And stay out of your bank uniform, find something else.'

Bennett fancied himself in a long coat and visited a few gent's outfitters. He finally picked one on sale at Newcombe in Marylebone, spending a lot more than he planned. He was sure it would be worth it though, especially once Violet saw him in it.

48

Peter De Fries checked in the mirror. Yes, he was the model of a company director ready to visit his bank. Ash not being available was unhelpful, but he thought a separate meeting might be a better idea anyway; it wouldn't lead back to their man. He had chosen the name Charles Hunter for his Tragopan directorship and used it to make the appointment. His story was ready, and he was pleased with his preparation.

Earlier in the day, Mac, his contact in Joburg, had called again.

'There's something going on for sure. My man says the drilling stopped a couple of weeks ago and the mining teams are only working in the sheds now, but there are rumours of a big find.'

This last piece of news was enough to persuade Malan too. With the bank meeting arranged, he gave De Fries a lecture on the importance of brevity during the appointment.

'Remember, the less you say the more people will think you know. Make sure you appear confident they'll offer the loan and the meeting's just a formality. Don't appear too grateful.'

De Fries picked up the briefcase. Inside it were the charts and samples from Jacobus Koss. They had debated the merits of taking the test results to the meeting, as Malan had concerns this might make it too newsworthy. In the end they decided De Fries should show them. 'Nothing like physical evidence and in any event, it's factually correct,' he said, and Malan had agreed.

Arriving at Swan Lane, De Fries checked his watch as he crossed the foyer. He smiled at the receptionist. 'Charlie Hunter, I have an appointment at 11:00.'

The woman inclined her head at the chairs lined along the marble wall. He watched as she called through to the offices behind the foyer, then he walked over and took a seat.

De Fries heard a sigh high above him, and looked up into the vaulted ceiling, but there was nothing there. A few minutes later the clack of shoes bounced off the marble as the receptionist approached him.

'Mr Stone will see you now,' she said. He rose and followed. After several turns in the corridor, the woman rapped on a large wooden door, opened it, and ushered De Fries forward. 'Here we are.'

A youngish man, arms folded neatly in front of him, was waiting at the table. He got up and motioned De Fries to a chair.

'Good to meet you, Mr Hunter, Nigel Stone. Can I offer you a coffee? How can I be of assistance?'

De Fries opened his briefcase and took out the charts and sample tube. He made no effort to speak in anything other than his normal voice and began his explanation. He had worried there might be some awkward questions, but to his surprise the discussion was straightforward. When he laid out the charts and displayed the samples, the man

234

made no pretence of understanding the information but was goggle-eyed at the collection of glinting rocks.

The meeting continued apace. They completed the formalities and when it came to the size of the loan, De Fries remembered to use the matter-of-fact demeanour Malan had emphasised. This was a success and an agreement to increase the loan went through without hesitation. It was then that Stone, slightly embarrassed, furrowed his brow.

'I'm sorry, Mr Hunter, there's one small matter. It's the size of the company's loans. With this one, they total more than £20,000 in sterling terms.'

'Yes indeed.' De Fries remembered to stay matter-of-fact.

'Well,' Stone hesitated. 'With the total over this amount, we need both director's signatures. Is Mr De Cock available to come in and sign too?'

De Fries thought fast. 'No, he isn't available today.' He made an irritated noise in his throat. 'This isn't helpful at all,' he added in his best business tone.

Stone bit his lip. Then a thought seemed to occur to him. 'We could deliver the documents to you by messenger for signature, if that's acceptable?'

'Messenger, by all means,' De Fries said.

'Then we'll bring them to your office, Mr De Cock can sign them there,' Stone added.

De Fries sensed Stone's relief. 'Just deliver them to the address shown on the paperwork,' he said flatly.

'Certainly, Mr Hunter. We should be able to deal with this tomorrow.' With the meeting finished the two men shook hands. De Fries left the branch, his work as Charlie Hunter done. The receptionist watched him as he walked through the foyer. Pity, he thought, on another day he might have stopped to chat.

De Fries left the bank thinking hard. He tried to calculate the profits in his head but gave up when the maths got too complicated. There was no doubt, he thought, even Charlie Malan would have to agree this was quite a find.

49

James Bennett's heart was racing. He pulled his hat down and watched De Fries exit the bank. He was disappointed not to be able to climb into a taxi and instruct the driver to 'follow that cab,' like they did in the films, but the man was only walking, so he settled to the task of tracking De Fries on foot.

Bennett watched De Fries cross Lombard Street. The pavements were busy with office workers on their lunch break, and the messenger held back, mixing in with the crowd. Weaving between the traffic, he tried to imagine he and the other man were joined by a length of invisible rope. De Fries walked quickly, and Bennett had to work hard to keep up, all the time making sure he stayed out of sight. As they turned into King William Street, he passed his reflection in a shop window. Yes, the hat and coat made him quite the sleuth he thought.

Eventually, on the edge of the City De Fries turned into 'Ephraim Street,' a line of terraced houses, some of which appeared to serve as small business premises. Bennett found a position next to the telephone box on the corner and watched as De Fries stopped at a faded blue door. The engineer checked around and entered. Bennett waited.

After a few minutes he stepped away from the telephone box and walked as slowly as he could down the street. He reached the blue door of number thirty-two and allowed himself a sideways glance. To his surprise the door was open, and he could see the figure of De Fries with his back to him, standing in the hall. Bennett bent down to retie a fictional loose shoelace, risked another glance, and saw De Fries tuck something into a pocket. He straightened and continued walking, keeping his eyes focused on the pavement, and then turned the corner back into the main road.

So, another address he thought. He found a shop window and stood in front of it, watching the street behind him in the glass. How could Erskine and the others use this latest information? He would report back and see what they made of it.

The man's reflection passed the window. The figure still had the same purposeful stride, although Bennett thought he now detected the smallest hint of a limp in the man's gait. He waited and then moved off too.

Their paths took them out of the financial district and crossed the western perimeter into Holborn. De Fries turned into Eagle Street and entered another house. This time Bennett was able to stand undetected in a jeweller's shop doorway. He watched through the window, which glinted with trays of rings and bracelets. The door of the property was open, and he saw De Fries come out after a few minutes, patting his pocket down.

Bennett checked his watch; he had been following De Fries for over two hours and decided it might be risky to continue with his tailing. After all he thought, any man, particularly one who had reason to be suspicious, would become aware of his companion eventually.

He hadn't used any of the allowance given to him for 'mission expenses,' as Sir John called them, and he opted to spend it all on a taxi back to Sir John's house. He waited until De Fries was out of sight and then hailed a cab. He wasn't sure how he would feel about being just a messenger once all this was over.

50

'All done. The money's on its way,' De Fries announced triumphantly.

Malan looked steadily at his partner. 'You're very sure of yourself. There were absolutely no hitches?'

'None.' De Fries hesitated and his voice became reedy. 'There are some more signatures needed though.'

Malan spoke quietly but the tone was like distant thunder. 'When,' he rumbled, 'when are you going to fix that.'

'It's not me, it's us. They need both our signatures on the loan, they said...'

'No. You know I can't go back to the bank, there are too many people who know me as Rand Mining.'

'It's fine,' De Fries said, recovering. 'They're going to send a messenger over with the new papers. He'll wait while we sign and then take them back to the bank. Once he gets back, they'll release the funds. There's no way a messenger would suspect anything, and we can both be there when he arrives.'

Malan looked incredulous. 'You haven't arranged for delivery here...'

'No, of course not. It's going to be at Ephraim Street tomorrow. The messenger will be going there, if you remember, it's the registered office of Tragopan.'

Malan visibly relaxed. 'OK, decent plan.'

De Fries nodded. 'It keeps us away from the branch, and the messenger will only be there a few minutes, there isn't any real risk. We're going to have to make it seem busy though, it needs to feel like there's business going on. We should take some files over and bring Miss Brand with us.'

'When did you say all this is to happen?'

'Tomorrow. Then it's get the money to Koss and off to Paris to wait for our slice of the platinum profits.'

'Aren't you forgetting something?' Malan growled.

'Collecting letters from the other addresses?' De Fries was pleased with himself. 'I've done that too.'

'No, the other thing.'

This time he looked blank.

Malan sighed.

'If you recall,' he said heavily, 'we wanted to leave the bank in a mess too.'

'Well, several million Rand of irrecoverable loans should do that,' De Fries snapped defensively.

'That won't take long to unravel.' Malan was up on his feet, his thick muscular frame exuded physical power. 'We need to get that bank run restarted. A collapsed bank will be much harder to untangle than a few unpaid loans.'

De Fries dropped into the chair opposite Malan. 'Well, it hasn't happened, so what do we do? It was *your* part of the plan after all,' he eyed his partner reproachfully.

For a moment, Malan's face went black, but with an obvious effort, he kept his mood in check.

'I'm going to see Crawley and give him a kick up the backside. He's supposed to be fixing it, that's what we pay him for.'

Malan paused.

'I tell you what,' he conceded, 'You focus on getting the money to Koss and I'll take care of the rest.'

De Fries nodded. 'Will there be any more casualties?' he asked uncertainly.

'Not as long as the job gets done.'

The afternoon wore on. De Fries could hear Miss Brand arranging a long-distance call to Jacobus Koss.

Malan got ready to visit their contact, Rupert Crawley. Malan had come across the man on one of his visits to the London nightclub circuit. Crawley had a reputation as a share tipster, with a column in the evening paper, and seemed able to influence the stock market. He also discovered that Crawley was a regular cocaine user and had expected to exploit the man's expensive habit. At the time this had seemed like a good fit for their plans, but he wasn't so sure now.

The journey from Rand Mining to the heart of Mayfair was a short one, although Malan often took the taxi. This time he walked, keen to avoid leaving evidence of his journey. He made sure he arrived at the Crawley's apartment block, Rembrandt Court, well before the appointed time. Entering the lobby, he sat in the waiting area and watched the lift. He had been there before and knew Crawley's penthouse was on its own floor. No one else came into the building, and after a few minutes Malan got up and walked to the buzzer.

'Crawley, it's me, I'm coming up.'

There was no answer, but the light for the penthouse floor flashed up and a series of metallic sounds were set off inside the shaft. The lift door opened, and Malan got in, checking back out into reception as he did so. The lift made steady progress back up to the penthouse level and opened opposite the entrance to Crawley's apartment. Malan got out. A flushed looking man wearing a cravat and holding a large glass was leaning against the door frame. The Afrikaans regarded Crawley with disgust.

'Malan, good to see you. How's that rather delicious secretary, I must pop in and see her again soon. Can I offer you one?'

Malan ignored Crawley and pushed past him into the flat. He stood hands on hips, surveying the room. The penthouse was full of expensive mahogany and leather furniture, and the floor was ankle deep in heavy cream carpet.

'Is this what we pay you for? Because if it is, we damn well expect results.'

'Steady on old man, don't want to intrigue the neighbours.' Crawley said reproachfully.

'There aren't any,' Malan growled. He walked out onto the balcony and very obviously studied the pavement seven floors below. 'Although I can easily get you closer to them if you wish.'

'Look old man,' Crawley addressed Malan's back plaintively. 'We almost got it up and running last time. My contact gave it his best shot, but for that meeting it would have worked.'

Malan continued to stare over the rail.

'You assured us your influence was sufficient to get the job done,' his Afrikaans accent was now much more pronounced. 'It seems it wasn't.' He turned.

Crawley flinched as Malan stepped forward.

'I can get my contact to give it another go,' he offered hurriedly.

'That would be a smart idea,' Malan rumbled again. 'Or we'll want our investment in you refunded, one way or another.'

Crawley's flushed face paled.

'Difficult,' he began, but then tailed off as Malan crossed the room. 'Actually, I was going to ask if you could see your way to advancing some more funds.'

Malan took another step forward and stood on the points of Crawley's crocodile shoes. His arms stayed by his side, but he clenched and unclenched his fists.

'No more money, just results,' he snarled.

Crawley made to step back into his own space, but the weight of Malan on his toecaps forced him out of his shoes and he fell back, catching his head on a coffee table. It was a glancing blow but drew blood. He tried to pull himself up. The wound dripped over the expensive carpet.

'Listen you Neanderthal,' he hissed. 'Don't try and intimidate me. One word to The Exchange and the police will be down on you like a knife.'

Malan stood over Crawley, who was still struggling to his feet. He planted a vicious kick on the bleeding figure. Crawley collapsed to the floor again.

'Just get it done. I don't give a damn how, but get it done.' He stepped back and Crawley levered himself up on the nearby desk.

Crawley winced and held his ribs. 'Give me a chance old man, give me a chance.'

Malan turned, walked to the door, and stepped out into the corridor. No one else had called the lift and it was still open. He could see Crawley's apartment reflected in its mirrored back wall. Crawley was already setting up a line of cocaine on the kitchen worktop. Incensed, Malan spun on his heel and almost ran back into the penthouse.

'You useless gat. That gets us nowhere.' He pushed Crawley violently away from the worktop and its contents. 'You've snorted all we're going to pay you, just get on with the damn job.'

Crawley reeled but regained his balance.

'I've told you; I'll get it done!' he spat, blood trickling down from the side of his head. He wiped it out of his eyes and flicked it at Malan. As he did so, his right hand almost knocked over a brass figurine on the desk. His eyes widened and he closed his fingers over it, swinging it hard at Malan. The clumsy movements were easy to avoid for the seasoned brawler and Malan swayed away from them. The Afrikaans swung his shovel-like hand into Crawley's jaw. There was a crunch and Crawley staggered back, tripped over a low table, and fell onto its thick mahogany top. His head hit the heavy wooden slab with a sickening pop.

Malan had seen plenty of dead men in his time, and not all of them in the gloom of a mine shaft. The angle of the body told its own story.

The Afrikaans took a moment to control his breathing and then surveyed the flat. He retraced his steps from the point where he had entered the block. He thought hard; he knew he'd touched the door handle but couldn't think of much else. Making his way out of the penthouse, he closed the door softly, wiping away his touches as he went. He cleaned the lift buttons and the handle of the entrance to the building, remembering to check the lobby on his way out.

Strolling back to the Rand offices, Malan went over the implications of Crawley's death. While he accepted it was unwelcome at this stage, the man was useless and likely to prove unreliable. It occurred to him Crawley might have leaked the plan to bring down St Martin's if successful, given his role in it. He remembered Crawley's comments about Miss Brand, at least she would be pleased, he thought, and suppressed a laugh. By the time he neared Rand's offices he was ready for De Fries.

51

De Fries remembered them finding Ash at the start. It was Malan who picked out the ambitious clerk.

'This is the guy we need, Pieter.'

Malan had struck up a conversation at the Swan Lane branch. It had taken a few 'accidental' meetings, a few drinks after the branch closed, but Malan was right.

The loans they arranged, increasing in size and value, propelled their recruit's career and he was already closing in on a manager's position.

He turned out to have other uses too.

The first time it happened, Malan briefed De Fries after the call.

'Ash's been on the phone. He thinks someone's on to us, a guy at the Embankment branch.'

'How does he know?' De Fries queried. 'He doesn't even work there.'

'Yes, but he does the rounds now, thanks to us.'

'Goes to other branches?'

'He's done well; they're grooming him for bigger things. He drops in on the other City branches, some kind of training.'

De Fries frowned. 'What's been said, what've they found?'

'I don't know the details, but someone at the branch raised it with him. So far, Ash's managed to keep it between the two of them; the guy didn't want to look stupid; we're a key account.'

'Should we back off? Maybe Ash can persuade him it's ok.'

'We're past that,' Malan said. 'We need to deal with it. I don't fancy our chances if we keep Kempez waiting much longer. We need that loan.'

'So, what do we do then?'

'The obvious,' Malan retorted. He looked levelly at De Fries.

De Fries shrank under Malan's stare.

'Charlie, we said no. Not after Antwerp.'

'Too bad my vriend. This is urgent. Kempez won't wait.'

And so it began, De Fries thought. The never-ending slaughter. With Charlie, there was always a reason and only one solution. He realised that by now. He didn't ask, he didn't want to ask, the problem, whatever it was, just went away.

He always knew when it was done. Malan went missing for a few days, and when he came back, he went on some kind of bender. De Fries had hoped to avoid it in London, stupid he thought, there was never any chance of that.

But he drew the line at a woman.

After Malan had dealt with the Embankment problem, the loan came through. De Fries was relieved; they were nearly there, and Malan had Kempez kept at bay.

'There's more where that came from,' the Afrikaans told their contact. 'You'll get all your money, don't be hasty.'

Things seemed to be going well, Kempez was quiet, and the money rolled in.

But then Ash called again. 'It's someone at Blackfriars.'

'A woman? How's that?' De Fries heard Malan on the phone. He flinched.

Ash said something and Malan laughed. 'That depends. What's she like?' Another laugh, De Fries broke out in a sweat, he could feel it.

'Can't be helped,' Malan said after the call. 'She shouldn't poke her nose in men's business. It'll be an easy one though.'

De Fries decided.

'I'll do it.'

Malan looked at his partner in mock astonishment.

'Hey, my vriend, respect to the engineer.' Malan put his hands on De Fries' shoulders, 'At last, some balls. I never thought... what'll you do?'

'Don't ask,' De Fries said flatly, 'I never ask you.'

'True my vriend, true. Do you want any tips?'

De Fries felt sick again.

'Get me the details,' he said. 'That's enough.'

52

Erskine, Amanda, and James Bennett were in the billiard room at Redshanks. Erskine was in full flow.

'So, they pretend to have companies in London and South Africa. Only one company exists and that's here. Now they just need the extra funding for the platinum mine, and they'll be off.'

'They might lose their nerve and run for it,' Bennett said, 'how do we know they'll hang on to collect the extra loan?'

'Oh, they will.' Amanda was confident. 'There's a big payoff coming if they can get to that platinum.'

Erskine grinned at James Bennett.

'Big day tomorrow, James.'

'Amanda,' Erskine continued, 'just how did you get Jacobus Koss to come in with us?'

'The things people will do for two per cent of a platinum find; you wouldn't believe,' she smiled.

Erskine was intrigued. 'The samples. Are they from your new mine or elsewhere?'

'That,' smiled Amanda, 'would be telling too much just now.'

'What's the next step?' asked Bennett.

'We go back to Ephraim Street and get them to sign the loans, don't forget they'll be using their fraudulent identities. At that point they will have committed a crime, and the police will be involved. Then we can begin to untangle this whole thing,' Erskine said.

'   'But nothing we've found so far explains the disappearances.' said Amanda exasperatedly, 'how do we unravel those?'

'My hope is,' said Erskine, 'my hope is that once the police have them, between us, we can squeeze out the complete story. Even if we only get one, it may unnerve the other. Fingers crossed; everything will come out.'

The three of them were still talking when Sir John entered the room.

'Hello,' said Amanda and then stopped abruptly.

The host's face was white.

'The police have found a body. The man's wearing a St Martin's Bank tie.'

53

De Fries had been surprised at how easy it was. Kempez was happy to help once he promised the Chilean a bonus. 'As long as you don't tell Charlie. This has nothing to do with him.'

'Always ready to help a customer, especially now he's paying again.' The South American's tone had been friendly. For now, at least, De Fries thought.

He had to wait a few days. Then, on one of his rounds, he found a note pushed through the door at Ephraim Street.

Hecho, it said. De Fries knew enough Spanish to understand *Done*. He checked under the doormat; they had put back the keys.

He hadn't been looking forward to this part. But at least she was still alive. He set off for Holborn.

De Fries heard a sob as he turned the key. He wore a mask, and he knew he couldn't speak, but there was no going back now, too much had happened. Keeping the woman here was a risk, but he had to assume someone would find her once they got out of London. Maybe he could get Koss to tell the police he thought. Charlie would be mad as hell. Ash wouldn't be happy either, it kept him in the frame.

The man was coming down the stairs, she could hear him. The lock rattled. Through the gloom she watched the handle turn. When the door opened, she saw at once it wasn't the same figure. The person was taller and had a different mask on. She eyed him anxiously as he approached, but he made no move to touch her. There was water in the tin again though, and some bread too. She pulled the rope, there was just enough slack to reach the food.

He looked down at her and reached inside his jacket. She watched his hand, but it only pulled out a piece of paper. He unfolded it and held it up. *Just a few more days,* it said.

Until what, she thought. Something in her expression must have registered with him. He waved his hand dismissively and then pointed at the door. It was hard to take in. What had she done, why was he interested in her kidnap? Her mind raced. The man closed the door again and disappeared back up the steps. There was hope now, she thought. But then maybe it was just a way of keeping her quiet.

54

The latter reaches of the Thames at low tide were a grey, soulless wasteland. Monochrome gulls scuttled their way across the mud, pausing sporadically to wail at each other across the estuary. Rats scurried along its margins picking at the debris, and jagged wooden piles rose like broken teeth through the mudbanks. The river, unravelling into a myriad of thin, muddy streams, made its way between the mounds out to the sea. There was no hope left here, thought Erskine, all life had expired. The London further upstream had abandoned it. Once a mighty force, the Thames here was grey and exhausted.

Erskine and Sir John made their way down onto the mud. There was a small group of men, some in police uniform, gathered at the end of a line of piles that stretched out into the estuary.

A man in a long coat detached himself from the group and met them as they approached.

'That's far enough gentlemen,' he called. 'It's not a pleasant sight.'

Sir John identified himself. The man nodded his respects. 'I'm afraid it may be one of your people, Sir John.' He looked at Erskine.

'Robert Erskine. Sir John has asked me to investigate some matters at the bank. Can I see the body?'

The man hesitated.

'This is a matter for the Metropolitan Police, sir. A gentleman such as yourself shouldn't have to get involved.

In any event I doubt whether a drowning would be related to anything you're looking into.'

Sir John cleared his throat.

'Would it be possible for Mr Erskine to look at the body? He's well used to such matters.' He played his trump card. 'Lord Trenchard is a good friend and as Head of The Metropolitan Police, I'm sure he would think it appropriate, officer.'

'Inspector Lumley, Sir John, from Lehman Street.' The Inspector seemed to be weighing up his options. He was a tall man with oiled down black hair, greying a little at the temples. His features were angular, and his eyes were alert and bright. The effect, thought Erskine, was that of a heron assessing his surroundings.

'Just a few minutes then, Mr Erskine.'

Erskine took a few steps along the edge of the mud. A constable was sat on the bank, levering himself out of some thigh waders.

'Can I borrow those?' he asked. The man gestured at the heavy boots.

'Be my guest.'

Climbing into the waders, Erskine made his way out to the group around the piles. His arrival went unnoticed by the other men who were studying the corpse. The body had evidently arrived at its final resting place face down, but they had turned it over for inspection. The man's clothing was run through with mud, but the necktie had been prised out from the sodden mess and Erskine could see the crest of St Martin's Bank on its knot.

Another man removed the contents of the jacket and opened a saturated wallet.

'His name's Ash,' he said soberly, 'poor devil. These were in his pocket too.' The officer held up a set of keys and a small tin.

To Erskine, the officer's use of the present tense somehow gave the body identity for a moment. He studied the prone figure, taking in incidental details, but then stopped. The puffy grey right hand was closed around something, and he moved forward to take a closer look. His interest alerted the officer.

'What occurred here I wonder?' The policeman wiped the outstretched hand, removing some of the mud, and revealing a clump of coarse fibre. He prised open the fingers of the corpse and examined the find.

'May I see?' asked Erskine. The officer offered the clump. Erskine turned and held the fibre up to the pale sky; at the same time, he separated a few strands and slipped them into his pocket.

'Thank you. Grisly, isn't it.'

'Drowning, one of the worst ways I always think.' The officer took back the clump.

Erskine returned to the riverbank and found Sir John talking to the Inspector.

'This is likely to be one of your missing employees,' the Inspector was saying.

'I'm afraid it is,' Sir John spoke quietly. 'It's Ash, he went missing some days ago.' He stared despairingly out across the mudflats. 'Lord Trenchard knows the full picture; I've kept him up to date, Lumley. I had hoped these disappearances would be explained without...' His voice trailed away.

'I have to say, Sir John, this looks like an accidental drowning, not murder.'

'Well, he did work at the Swan Lane office, which is on the river,' Sir John sighed.

The Inspector brightened a little.

'That adds up, but we won't make any assumptions just yet. Let's wait and see when we get back to the mortuary. I'm bound to say though, I don't expect to find anything suspicious.'

Erskine and Sir John made their way back out of the mud. They walked in silence until they reached the road.

'You saw the tin?' Erskine said. Sir John nodded. The waiting cab coughed into life as the two men approached. Climbing back into the warmth of the taxi they unbuttoned their coats, shaking the damp from their clothes.

The cab made its ponderous way back to Redshanks. As they passed The Slow Pony, Erskine remembered the fibres in his pocket and took them out.

'I found these in Ash's hand. What do you make of them?'

Sir John held them up to the light. He reached into his jacket, and took out a handkerchief, wrapping it around the fibres before rolling them clean in its folds. He laid them out again on the seat between the two men.

'They look like horsehair,' he said.

55

For Knapp, the excitement of joining the investigation was beginning to wane. Sitting watching the street had felt like critical work, but he'd had nothing important to report for a while now. There was plenty of activity at Rand's offices, but it seemed to Knapp that it was all much the same day to day, and this morning was especially quiet. Having reached lunch, Knapp stepped out of the coffee shop and was stretching his legs, when the door to the building accommodating Rand Mining's offices opened, and a large swarthy man set off at pace. Knapp pretended to be interested in a shop window and watched as the man strode past him in the direction of Mayfair.

Knapp was sure the man was one of the characters he'd been told to watch out for. They'd never met, so he knew he had the advantage over his target and made a snap decision to follow him. Knapp acknowledged this was not strictly within his brief, but, he reasoned, tracking a key player in the investigation should be helpful and might lead to further clues.

Knapp fell in behind. He kept a safe distance, but the man did nothing to suggest he was suspicious of anything. Eventually they reached the leafy streets of Mayfair, where his quarry stopped outside an apartment block. This time he did check around him, but Knapp kept walking. As he passed, Knapp risked a glance and again noted the man's muscular build; not someone to be taken lightly, he thought.

He watched the figure enter the building. Knapp crossed the street and sat on a bench under a Plane tree. The spot gave him an unobstructed view of the block and its entrance. A large sign over the revolving door told him the place was Rembrandt Court. Rembrandt, he thought, well, the block was no oil painting.

Time passed slowly, and Knapp was thinking about entering the building when the muscular figure's head appeared over the penthouse balcony.

Knapp was pleased; now he knew which apartment his quarry was in. He decided to wait until the man left, then go into the block to see who or what his target had visited. He was debating what excuse to use for his call when the man appeared at ground level and set off back towards the City.

Knapp waited a few minutes and then crossed the street into the block. The foyer was silent. Knapp checked for the stair exit and then inspected the lift panel in front of him. He pressed the topmost button. Maybe, he thought, this was a second office, a place to hide other evidence of their fraud.

Knapp pressed again, but there was still no reply. Climbing the stairs was no trouble for a fit gardener, but at the top he found the penthouse level had its own locked door. Knapp cursed to himself at such an obvious 'miss' on his part.

After a few fruitless minutes, he was ready to give up when something else occurred to him; even the penthouse needed a fire exit. He went to the stairwell and found he was in luck. An iron ladder outside passed by the window and up onto the penthouse balcony. Walking back down one flight he found the fire exit door and opened it. Trying not to look down he made his way gingerly along the fire escape, past the sixth floor and up onto the balcony. From here he thought, he would at least be able to look through the penthouse windows. There was a chance too, the door from the balcony to the flat would be unlocked. Knapp stepped onto the patio and peered through the glass doors into the flat. He wiped at the damp panes.

The penthouse was a battle scene. Broken ornaments lay on the floor and there was furniture rammed up against the window. A shoe lay on its own in the centre of the room and there was something, possibly blood, on the carpet. He put his face hard up against the glass and scanned the whole room, then froze. The motionless body of a man lay across the coffee table. His head swam as he took in this new, ghastly information. He abandoned his inspection and sat nauseous and shaking on the balcony. He knew he had to get back and report to the others but didn't trust himself to descend the ladder.

He had been there for a while, how long he wasn't sure. The shock had receded enough for him to tackle the climb down the fire escape, and with one more glance back at the penthouse he began to descend. He made it to the lift level and into the lobby. Back out on the street he looked up to the penthouse balcony, but there was no hint of the dreadful scene seven floors above. He reasoned that other than those who had business there, no one would raise the alarm in the short term.

All thoughts of bravura had left him. He walked, then caught a bus back to Aldford Street. He reached the safety of the coffee shop and began to feel less shaky. He gave himself a minute and then went to the telephone box to report his shocking news.

56

Erskine recounted Knapp's discovery to Inspector Lumley and put the phone down. Although appalled, the Inspector had underlined that there was nothing to connect Ash's body with the one in the Mayfair penthouse. Erskine was sure there would be in time, but he accepted that a professional police officer would be cautious about making any connection, and in the absence of anything obvious, he didn't pursue the point.

The telephone rang almost as soon as it was back in its cradle; Erskine raised the receiver. It was Inspector Lumley again.

'I'm going over to the flat,' Lumley said. 'We'll put a watch on the Rand offices too, but we've talked it through here and aren't going to pick up the attacker just yet. There are no witnesses, and we need to speak to the gardener before we make that decision. And you never know, this morning's events might trigger something.'

Erskine reflected. They needed to find more to link the disappearances with the two bodies, and a pause in the police proceedings was helpful. If the Afrikaans were under surveillance, he, Amanda, and Sir John could continue their own work, although they would have to move faster than up to now.

He glanced up at the calendar in Sir John's study. There could only be a few days before the plotters left.

'I'll ask Sir John to make Knapp available for an interview. Do you want him to come to the station, you didn't say earlier?'

Lumley was conciliatory,

'If it's acceptable to Sir John, I'd prefer to speak to Knapp at the house. He isn't a suspect, and we want to get the most out of him; I find it helpful if the witness is on home ground; it's less intimidating for them, and they sometimes loosen up a bit.'

'Good idea.' This piece of insight showed Lumley in a different light, thought Erskine. Up to now he'd assumed the Inspector was all about procedure.

'I'll arrange it with Sir John and call you back.'

Before he could put the telephone down, Lumley continued.

'Mr Knapp is still on watch at the coffee shop I assume. I'll send Plender along to take over, our man's excellent, and I expect your chap could do with a break.'

'Not to mention a large scotch I should think,' said Erskine.

The call over, Erskine went to find the others. They were in the orangery. Amanda had her arm around Sir John's shoulders. The host was a grey shrunken figure.

'What's the plan?' Amanda asked, 'are we going to move on the offices?'

Erskine explained the agreement with Inspector Lumley, he looked at James Bennett.

'Yes,' he said. 'We'll visit them at the address of this non-existent Tragopan company, along with a few of his majesty's finest. While I think of it, Inspector Lumley would like to debrief Knapp here, if that's alright with you, Sir John.'

His host stirred. 'Of course. But I expect he needs a chance to recover after today.'

Erskine nodded. 'One of Lumley's men is going over now, and we should have Knapp back here by late afternoon. The Inspector can come here tomorrow.'

'I'll send a taxi for Knapp,' said Sir John.

Amanda turned to James Bennett. 'Well, James, when Inspector Lumley comes over, we can plan the document delivery too.' She smiled, 'Your big moment's almost here.'

James Bennett's heart missed several beats.

An hour passed during which Erskine and Amanda went through the circumstances of the two deaths. They were both now resigned to finding the other three bank employees post-mortem. Having seen how Sir John reacted to the loss of one employee, Amanda was concerned, not just for the victims but also for the health of the bank's chief executive.

'He's taken it very badly,' Amanda whispered to Erskine. 'But what happens when we find the others?'

Erskine grimaced. 'I agree,' he said sombrely, 'he's going to need support.'

Sounds of an arrival on the drive made their way back through the house to the orangery. Sir John brightened a little. 'That will be Knapp, let's go and make him welcome.'

The shock of his discovery had severely shaken the gardener, but the taxi journey had given him time to recover some of his nerve, and Knapp was feeling more robust when the investigators met him in the hall.

'Come on through dear boy,' Sir John was sympathetic. 'You've had a hell of a day. I'm afraid you're going to have to tell us everything and then repeat it to the police inspector tomorrow, but please don't leave anything out.'

Sir John showed Knapp to a seat in the study and offered him an enormous scotch. He accepted both and settled back to recount his story. Sir John and Amanda sat down whilst Erskine paced. James Bennett stood to one side, attentive.

As Knapp reached the discovery of the body, Sir John interjected. 'And you have no idea who this man was you say?'

'But you mentioned Mayfair,' Erskine said, 'so a man from affluent circles. And what's his connection with Rand Mining?'

'Well mining and money go together,' said Amanda. 'This has the signs of a row between investors and owners, or something along those lines.'

'Perhaps an argument that got out of hand?' Sir John suggested.

'Or a broken promise, money that hasn't been paid,' Erskine added. 'Don't forget they seem to have cash flow problems and Amanda has just floated the chance of a platinum mine under their nose. Lumley should have the man's identity soon. Hopefully we'll have a better picture tomorrow.'

Knapp finished his account and drained the last of the scotch. 'If it's alright with you sir, I'd like to go home now.'

Sir John nodded. 'Will you be alright to walk back to the village or shall we arrange something?'

'I'll be fine now sir.' Knapp raised himself out of the study chair. 'I'm going to walk; it'll help clear my head.'

Erskine was sympathetic but also serious. 'Please, Knapp, not a word to anyone, just for the moment. We need to keep this away from St Martin's, at least until we have more to go on.'

After the day he'd had, Knapp was sure the last thing he wanted was an evening in The Slow Pony. That would come another time, and he thought, what a story he would have to tell.

'Don't worry,' he said, 'straight home to bed for me.'

57

Even by his standards, Inspector Lumley was up early. He was always one of the first to arrive at the station and spurred on by the prospect of a visit to Redshanks House, he had made a special effort. The home of Sir John MacGregor was known to be quite a 'pile' as Plender put it, although for Lumley it was not the house but the garden that held the attraction for him.

The April edition of *Best Homes and Gardens* had carried an article on Redshanks, featuring the Rose Garden as a highlight. Lumley, a keen gardener, had this partly in mind when he suggested interviewing Knapp on site. As the squad car rattled and bounced up the drive, he reminded himself that there would be no display at this time of year. He was keen to see the structure of the garden though, and, he hoped, extract an offer from Sir John to return in the spring.

Rather than the expected houseman, his host greeted him at the door.

'Thanks for coming over, Lumley. Knapp's in the study, I'm sure you're better seeing him here rather than the police station, given everything that's gone on.'

Inspector Lumley entered and found Erskine present, along with a woman he didn't recognise and two men, who appeared to be workers of some kind.

Erskine came forward and introduced Amanda and James Bennett.

'And this is Terence Knapp, Redshanks' Head Gardener,' Erskine said. 'He's also been helping with our investigation into Rand Mining and the staff disappearances at St Martin's.'

'A busy fellow,' Lumley smiled encouragingly at Knapp. At this stage he thought it unlikely the disappearances and drowning were directly connected to the death in Mayfair. He had to concede though, it was quite a coincidence that both were, in some way, related to the investigations by the people in this room. They had quite a capacity to involve themselves in unpleasant events, he thought. He wondered what their background was.

Knapp took Inspector Lumley through the previous day, starting with his decision to follow the man from Rand Mining across London to Mayfair.

'We think that must've been Malan,' said Amanda, 'from the way Knapp described him.'

'Another Afrikaans on your suspect list then?' Lumley asked.

'The point is all roads lead back to Rand Mining.' Erskine folded his arms across his chest. 'When you've finished debriefing Knapp here, Amanda and I will take you through it.'

Lumley saw there was nothing for it but to hear them out. He knew how easy it was to be drawn into conspiracy theories, he had advanced a few of his own over the years. He expected little in the way of factual evidence, but the group in the study were no fools, and there might be something in their account, even if they were wide of the mark.

He spoke up. 'We know the identity of the man in the Mayfair penthouse at least. There's no harm in sharing it with you. His name was Crawley.'

Sir John frowned. 'I know that name, but where from?' his voice tailed away in thought.

'He was some kind of stockbroker as far as we can tell,' Lumley explained, 'and he had some expensive drug habits, judging by the contents of his flat.'

Sir John's expression cleared. 'Yes, I remember him, Rupert Crawley. He has an association with Bowen and Skier, the stockbrokers in Cheapside. But what they have to do with Rand Mining I wouldn't know.'

'Do they use the bank?' Lumley asked.

'No, not ours,' Sir John was definitive. 'That firm came up after the crash, but they have a bit of a,' he hesitated, 'they're a bit too racy for us, but I must say they're successful.'

'Anything illegal?' Amanda asked.

'No, I don't think so, just not our type of institution.'

'You mean not at least a hundred years old,' she laughed.

Sir John inclined his head. 'You may have a point.'

Over the next half hour, Knapp gave Lumley his account.

'I'll need to go through this a bit more carefully with you,' the Inspector said, 'but we can do that later.' He closed his notebook and turned to Erskine and Amanda. His manner was friendly, even if there was a hint of resignation in his tone.

'You'd better set out your thoughts for me too, then. Let's get it all out on the table.'

Sir John excused himself. 'You don't need me for this. I've some telephone calls to make.'

Erskine and Amanda described all the threads of their research. Erskine went through the disappearances, the fraudulent loan applications, and Rand Mining's recent chequered history. When he got to the subject of the colour coded analysis of the accounts, and how this led to the identification of the suspect companies, the Inspector was impressed.

'Excellent work, I must say. But how did you manage to link the disappearances to Rand? I can see the drowning at the estuary might be something to do with all this. They appear quite capable of murder if they're responsible for the events in Mayfair, but all four?'

For the first time James Bennett spoke up. 'It's the mints sir, you see. They had them.'

The Inspector, who had almost forgotten the young man in the study, looked quizzically at Bennett.

'Mints, what mints?'

Amanda broke in. 'Yaram mints.'

'I've never heard of them.' Lumley was mystified. 'Go on though.'

'The point is,' Amanda continued, 'three of the missing employees, Hubert Heath, Harriet Simpson, and Leonard Ash, all of them had a tin of Yaram mints. You remember Ash, the body in the estuary, he had them in his pocket. The sweets are South African, and there's only one way they could have received them, you can't buy them here in London.'

'From a South African customer.' Lumley said thoughtfully. 'So even though the loans were made to different and supposedly unrelated companies, they must have been arranged by the same person visiting different branches.' The Inspector was silent for a moment. 'What about Stevens?'

'He had Tragopan's phone number written on his blotter,' said Bennett.

'Some good circumstantial evidence, well done. If you're correct, then I'm afraid this doesn't bode well for the other missing people. But what was this man, Malan, doing in a Mayfair penthouse, possibly murdering a London stockbroker?'

Sir John returned. As Inspector Lumley finished speaking, he got up again. 'Just a moment,' he said, and left the study.

Erskine resumed. 'We think the loans have got Rand Mining out of a hole, although we don't know any details. Thanks to Amanda and her contacts in South Africa, we've managed to get them to extend themselves one more time. But this time we're ahead of them.'

Erskine set out the planned interception of De Fries and Malan, and the arrangements the two had made to sign the fraudulent loan documents.

'Between us we can lead you to an arrest for fraud,' he continued, 'but so far we can't help you with any evidence for the disappearances.'

'Or the possible drowning,' Lumley agreed. 'But with an arrest they may begin to unravel. It does happen.'

'Now we set the trap,' Erskine said grimly. 'And that's where this young man comes in.'

Once more the attention of the room swung around to James Bennett.

58

He was reluctant to acknowledge it, but Terence Knapp was exhausted. The events of the past two days, thrilling and appalling, had left him relieved to get back to his duties as a gardener. Inspector Lumley had been sympathetic with his questions given Knapp's ordeal, but he was also a professional police officer with great attention to detail and he had found the process draining.

Now Knapp was back at Redshanks, with the prospect of a chat with Mary and a ready supply of tea and biscuits. On home ground again, his expert eye ranged along the radishes and winter kale that marched across the kitchen garden, within easy reach of Mary's creaking back. He nodded in satisfaction and went in search of the cook.

Mary was conducting an orchestra of pots, which bubbled and steamed in appreciation. The windows at the far end of the kitchen dripped with condensation. As he entered, and without turning away from her culinary concert, she greeted him with more than usual interest.

'Well now Mr Terence Knapp, where on earth have you been? It's unlike you to leave that garden unattended for so long.' Then, in a tone intended to convey intrigue, she said, 'Bridges says there's talk of murder and mayhem; what *have* you been up to?'

Knapp leant against the brick wall of the kitchen and shifted his shoulder blades back and forth against the rough surface.

'Well,' he paused for dramatic effect, 'I'm sworn to secrecy, at least for now.'

'By Sir John I've no doubt,' Mary was disappointed.

'By Chief Inspector Lumley of his majesty's police.' Knapp bit his tongue.

Cook was sufficiently impressed to pause in the middle of a vigorous stirring, and she swung around. 'So, it's true, there *has* been a murder,' she said deliciously. 'Whatever shall we think of that?'

Knapp moved away from the wall and adopted what he considered to be a more professional tone. 'I've nothing more to say,' he narrowed his eyes, 'just be careful, that's all.'

'I doubt there'll be any murders in my kitchen,' Mary harrumphed. She turned back to her preparations, 'unless it's the mice.'

'No biscuits today, Mary?'

'There might be later.' She supped a spoonful of whatever the pot held, made a 'room for improvement' kind of noise and reached for the salt.

Bridges appeared at the door. 'The Inspector will be staying for lunch.'

Mary sighed, 'How many is that now?'

'Altogether that's five,' the Butler confirmed. 'Knapp, you're to join them after lunch.'

'Well now, Terence, you *are* moving up in the world. You'll be asking for an assistant next. Too busy to get your hands dirty soon, I'll be bound,' Mary said.

The household knew of Knapp's abilities as a gardener, and they all liked him. His title of 'Head Gardener' did sometimes give rise to amusement as he was the only gardener. 'Still,' as Knapp himself said, 'that does make me the Head Gardener too.'

Knapp was pleased with his inclusion and wondered what his role might be. He nodded to Bridges and left the kitchen. Taking the path along the perimeter of the walled garden, he walked around the rose beds that led down to the Thames, pocketing his pruning secateurs on the way.

Knapp's route took him past the last of the flower beds, before crossing the lawns that ran down to the river's edge. He liked the spot as he could look at the gardens and the house as one.

He was enjoying the view when he became aware he was not alone. To the far left, just on the edge of the garden, a large black horse was standing, head raised, looking up at the house. Knapp thought he recognised it as the animal from the opposite bank. He was surprised the beast had got into the grounds, it gave weight to Mary's assertion that there was a gap or failing in the fence. Knapp set off toward it, intent on a closer inspection of the boundary and any repairs that might be necessary.

As he approached, the animal turned to study him. The grey vapers from its nostrils hung heavily in the damp air. Knapp stepped around the beast and began to walk parallel to the fence, inspecting it for broken panels. He was pleased that, despite walking the full length of the boundary, he could find no gaps or any other signs of damage. He was also puzzled. There was no sign of how the beast entered.

Knapp turned to make his way back along the fence and down to the river. To his surprise he found the horse had followed him silently up the line. It stood close behind him, and Knapp had to take a pace back to give himself some space.

'Well now fella, how did you manage that,' he muttered. The horse lowered its head and nudged at Knapp's legs.

'Let's check back that way.' Knapp spoke to his new companion and began to walk towards the river. The animal followed. For such a large horse, Knapp thought, it made almost no noise. They walked down to the edge of the Thames without finding any holes in the fence. Knapp was now doubly sure there were no weak points in the boundary. He turned to his equine companion, hands on hips.

'How did you get in here I wonder?' he asked out loud. 'You're either a will of the wisp or a powerful swimmer, that's no pond out there.' He gestured at the steely grey Thames running powerfully behind them. The animal nudged his legs again but made no sound.

'Well, we'll have to look again, that's all there is to it.' He shrugged his shoulders at the beast. 'But I'd better get back to the house, they must be close to finishing lunch.' Knapp patted the horse and turned away.

59

Lambourne Tucker crossed the stile. On leaving The Slow Pony, he'd decided to take the route home along the towpath rather than the road. He enjoyed the walk by the river, even though it took him longer. He also had half a mind to call in at Redshanks to see if any work needed doing. The rumours about non-payment, long since dispelled by Sir John's actions, were of no concern and he was pleased with himself. After all, he had never really doubted a man who'd provided him with so much work over the years. Yes, he told himself, he would call in. With luck that cook would have been baking too.

The towpath ran on the opposite side of the bank to Redshanks. There was a weir upstream of the house that spanned the river. On top of the weir was a narrow footbridge and Lambourne made for this with an easy stride. The river's course was straight, with nothing to inhibit it after it passed over the weir, and the current was powerful. Redshanks lay about a mile along the route and Lambourne could see the house across the fields some time before he reached it. To get there he had to walk past the property and continue upstream to the weir, before crossing and walking back to join the drive up to the house.

As he passed Redshanks on the opposite bank, he saw Knapp with a large horse, walking in the garden. He was about to shout a greeting but decided against it. He knew Knapp was an excellent gardener, but his reputation as something of a perfectionist meant it wasn't always wise to interrupt him.

Lambourne reached the weir and crossed over the narrow walkway, stepping down onto the path that intersected the driveway up to the house. Instead of arriving at the main door, he turned off across the lawns and up to the kitchen garden. The smell of baking drifted from the house, reminding him of his mother's wonderful boyhood cooking. He reached the open kitchen door and tapped on the lintel.

'Biscuits later,' cook shouted over her shoulder.

'That's good. I'll get some then,' he said.

She turned, hands on hips. 'I thought you were Terence. What brings you here stranger.'

'I was wondering,' Lambourne ventured, 'if there was any work needs doing on the house. You'd be best to know.'

'Well, there's an interesting question. Why the sudden visit after all this time?'

'I just thought I'd be helpful,' Lambourne said defensively.

'You thought you might get paid after all,' cook remarked dryly. 'I know how many beans make five.'

'Very perspicacious,' Lambourne retorted, 'but I never believed the gossip anyway.'

'I've nothing, but I could ask, if you can wait a bit.' She seemed struck by a thought. 'I told Terence there must be a hole in the fence down near the river. Maybe you could fix that.'

Lambourne brightened. 'Thank you, Mary, just the ticket. I saw him just now; I'll go and ask.'

'Better make it quick, mind, he's moving up in the world and it won't be long before he'll be above bandying words with the likes of us.'

Lambourne inclined his head. Mary lowered her voice. 'Murder. Proper grisly murder.'

Lambourne was stunned.

'Can't say more.' She drew herself up. 'We've a chief inspector here for lunch too. Got to get on.'

Lambourne Tucker struggled to contain himself. This was one to tell Silus. Maybe he would get more from the cook when she wasn't so busy. He decided to find Knapp first and then return for the biscuits.

'I'll come back later,' he said. 'I'd better speak to Knapp about that fence. By the way,' Lambourne asked, 'when did Sir John buy the horse?'

'Back, is it?' said cook. 'The sooner that fence is fixed the better. That animal doesn't belong to this house.'

60

De Fries was shaking. 'Dead? What the hell were you thinking? Dead? Are you insane? You've screwed up everything.'

Malan was belligerent. 'It screws up nothing. No one knows who did it and there's no chance of connecting it to us. Get a grip man. It's a bit messy, but we only have a few more days in London, then we can clear out.'

'We have to go now.' De Fries' voice had lost its sophistication and was thin and reedy. 'We can't take any more risks.'

Malan kicked out at a wastepaper basket at the corner of De Fries' desk and sent it flying. 'I told you; it's not a risk. I'm not giving up shares in a platinum mine just for getting rid of Crawley. Where's that money, is it in yet?' Malan levelled his stare at De Fries and by force of will, steadied him.

'You know we need the signatures for the money,' De Fries said tightly. 'Which reminds me, we need to take Miss Brand with us. Have you told her about Crawley?'

'On the way in just now. I said he'd met with an accident, and she didn't have to worry about his attentions anymore.'

The telephone rang. Both men stared at it, De Fries picked up the receiver. The operator asked if he would take the call.

'Hello, Jacobus.' De Fries spoke slowly. 'Yes, the funds will be ready soon, where should we transfer them?'

Malan advanced and stretched out his hand. De Fries passed him the receiver.

'Jacobus, I never thought I'd hear from you again, it's Charlie Malan.'

'Malan, you devil, our paths cross again. Cross again. I should have realised; you're never far from the smell of money.'

Malan snorted. 'Goes for you too. A platinum mine, that's quite a find,' he lowered his voice. 'We've seen the samples,' he rumbled, 'but let me tell you my vriend, if this turns out to be a dud, you will be watching over your shoulder for a very long time.'

There was a chortle. 'I wouldn't expect anything less from you, Charlie. Although, from what I hear, you've had to use some fast footwork of your own recently.'

Malan's eyes narrowed, and he stared across at De Fries. 'What do you mean, Jacobus?'

'Just your South American contacts have become a little more, a little more fractious.'

Malan relaxed. 'You can't please everyone all the time. But you'll find they're happy now.'

'Just as well. They can be unpleasant partners if things go against them.'

'When will we get the shareholder papers?' asked Malan.

'Our man in London. He'll hand them over once the money is in our account. You said that would be soon?'

'Just a few days.' Malan was careful to sound matter-of-fact. 'Have we got the details, Pieter?'

De Fries nodded. Malan handed back the receiver.

'We'll call you as soon as we're ready. Speak soon.' De Fries was nominally back in charge now. He put the receiver down.

The two men looked at each other. De Fries spoke first.

'I'll get Miss Brand to call the bank. She can tell them to send the messenger to Ephraim Street for eleven tomorrow. We should get working on the rooms to make them look used. And we need to be there well before the bank guy arrives.'

61

'As we thought,' Erskine said. 'They couldn't risk Malan returning to the bank, so we've offered to take the documents to them.'

'How does that help us?' Bennett asked uncertainly.

'Because James,' explained Amanda, 'when they sign the loan documents, they will have to use their fictitious names as directors of Tragopan Exploratory. Once they sign using those names the Inspector can arrest them for fraud.'

Bennett nodded. 'But it still doesn't connect them with the disappearances. Well, any more than what we have already.' He tapped a tin of Yaram mints on the table.

'That's true,' Inspector Lumley acknowledged. 'But once we get them on the fraud it gives us a chance to go through the whole shooting match and see if your team's theory is right. If they've got rid of the missing employees there will be something to give them away, there's no doubt.'

Sir John left the investigators to it. He wanted to be on his own for a while and went into the living room. He called for Bridges and ordered a coffee. He was sure there was something else he should be doing, something to help the investigation.

He had developed an instinct for things that might damage the bank. Over the years this showed itself in different ways. Sometimes it meant turning away a potential customer despite the value of the account. Other times an investment opportunity that might have made a lot of money for the bank just didn't sit comfortably with him. There was a kind of unease which settled on him and from the moment he received news of the death in Mayfair, something had been tugging at him. It was unusual, he conceded, to experience this at home in Redshanks. The feeling usually manifested itself at the bank. His nagging worry that something was wrong often felt like it transferred from the walls of St Martin's to his own thoughts. He could feel it in the air of its chilly marble corridors.

Not here at Redshanks though. Never amongst the dusty oak bookcases, the demure lounge or the cosy quiet of the study. Not until now. So, he thought, what had changed?

Sir John shook himself and crossed to the telephone. He picked up the receiver and dialled. A voice at the other end answered, 'Saviour and Bell, how may I help you?'

***

A dozen miles east, high in the vaulted ceiling of St Martin's head office, there was a marble clad sigh of satisfaction. The spirits, not for the first time, had prevailed on a chief executive to act.

62

'Toby, it's John MacGregor. I'm sorry to call again, but I wanted to run something past you. Do you have a minute?'

'Yes of course, how can I help?'

'The rumours about St Martin's, we never got to the bottom of it did we? Does the name Rupert Crawley mean anything to you?'

'Yes, in a way. He has something of a reputation as a share tipster. Personally, I wouldn't trust his judgment, he's just a gossip monger in my book.' There was a pause. 'Are you suggesting he's the source of the problem?'

'Could you do some quiet detective work to see?'

'Of course, I'll get back to you. He may be involved, it's not impossible. Why do you suspect Crawley?'

'The penny took a while to drop, but then I remembered he was part of our world. He sometimes published his commentary in 'Investors News' and there was one on banks earlier this year. His views carried some weight; our shares took a bit of a hit after the article.'

'I remember.'

'But before you do, you need to know what's happened to him.' Sir John hesitated, 'he has met ah, a misfortune.'

'What kind of misfortune?'

'No point in beating about the bush, it looks as though he's been murdered.'

There was a palpable sense of shock at the other end of the line.

'How on earth? He isn't the only gossip out there. Unhelpful yes, but I doubt anyone would kill him for it.'

'We don't know,' said Sir John, 'but it might be he was in over his head on something. It's a dreadful business.'

Toby was earnest. 'John, you aren't caught up in this are you?'

MacGregor managed a hollow laugh. 'No, I can promise you, Toby. We haven't resorted to bumping off the naysayers, at least not for the last hundred years.'

'But murdered you say, how has that involved you?'

'It's a bit complicated, but let's leave that for now. Can you do the digging and then we can compare notes.'

Toby Saviour needed no encouragement. They agreed to speak the next day, but the phone in the drawing room rang less than an hour later.

'That was a good hunch, John.' Saviour sounded worried but also intrigued. 'The rumours seem to have come from his side of the City. But no one has him down as mixed up in anything that could lead to murder, that's a world away from his line of work.'

But it was all Sir John needed. He rejoined Erskine and the team.

Inspector Lumley seemed impressed. He leant forward slowly and peered at the others. The heron again Erskine thought.

'It does give us the link back to the bank,' Lumley tilted his head on one side. 'No doubt he was a mischief maker, but how does this end up as murder? Somethings gone very wrong.'

'Nevertheless, that's what's happened,' Amanda said. 'If these people can make bank staff disappear then nothing's beyond them.'

Erskine was watching Bennett. 'James, we may have to rethink our plan. We know for certain, or pretty much, they're capable of murder. There's a lot at stake for them here.' He turned to Inspector Lumley. 'We can't send James into a situation like that on his own.'

James Bennett had clearly decided to speak up before thinking too hard about what might follow. 'I'm ready to try, I've done this kind of thing lots of times before.'

'What d'you mean?' asked Lumley.

'Taken documents to customers for signature.' Bennett hesitated and glanced at Sir John. 'Some of the customers are a bit, well, old. I go to them when there are routine things to sign, they don't like making a trip to the bank if they don't have to.'

Erskine frowned. 'James, this is hardly a standard run. Lumley, couldn't we dress up one of your men as a bank employee and get him to take James' place?'

Erskine thought the messenger seemed crestfallen and relieved in equal measure.

'Do you ever get asked about the documents, James?' asked Amanda.

'Sometimes. They mark the papers up to show where to sign, but if you're not careful signatures get missed. I check them as the customer hands them back.' He glanced at Sir John again. 'I don't look at the details, but it saves a return trip.'

'So, we need to make sure that whoever does this, they get all the signatures as well as being convincing. We can't afford to slip up.' Amanda said thoughtfully.

'I think we should stick with James as the messenger and have one of my men as a second,' Inspector Lumley agreed. 'Eliot should fit the bill. I'll get that set up.'

'Armed, I would think?' Erskine asked.

'Certainly.' Inspector Lumley was grim; he began to collect his things together. 'I should get back.'

Not for the first time that week, James Bennett pinched himself.

63

Lambourne Tucker left the warmth of Redshanks' kitchen and turned back down the path toward the river. He was keen to catch Knapp; a chance to do some more work at the house wasn't something he wanted to pass up. He scanned the lower section of the flowerbeds but couldn't see the gardener or the horse. He walked down the entire length of the lawns and reached the end of the small jetty that served as a mooring for Sir John's boat. Even a few feet from the bank the Thames was already deep. He gazed idly into the river; the autumn rain muddied the water, and it was impossible to see into its depths.

Looking upstream, on the end of the jetty, Tucker felt as though he were standing on the river. From here, he sensed the full power of the Thames. The dark, oily water circled and tugged at the wooden stanchions of the platform. The current raced under the structure, and he watched the flotsam from the weir collect against its piles before spinning off downstream again.

He sighed and thrust his hands into his pockets. The opportunity to pick up some work from Knapp was gone. He wondered if he could ask the cook to put a word in for him. A pinecone lay on the wooden walkway, and he kicked it into the swirling waters. He watched as it spun in the current around the jetty.

Then, from under the platform, a shape exploded vertically out of the surface of the Thames. Water, mud, weed, and flotsam rained down on the jetty before the figure, unmistakably human, crashed back into the river. A vortex of muddy water below it betrayed another form, powerful but unseen, which sent out a bulging black tidal wave.

The figure resurfaced, and gasping, made for the jetty. It wrapped an arm around the wooden pilings, whimpering with fear. The wave circled back, coming closer to the jetty before turning again and accelerating out into the depths. The wave subsided behind it and the Thames was oily smooth again.

Tucker, motionless with shock, took in the sodden form under the jetty. He could see blood running from the hand grasping the pile. The bright crimson ribbon ran down the man's arm and joined the current. The figure turned and shook the mud from its head. A face even more shocking for its familiarity, stared up at him, pale, frightened, and incomprehensible.

'Knapp, hell, what was that? Hang on, I'll get you.' Tucker crossed the jetty and grabbed at the rope that lay curled around the mooring post. He lowered it, and, lying flat on the edge of the walkway, eased himself out over the edge as far as he dared. Knapp eyed the water around him and then made a lunge for it. For a moment Tucker thought his friend would be swept back into the current, but with a yell of pain Knapp released his hold on the pile and wrapped the lifeline around him.

Tucker pulled on the rope and brought the exhausted man alongside. He tried to lift the gardener out of the water, but in his sodden clothes Knapp was too heavy. Loss of blood, shock, and the adrenaline sapping horrors of the last few minutes drained both men of any strength. They laboured, sucking in air, unable to move or comprehend what had happened.

'I have to get help,' Tucker gasped. 'I can make you fast here, I won't be long.' He gestured at the mooring post.

'For Christ's sake don't leave me.' Knapp was desperate. Wild-eyed, he stared desperately into the depths. Tucker hesitated, but then a voice, familiar, chiding, and wonderful, called down the jetty.

'Lambourne Tucker, what on earth are you up to? Poaching? I'm not cooking any fish from this river.'

Tucker, on his knees, turned to see the figure of Mary, standing hands on hips, looking down the jetty at him.

64

Knapp had finished his account. The exhausted gardener, pale and shaking, was in the study, wrapped in a blanket, a huge white bandage covered his right hand.

Erskine was the first to recover his voice.

'A horse, you say, a large black horse.' He shivered involuntarily. 'But this thing, whatever it was, just walked backwards into the water. Without hesitation.'

'But where is it now? It can't just submerge, just vanish, it has to come up for air.' James Bennett spoke up, deference to the others lost in the horror of the moment.

'I saw it go,' Lambourne said hoarsely, 'at least I think that's what it was. It just moved out, disappeared into the river.'

'And it had you trapped, you couldn't get free?' Erskine asked again.

'Yes.' Knapp whispered. 'My hand was stuck to its nose. It just walked back into the river. I couldn't get back, I... I just went under.'

Amanda looked at the white bandaged lump. 'To have the presence of mind to do that, even though you were drowning...' Her voice tailed away.

'Two fingers gone. Thank goodness for those secateurs though.' Erskine squeezed Knapp's shoulder.

Knapp managed a weak smile, 'I know how the roses feel now.'

'That's the spirit,' said Amanda. 'But what on earth was it?'

65

Number 32 Ephraim Street was an unimposing place for the head office of an engineering company. But then of course, James Bennett told himself, there was no company, just, what was it Amanda called it? 'A brass plate.'

He and Officer Eliot had passed the house in an unmarked police car a couple of times, 'to get the lie of the land,' Eliot said. Eliot wasn't a bad cove, James thought. He listened attentively to James' explanation of how the signing arrangements worked, and Bennett saw him make notes. Inspector Lumley and Erskine were careful to stress that Eliot and James were 'in charge' of the process up until the moment they secured the signatures.

'Once you exit the property with the signed loans, we'll come in hard,' Inspector Lumley explained. 'We're arresting them on suspicion of fraud, but I hope we can get much more once they're under questioning. They may be ready to confess to the false financing but be wrong-footed by the murder enquiries, especially the Crawley angle. Remember, they don't know Malan was seen. If we work at it, they may unravel and give us the whole thing.' Lumley sighed. 'I know we want them for the disappearances too, but you can only hang once, so, if necessary, we'll focus on Crawley.'

'Understood,' Erskine said. 'Let's hope for the whole show though. Sir John will rest easier if we can manage it, not to mention the families.'

'As will we,' Lumley agreed.

The autumn morning still had a hint of warmth despite the mist. Inspector Lumley, Erskine and the Inspector's men met at Lehman Street for a final briefing.

'I'm going to post one of my men at the top of the street,' Lumley said. 'He'll be waiting at the bus stop, keeping an eye out for the Afrikaans.'

James Bennett and Eliot, both clad in St Martin's messenger jackets and caps, readied themselves for their trip to Ephraim Street. Eliot smiled when presented with the bank's tie to wear.

'Very smart,' he observed. 'Will I have to give it back? It's better than the one they give you in CID.'

Nigel Stone handed over the loan papers.

'The forms were prepared in the name of Tragopan Exploratory, and the signatory's names are listed as Hunter and De Cock,' he told James Bennett.

By mid-morning, the mist had lifted. James Bennett and Eliot, in full bank messenger character, were dropped off by car, half a mile from the address. James had been full of adventure when they started the journey, but now he was nervous; Eliot showed him the gun tucked inside his jacket. James tried not to grip the large manila envelope too tightly. He laid it on his lap to avoid crumpling on the journey, but now it was his to carry. Never, he thought, had such a small load felt so heavy.

The two messengers passed a large blue car and a van. A tall man was standing on the pavement, reading his morning paper. He had a motionless heron-like quality and paid them no attention.

At the top of Ephraim Street, a man was waiting at the number 15 bus stop. The bus arrived on its route to Aldgate, and Bennett was surprised to see the passenger step back as it approached.

'Lovely morning,' he said as they passed. The two messengers continued their way down the street.

Bennett and Eliot reached the familiar frontage, and James pressed the bell as firmly as he could manage. After an age, the door opened, and a smart woman appeared. She glanced at them disparagingly.

'From St Martin's? This way.'

I wonder if she's in on it, he thought.

The woman walked back into the house. 'In there,' she waived them into a room on the left of the corridor. Bennett and Eliot found themselves in a drab, sparsely furnished room with three upright chairs grouped around a table partly covered in paper files.

The secretary held out her hand toward James Bennett and the manila envelope.

'I'll take that.'

'It's better,' said James, 'it's better if the gentlemen sign them with someone present. For the witnessing, you see.'

'I can do that,' the secretary said flatly.

James Bennett cast around. 'If we could arrange to do the signing here,' he nodded at the table, 'I can check we haven't missed anything.' The secretary seemed about to say something but turned and left the room instead. Moments later, two men entered. One, a thick set muscular man with a heavy tan, was silent, but the other, taller, and well dressed, gave them a thin smile.

'Gentlemen, good morning. Are the papers ready?'

'Just a few signatures, sir,' said Bennett, 'the places are marked.' The Afrikaans sat down opposite. Bennett offered the secretary his seat.

The two men seemed confused, and the woman hesitated.

'For witnessing the signatures,' he added.

Bennett glanced at the heavy-set man who was sucking something. He watched the man calling himself Hunter reach into his jacket and produce a fountain pen. Hunter removed the top, and leaning on an elbow, waived it expectantly above the pages. 'Where?'

Bennett took the two men through each document. First one, then the other signed in each space where the names Hunter and De Cock appeared. The secretary added her signature as a witness each time.

'Can you print your name under the signature please,' Bennett asked the woman. He leaned forward.

'Thank you, Miss Brand.' Bennett thought he caught a flicker between the two men at the table, but it was there and gone in a moment.

The well-dressed man sat back. 'All done?' he asked.

'Yes sir, thank you.' Bennett's hands shook as he gathered up the papers. He glanced across and then tapped the documents together on the tabletop. Now all he could think about was reversing out of the room, but he kept his mind on the job as much as he could.

There was a pause, and then for the first time the heavy-set man spoke up.

'When will we have the money?' The man calling himself De Cock had a thick accent, completely out of place with the surroundings, Bennett thought. He knew if he tried to speak he would be hoarse, and pretended not to hear the question.

'Well, the money, when'll we have it?' the man asked again.

James prepared himself, his throat was still dry, and he coughed before speaking.

'Well sir, in my experience, once we get back to the branch it doesn't take long, so probably by tomorrow morning.' The man grunted. He stopped sucking whatever it was and reached into his pocket, producing a small tin. He helped himself and then, as an afterthought, offered it to James.

The Yaram mints jostled against each other, filling the small shiny confectionary box. Bennett took one. 'Thank you,' he managed. His heart was pounding. The group at the table rose and he and Eliot took their grateful cue.

Miss Brand motioned toward the door, 'I'll show you out.' James followed her down the hallway, Eliot just behind him. At the door she released the catch and stood aside.

Bennett and Eliot stepped out into the daylight. They had barely taken a step when Inspector Lumley, Erskine and a group of constables pushed past them in the opposite direction.

The tall Lumley was first to the door, folding his hand around the leading edge as Miss Brand closed it.

'Thank you, Miss.' He held the door open, and the woman tipped back into the hallway, powerless and open-mouthed. Bennett watched as Erskine and the others pounded past him and down the corridor. There was a shout, then a crash. A thick Afrikaans accent boomed an obscenity. Another voice, high and reedy, wailed in protest.

Lumley handed the woman over to a constable and entered the room. A chair was in splinters on the floor and one of his officers was picking himself up, blood dripping through the fingers over his mouth. Four other constables held the two men. The tall one was pale, but his companion was belligerent. He shrugged and rumbled at the grip of his captors then spat on the floor in front of Lumley.

'What the hell's this? You people have no right to manhandle us. You're going to have to explain yourselves and bloody quickly.' He pulled again at the men holding him in check.

'Malan, isn't it? I'm an Inspector of His Majesty's Police.' Lumley regarded his captives with satisfaction.

'You know this man already of course,' he gestured towards Erskine, who was standing to one side.

De Fries' face was incredulous.

'You! What the...?'

'Shut it,' Malan thundered. The pale man stopped, but his eyes were wide, and they flicked from Lumley to Erskine and back.

'Pieter De Fries and Charlie Malan. Those are your real names I believe,' Lumley went on. 'We are taking you in for questioning, and you will be charged with fraud, and,' he nodded at the constable still holding his face, 'assaulting a police officer.'

Lumley, helped by Erskine and the constables, herded the whole group back down the corridor. Malan thrashed and gouged his way down the hall, kicking holes in the thin wall. Outside, Eliot and James Bennett watched from the far side of the street. Malan saw them and spat on the pavement.

The Inspector and Erskine examined the signed documents.

Erskine pointed at the printed name of the witness. 'They didn't brief her properly. No alias for the secretary I see.'

'Might be useful,' Lumley agreed. He walked across to the would-be messengers.

'Well done. Eliot, get back to the station and out of that uniform. Mr Bennett, you will need to go too and make a full statement.'

'Mr,' thought James, that was a step up.

Erskine joined the group. 'A good morning's work.'

'The next step is to divide and conquer. It's the only way we're going to move these charges up to murder,' said Lumley. 'And we need to catch them out with something they don't expect. My money is on the tall one. We should start with him.'

66

Erskine put down the telephone. He'd briefed Sir John and Amanda, who were back at Redshanks. They agreed Amanda should travel over to Lehman Street police station with the gardener and collect James Bennett once he was ready.

'Knapp's been through a lot,' Sir John said. 'We should keep him company for a few hours, just in case. Besides, he might remember something from this morning, and we should be there to note it.'

'I can't wait to see it all,' Amanda said excitedly, 'I'm leaving for Lehman Street.'

Erskine wanted to check on Knapp, and he guessed there was no need to ask James Bennett if he was happy with the arrangements.

In the Lehman Street station interview room, Inspector Lumley could see that De Fries had begun to compose himself. No doubt, he thought, the man had decided the prospect of a modest sentence for fraud was as nothing compared to the punishment that would have been handed out by the gang they owed money to. Lumley was sure De Fries had told himself that his was a light touch, given the circumstances. The slip with Miss Brand's witnessing of the false signatures was a mistake, but De Fries would assume Lumley had enough without that, and he would know he wasn't going to prison for long. He might even avoid it altogether, if forging a few documents and redirecting bank funds was all they could come up with.

The tall Afrikaans stared across the table. The loss of a chance at the platinum mine was disappointing, but he accepted that it was gone now. With a bit of luck, he thought, he would still be in Paris, with or without Malan, in the not-too-distant future. All this without the South Americans on his back, as originally planned.

'So, officer, what're we talking about here?' De Fries held up his hands. 'Yes, yes, you're right, we have been keen to borrow funds from St Martin's, maybe a little too keen. But I don't suppose we're the first to get a bit ahead of ourselves that way.' De Fries flicked something from his suit. 'It's very dusty in here,' he tutted.

The Inspector was standing on the other side of the table. 'Well, you'll certainly save us a lot of time if we can deal with the fraud as a formality,' Lumley conceded. 'That should help your case when it comes to sentencing too. Shall I get my officer to take your statement?'

De Fries was magnanimous. 'Why not.' He spread his hands wide in supplication.

Lumley left the room. He met Erskine and the recently arrived Amanda in the station reception.

'De Fries is very cocky,' he said grimly. 'He's sure we haven't linked the disappearances to them. We'll get the fraud down and then start softening him up on the big-ticket items.'

'Will you need Terence?' Amanda asked. She looked at the gardener sitting in a chair against the reception wall. Knapp raised a bandaged hand. He was still pale, thought

Lumley, but he looked better than the last time he'd seen him.

'Yes, we need him to identify Malan.' Lumley was thinking hard; he spoke to his desk sergeant. 'Can you find Eliot for me.' A few moments later the detective, now in plain clothes but still wearing the bank tie, appeared from the back of the station. Inspector Lumley eyed the tie, then passed on. 'Eliot, take Mr Knapp,' he gestured toward the bandaged hand, 'and see if you can get him to identify Malan.'

'This is about the death in Mayfair?'

'Yes, and I don't much care if Malan knows why either, it might shake a few things loose.' Eliot walked over to the seated Knapp. The two men spoke briefly and then the officer helped Knapp out of the chair. They disappeared behind the front desk.

Lumley turned to Erskine and Amanda. 'Can you wait here; I want to see how our other inmate is doing.' The Inspector walked away in the same direction as Eliot and Knapp.

'There's a lot to take in,' Amanda said. 'We're making progress, but what in God's name came after Knapp? Could he be delirious, something in the garden, a wound like that, and the Thames isn't exactly clean...' She tailed off.

'It's not impossible,' Erskine was equally perplexed. His thoughts kept returning to the beast he'd encountered in the fog near Clapham Common; he shivered. 'But, if that's so, without medication he should be getting worse, and he isn't.'

'Do you think Lumley will get to the murder charge?' Amanda asked.

'There may be murder charges plural,' Erskine reflected. 'After all, we have two bodies and there are another three missing...' He stopped talking.

'Well let's hope,' Amanda broke off as the Inspector returned. There was a little more spring in his step. He's caught something, at least a sprat, Erskine thought.

'Knapp says Malan is the person he saw enter the flat and lean over the balcony, which means we have progress,' said Lumley.

'Good man,' Erskine said.

Amanda squeezed the Inspector's arm. He was clearly unused to this, but he smiled, nevertheless.

'Did Malan see Knapp?'

'No, that's our next step but we've saved it for now. We have some decent circumstantial evidence, but we need more than that.'

'Are you going to try for the other body and the disappearances?' asked Amanda.

'Well, there's a long way to go,' Lumley said. 'Still, we'll give it a try.'

An officer approached.

'Sir, we have the prisoner's signed statement covering the fraud.'

Lumley nodded. 'Let's pitch Malan with the Mayfair murder and try De Fries with the body in the estuary.'

67

Inspector Lumley entered the interview room. A seated De Fries looked up. The man smiled and lifted his hands together.

'I'm ready for my cuffs now. Assuming you feel them necessary for a desperate fraudster like me,' he smirked.

'All in good time, Mr De Fries. We're still chatting to Mr Malan about a few things. After all a trick like that needs a lot of planning.'

De Fries seemed inordinately pleased. 'Well, if I say so myself.' He stopped, obviously struck by the realisation there were two sets of conversations going on. 'Charlie has supported my statement then?'

'Not exactly, not yet anyway.' The Inspector studied De Fries. 'Does the name Hubert Heath mean anything to you?' There was a flicker on De Fries' face.

'No, why?'

'He's an employee of the bank. Quite up-and-coming it seems. He works at the Swan Lane branch. He's missing you see, and we wondered if you could help us with that.'

'Missing you say. Sorry, the name means nothing to me.'

'What about Simpson?'

'Not another missing man I hope,' De Fries raised his eyebrows. 'St Martin's has been careless.' Lumley thought De Fries seemed about to add something but then stopped.

'A woman actually.' Lumley felt his jawline ripple, but he stayed focused. 'It seems strange there are three missing employees, and all of them from branches involved in your fraud. Odd don't you think.'

De Fries looked thoughtful but then shrugged his shoulders. 'Sorry not to be more helpful.' He paused. 'You mentioned there were three people, perhaps I can help you with the other one.' He smirked again.

'Ah yes, my mistake.' Inspector Lumley, standing, looked heron-like again. 'The other one's a man called Leonard Ash.'

This time De Fries laughed. 'Ah yes, now he *is* one I can help you with Inspector. Mr Ash is our man on the inside. We couldn't have managed all this,' De Fries spread his hands wide, 'without his help. You should certainly find and arrest him.'

'Oh, we've found him. At the bottom of the Thames. Can you help us with that?' Inspector Lumley took one long deliberate stride forward and stood over De Fries. 'I'm thinking you can.'

The Afrikaans expression registered astonishment. His mouth opened but no sound came out. Lumley had to grab the Afrikaans to stop him falling off his chair. He held the man up by his collar and looked at the white face. De Fries was in a dead faint.

68

Erskine and Amanda stood in the corridor of Lehman Street, stepping aside occasionally to let the busy blue uniforms pass.

'I wish there was something more we could do; it all feels so sad and incomplete.' Erskine said. 'It looks like we've got the Afrikaans, but what about the people? Do we really have to wait until they wash up in the Thames?'

'Finding bodies in a river. Until it gives them up, I would think it's next to impossible,' Amanda said.

'But just imagine, just for a minute. What if there *is* someone still alive? We've interrupted their plans, and they're still stuck in London, what if they've not got around to,'

'Tidying up.' Amanda shivered. 'But where would they hide someone? It can't be at the Rand offices, that's too risky, and in any case, you might've turned up at any time.'

'Well, we've been to Ephraim Street, there's nothing there. Lumley's men have been all over it.'

'Wasn't there another address?' Amanda asked. 'When James followed De Fries, didn't he go to another house?'

Erskine was looking at her, his expression had changed, she thought.

'You're right, there was another place, it was after Ephraim Street. What was it? Where's Bennett?' Erskine looked around.

Amanda was already running down the corridor.

'Eagle Street,' Erskine shouted after her. 'I think it was Eagle Street, get Bennett.'

James Bennett walked back into Lehman Street reception. He could tell Violet everything now, he thought. He found a spot to lean on the counter and tried to look nonchalant. There were policemen everywhere he looked.

Amanda appeared and made straight for him. He took his elbows off the counter.

'James, when you followed that man, De Fries, you said he stopped off somewhere?'

'Yes, Ephraim Street.'

'Wasn't there somewhere else, another address?'

'There was another one.' He went back to the afternoon. 'I can't remember the name, but I could take you there.' He paused, 'Hang on, it was in Eagle Street.'

Amanda took James' arm. 'Come with me.' She walked Bennett up the corridor to Erskine.

'Robbie, you were right. It was Eagle Street. James can take you there now.'

'I'll explain on the way,' Erskine said. 'Come on, Bennett.' Amanda let go James' arm and almost pushed him into Erskine.

'Good luck boys,' she called. 'I'll tell Inspector Lumley.'

Erskine ran out of the station. Bennett, breathless, followed him into the street. Erskine was already hailing a cab.

'So, you think someone might be left, one of the staff may still be alive?' Bennett said, watching out of the cab window.

'Don't get your hopes up, James, it's a long shot. It's only because they were interrupted by our investigation, we're hoping they might not have got around to silencing everyone.'

The taxi was lumbering through Holborn, when Bennett jumped up, almost banging his head on the cab roof.

'We're here,' he exclaimed. 'Driver, take it slow, it's down here on the left somewhere.'

Erskine watched as the messenger counted off the houses.

'Not that one. No, not the one after the post box. I can see the jewellers.' There was a pause, and then suddenly he shouted,

'That's it, there, the one with the streetlamp. Quick, here driver, please.'

With a rattle the taxi pulled to a halt. Erskine sized up the property as he stepped onto the pavement.

'No keys,' Bennett said. 'I bet that South African's got them.'

'We'll have to improvise. No time for niceties,' Erskine said.

'That door's got a glass panel.' Bennett was looking around in the street. 'Here we go.' He picked up a piece of broken curb that was lying in the gutter and balanced it in his hand. 'Ok?' He looked at Erskine.

Bennett heaved it through the panel with a crash. They both looked at each other.

'We're burglars now,' said Erskine. 'Come on!'

Bennett opened the catch from the inside and Erskine followed him in. They stood still for a minute.

'Well, if there's anyone here, they're deaf,' Erskine said.

The hallway was cold and musty. Erskine tried the light switch. A pale yellow bulb came to life at the far end of the corridor. 'Be careful,' he muttered, 'we're in enemy territory.'

They moved slowly down the hall, checking the rooms. Apart from a few battered sticks of furniture, there was nothing. Erskine put his head around the door at the end of the passageway, 'Kitchen, empty,' he called.

Bennett was standing at the foot of the stairs,

'Ready?' he asked.

But Erskine was looking at a small door in the side of the staircase. He tried the key, and the lock turned smoothly. He glanced at Bennett. 'That's been oiled.'

There was another switch just inside the door. He flicked it, and another pale light appeared above their heads.

Erskine could see a set of grey stone steps leading down into the gloom. Bennett's breath was warm on the back of his neck.

'Here we go,' he muttered.

'Did you hear that?' Bennett whispered. 'There's something down there, take it easy.'

The two men descended slowly. They were almost at the bottom when Bennett said, 'There it is again.'

'I heard it this time,' Erskine whispered. 'Hello? Anybody there?'

'Someone's crying,' Bennett said. 'Hello? Hello, we're not going to hurt you.'

The light from the stairs leaked past them and down into the cellar. The floor was pock-marked and empty, but Erskine could see what looked like a pile of clothes in one corner. He crossed towards it.

The shape moved and the sound came again. Bennett gasped and pushed past Erskine. He sank down in front of the pile.

'Miss Simpson, Miss Simpson, is it you?'

69

'Tell me, Inspector, what's the sentence for borrowing money from a bank using a fictitious company?'

There was no doubt Malan was sure of his ground, Lumley thought; he was bordering on the belligerent. He's planning along the same lines as De Fries. Admit to the fraud, take the sentence, and then move on to a bigger prize once released.

'I'm surprised a man of your seniority should bother himself with such indiscretions.' Malan waived his muscular arms expansively. 'Surely you have a junior officer around the place. Someone who could deal with such... trifles...'

Inspector Lumley had left the twitching De Fries, as he said to Eliot, 'to stew in his own juice.' Miss Brand had supplied some surprisingly useful information, and now he was watching his final prey. He stood motionless in front of Malan, with the Afrikaans seated at the interview table, stretched out in front of him.

'Fraud is a serious offence, Mr Malan.'

The financier snorted.

'But there are some other matters we need to speak to you about.'

The Afrikaans gave Lumley a steady glare.

'Your property in Eagle Street,' Lumley began,

'Never been there.'

'But you *do* have a property in *that* street?'

'De Fries looks after that, nothing to do with me.'

'We have people checking it now.' The Inspector waited for a reaction, but there was none.

'Go ahead, anything else?'

'Do you know anyone in Mayfair, Mr Malan?'

'Mayfair, no.' The Afrikaans traced the wood grain of the table with his fingernail. 'Much too rich a place for the likes of me.' Malan was superficially the same, Lumley thought, but his manner had tightened.

'You've never been there?'

'Oh, sure. I've been through it, our offices are close to Mayfair, but I've never spent any time there.' Lumley sensed Malan was treading carefully.

'You've never visited Rembrandt Court?'

'Where? No, never heard of it.'

Lumley watched Malan.

'Do you know someone called Rupert Crawley?'

'Not that I recall.'

'Strange.' Lumley stepped forward. 'Miss Brand thinks he might be familiar. And we have someone here who is certain he saw you enter that building.'

There was a pause.

'He also saw you lean out over the balcony of,' Lumley checked his notes, 'the penthouse, where Mr Crawley lives, or rather, lived.'

'Past tense?' queried Malan appearing confused.

'Yes. Regrettably, Mr Crawley met with an accident. About the same time you were visiting.'

Malan exhaled forcefully. When he spoke, his voice was thick and thunderous. 'I've already told you. I've never been

to Rembrandt Court. Brand is mistaken. As for your man...'
He snorted again.

Inspector Lumley persisted. 'He followed you there. All the way from your office in Soho.'

'Very diligent of him,' Malan retorted, 'but it wasn't me. Listen, how many floors is this place?'

'Six, plus one for the penthouse.'

'Then the guy your man saw, the one on the balcony, he would have been a long way above him.'

'Correct,' Lumley acknowledged.

'And your man would have been staring into the sky too.'

'Agreed.'

Malan's belligerence returned. 'Then how could someone identify a guy six or seven floors above him if he was squinting into the sky?'

'You have a point.'

Malan was close to triumphant. 'The dead man, the one in the flat. What interest would he be to me anyway?'

'He had a connection with St Martin's too.'

'Really.' Malan was dismissive. 'Well, just because some cokey has a link to the bank, doesn't mean I either know him or want him dead.'

'Tell me,' Inspector Lumley said. 'Tell me how you know he was a cocaine user?'

70

Inspector Lumley stood outside the interview room with Amanda. They could hear what sounded like a bull bellowing. Accent heavy obscenities and indecipherable Afrikaans bounced off the wall separating them from the prisoner.

'So, a falling out amongst the conspirators. They must've been working with Crawley to destabilise the bank,' Lumley said. 'Might unnerve De Fries if he hears that commotion.' He looked around for Eliot.

'Can you find a reason to walk De Fries past that,' he indicated the roars beyond the door. 'We can play on his nerves if we move quickly.' Eliot left and reappeared with the pale De Fries handcuffed to him.

'Mr De Fries, we have some more points we'd like to go over with the two of you.' Lumley said. 'We're just waiting for Mr Malan to calm down and then we'll take you through.' He nodded at the door in front of them. The roaring on the other side continued.

'I can't go in there. Not with that lunatic.' De Fries' voice was reedy.

Amanda took her cue. 'You can't do that Inspector Lumley. The man's a killer, he's admitted it. For goodness' sake think about it.'

Lumley made a show of being in two minds.

'It's illegal,' shrieked De Fries in a terrified falsetto. 'To put me in there. I had nothing to do with Crawley, he did that on his own, if I go in there, he'll think I told you.'

'On his own,' Inspector Lumley said. 'But the others...
the other employees, you knew about them didn't you.'

'That's not how it was,' De Fries was breathless. 'But ...'

'But these things happen, don't they? Especially when
Charlie Malan is involved.' Erskine was almost
sympathetic. De Fries didn't speak.

'Where are they, what have you done with those
people?' demanded Lumley.

The engineer stood shaking, lost and wide-eyed,
wanting the man behind the door to stay there and the
whole wretched process to end.

71

'Any news?' Lumley asked.

'Nothing yet,' Amanda said. 'I expect they've had to be careful. There could be anything there.'

The Inspector and Amanda were sitting in Lumley's office, a small space screened from the general station hubbub by frosted glass.

'What happens next?' asked Amanda. 'I assume they'll be charged?'

'My men are going through it all with them now,' Lumley said. 'We must do these things absolutely by the book. It's easy to miss something and give defence counsel a loophole.'

'What if they...' There was an increase in the noise on the other side of the panels and Amanda peered at the glass.

'Hang on,' said Lumley and pulled open the door; Amanda followed him out of the office.

Lumley and Amanda discovered a station in an uproar. Amanda, astonished, took in the extraordinary scene. Erskine and James Bennett, both in shirtsleeves, were carrying what looked like a long bundle of clothing. A pair of feet stuck out of one end and the top of a head was just visible at the other. As she watched, the two men sat the bundle down gently on a chair.

The Inspector and Amanda pushed through the crowd. Amanda grabbed Erskine.

'Who is it, Robbie?'

Erskine turned to speak.

'It's Miss Simpson,' James Bennet exclaimed breathlessly, 'we found her. At Eagle Street.'

Two police officers with a medical bag appeared and began to attend to the motionless figure.

'Is she alive?' Amanda could barely believe it.

'Just in time,' said Erskine. 'But she's in a bad way.'

One of the medics came over. 'The ambulance is here; we're off to Charing Cross with this one.'

Erskine nodded. 'Take it easy.'

The investigators watched as the medics carried Miss Simpson carefully out through reception.

'Nice work, Erskine,' Lumley said. 'A life saved. More than I'd expected.'

Amanda grabbed Bennett's arm. 'And James, you tailing De Fries, that was vital. We wouldn't have known about Eagle Street without your work.'

'Better call Sir John,' said Erskine. 'Some good news at last.'

Inspector Lumley gestured at his office. 'Through this way,' he said. 'Bennett, why don't you speak to him.'

'Looks like your messenger days might be over, James,' said Amanda. 'Violet will like you in a suit.'

72

Back at Redshanks, the investigators were with Inspector Lumley.

A week had passed. A week in which another body wearing a bank tie had washed up in the Thames. Sir John had identified Hubert Heath.

'Strangulation and by a powerful man,' the Inspector reported. 'Heath was big enough to fight back, Malan must've had his work cut out.'

Erskine, sitting next to Sir John, had his head in his hands.

'Once we'd broken De Fries it was easy enough to flush out the actions of those two,' Lumley said. 'And you were right.'

Erskine looked up. 'As we thought, Sir John, they arranged the loans to get Rand Mining out of trouble. They were up to their necks in debt with their so-called business partners from South America. They needed more money, a lot more money than you or any bank would lend them.'

'I see. And they hit upon the idea of multiple loans through fictitious companies,' Sir John was despairing. 'But why kill my people? What did they do to cause such retribution?'

'There was no retribution. They were simply too bright. They spotted what was going on and had to be silenced.' Erskine was grim. 'At least that's the case for Stevens and Hubert Heath.'

'Thank God you found Harriet Simpson.'

'What about Ash, though?' James Bennett spoke up.

'That's a different matter,' Erskine went on. 'Ash was their man on the inside. He made sure the applications went as smoothly as possible; he must have alerted De Fries and Malan when the others got suspicious.'

'Why kill him too? Loose ends possibly?' Sir John asked.

'That's Lumley's assumption. But De Fries says he'd nothing to do with that, and Malan's refusing to talk, at least to say anything worth writing down. The man is almost mad. Still, we have De Fries' confession that between them they murdered Stevens and Heath, and we can get Malan for Crawley's murder. We're still missing Stevens' body, but we know from De Fries he met the same fate. We also have Miss Brand's testimony. She's been extremely helpful, especially about Crawley's demise. We *will* get there.'

'To murder my people and dump them in the Thames. It's despicable.' Sir John was close to tears.

'Malan will hang, Sir John,' Erskine said quietly. 'You can be sure of that. And we will see how it goes for De Fries too.'

'Why would Ash get himself caught up in such a thing? He was one of our best,' said Sir John. 'It's so sad.'

'Greed,' Erskine said. 'Simple greed.'

'And if you sup with the devil...' Sir John shook his head. 'The bank will do something for the families. What to do about Ash, I'm not sure. At least he was a single man.'

'In a way, we were lucky,' Erskine reflected. 'If Malan hadn't killed Crawley, we might never have got De Fries to unravel.'

'And now I have some visits to make,' said Sir John bleakly. 'At least there's been some good news for Arthur Simpson, but it's not going to be easy for the Stevens family.'

'I'll come with you,' said Erskine.

They went to see George Steven's wife first. She was resolute, and they made a point of explaining that St Martin's would support her. Erskine could see Sir John was determined to see things through, and he knew this act of kindness would help his host and the widow.

They also visited Harriet Simpson, now back at home recovering. Arthur Simpson was close to tears, and his wife, Jean, threw her arms around St Martin's chief executive, 'a wonderful man,' she said. Another fruitcake appeared. When it came to leave, there were more hugs, quite a departure for St Martin's, Erskine thought.

73

The spirits at the bank were taking in the last few dreadful weeks. For over two hundred and fifty years, they had witnessed triumph and tragedy in the lives of employees and customers, and wherever possible, they stayed out of human adventures. They were safe in the knowledge that, from their perspective, the forces of good, for the most part, had won out and kept their institution from harm. There had been no collapse, and life at the bank could, as much as possible in such fast-changing times, return to normal.

However, something continued to trouble them. Over hundreds of years, they had become wary of intrusion from other forces and could sense when something new arrived; this was the case now. Something malign, a presence they could not resolve, had taken up residence in the City. Although they had some suspicion, they had not completely worked out its intentions or what it was. They were uneasy as they looked out across the square mile, watchful, waiting, and on their guard.

74

It was an unusual table for Le Homard, Erskine thought. Sir John and Amanda were there with him, but also present, wide-eyed with excitement, were a gardener, a bank messenger, and his girl. Erskine had bumped into James Bennett at St Martin's that morning.

'I've told Violet not to go on about the Mitford Sisters tonight, I don't suppose they're Sir John's cup of tea,' Bennett said.

'Don't worry, James, Sir John won't mind.'

'It's exciting, we have our very own evening with the posh set,' Bennett added. Erskine laughed.

They had invited the Inspector too, but Lumley made his excuses, agreeing to dine privately with Sir John another time.

'There's a lot more work to do before those two are convicted,' he'd remarked. 'We will get them, but I don't want to be part of a celebration dinner. That might not go down well internally, quite apart from running risks with the press and defence counsel.'

They were six friends now, thought Erskine. He watched them. Amanda, back to her businesslike best, was in full flow with Sir John, but also doing a wonderful job of helping Knapp, James Bennett and Violet relax in unfamiliar surroundings. His host was looking less strained too, he thought.

It had been an extraordinary few weeks, but he'd made it. No personal collapse, some very unhappy findings, but a successful outcome to the investigation itself. And a reconnection with Amanda. He wondered what would happen there. Would she complete her funding and go back to South Africa? If the discussions with Sir John were going as well as they seemed, the first part of the question was already answered. What would he do now? Maybe more investigative work would come his way, but preferably it would stop short of murder.

'Penny for them.'

Erskine turned. 'I'm sorry, Sir John, I was miles away.'

'What'll you do now, Robert? You can't come across cases like this every day?'

Erskine nodded. 'I was just thinking the same.'

Sir John leant forward. 'Although I'm bound to say, things might seem a little, well, slow after all this.'

'I'm hoping so.' Erskine said wryly. 'You know I'm always available if anything comes up. Something easier next time, though, if you can manage it.'

'Well things do crop up, they're mostly routine. We may well call on your services if you're still in London.' Sir John smiled and glanced at Amanda.

Across the table, Erskine watched Knapp in full flow, holding up his bandaged hand. 'And it had me. Walking back down into the water. There was nothing, nothing I could do. And then I thought of the secateurs.'

Violet was aghast. She put her hand to her mouth. 'Terence, you're such a quick thinker and so brave,' she gasped.

'It's only a couple of fingers,' James Bennett said, but then added, 'though it was quite something.'

'We still don't know what it was.' Erskine said.

'Whatever it was, I hope it's gone.' Sir John said emphatically.

Erskine remembered his encounter in the Clapham fog and the horsehair in the fist of the drowned man. Then there was Knapp's narrow escape from the river. He shivered despite the warmth of the restaurant.

Amanda leaned over and put her hand on his arm. 'Are you alright, Robbie?' she squeezed his hand.

Sir John summoned the bill, and Erskine looked on as the party said their goodbyes. Knapp and James Bennett, now companion in arms, and Violet, pink and garrulous, were talking excitedly.

'And I can show you around the gardens,' Knapp was saying. 'Not many get to visit them. We can have lunch at The Slow Pony after that.'

'I thought you'd had enough of horses,' James Bennett laughed. A shadow passed across Knapp's face.

'Don't worry, Terence, whatever it was is long gone,' Sir John said.

Erskine frowned.

'No need to frighten the man, Erskine,' Sir John whispered as they made their way toward the lobby.

Erskine felt Amanda's arm in his again, he turned.

'Funding secured?' he asked, Amanda grinned.

'As good as.'

'Back to Joburg, I guess?' he said as carelessly as he could manage.

'In time no doubt.' Amanda was still on his arm as they stepped out onto the pavement. The door attendant came forward.

'Taxi, Sir?' he asked; Amanda spoke first.

'Whites, please.'

Erskine glanced back at the group on the pavement. Sir John was speaking enthusiastically with the others and showed no sign of leaving them. He had evidently called two taxis.

'Roses, no doubt,' Amanda said. 'What a nice man. Perhaps there will be more work to come.'

The taxi arrived and the attendant opened the passenger door. Amanda smiled at Erskine.

'Shall we?'

75

The beast, at least for the moment, was content. Although far from home, it had taken to its new surroundings. From time to time, it ventured out into the world of commerce. The banker or broker, dealing with the new customer, would remark after the meeting how unusual it was to meet a man so smartly dressed but with such long flowing hair.

Accounts were opened, investments made, and transactions completed by the quietly spoken customer with the lustrous jet-black mane. Yet the curious, given time, might have noted these meetings always occurred in branches near the Thames. Even more noteworthy, to those of a nautical mind at least, would have been their timing, which coincided with high tide in the reaches that ran along the southern perimeter of the City of London.

But there were no onlookers. The staff's interest in their new account holder ceased at the end of the working day. Making their way home, they mentally filed away these events and looked forward to their supper. At most, the encounter might come up in conversation with their spouse under 'How was your day?'

So, the Kelpie, for that is what it was, with no chance of detection, possessed of an endless, merciless patience, became part of the life of the City.

From time to time the London evening paper would report on the drowning of another soul walking the City towpaths. Life by a river has its hazards, and there was no special cause for comment. No one asked why the drownings were never seen, or commented on the enormous hoof prints on the bank at each site.

The Kelpie had other plans.

Like the spirits in the vaulted ceilings of St Martin's, it kept watch.

And waited.